APRICOTS

APRICOTS

a war novel

JOHN E. HOLLOWAY

Indigo River Publishing

Indigo River Publishing
3 West Garden Street, Ste. 352
Pensacola, FL 32502
www.indigoriverpublishing.com

Editors: Earl Tillinghast, Liesel Schmidt
Cover & Book Design: mycustombookcover.com

Ordering Information:
Quantity sales: Special discounts are available on quantity purchases by corporations, associations, and others. For details, contact the publisher at the address above.

Orders by US trade bookstores and wholesalers: Please contact the publisher at the address above.

Printed in the United States of America

Library of Congress Control Number: 2019946791

ISBN: 978-1-950906-12-3

First Edition

With Indigo River Publishing, you can always expect great books, strong voices, and meaningful messages. Most importantly, you'll always find . . . words worth reading.

"These guys won a war, and they don't even get a cold beer before crossing the Atlantic to go back to another one in Beirut."

Lt. Col. Ray L. Smith, USMC

Life Magazine, December 1983.

Disclaimer

Although some chapters refer to actual historic figures like Ronald Reagan and Maurice Bishop, all of the other characters are fictional. If the story was staged within larger military operations, it would have been possible to use fictional units and operations; but that was not possible here, where only one Marine battalion was involved. Most of the action follows the Marines of 4th Platoon, A Company, Second Assault Amphibian Battalion, which was attached to Golf Company, Second Battalion, Eighth Marines. While those units were involved in the Grenada and Beirut operations in 1983-84, they have been populated in these pages by fictional characters.

Contents

Chapter One

The Washington Post
"Iranian Denies Flurry of reports of Christmas Hostage Release."

December 12, 1980—"The head of the Iranian hostage commission today denied a new flurry of reports that Iran decided to free the 52 American hostages on or before Christmas. The official ... also denied a report that the United States and Iran have agreed to a compromise settling one of Iran's four demands for release of the hostages who spent their 404th day in captivity."

The Washington Post

"Syrians Attack 2 Villages in South Lebanon"
December 1980—"Lebanon Says 15 Killed, 13 Hurt in Israe-
li Raid on PLO Position… Israel said it destroyed two vehicles
carrying guerrillas, killing a number of them, and that gunboats
shelled the area 45 miles north of the Israeli border." … A Syrian
communiqué issued in Damascus said Israeli tank concentrations
in south Lebanon were hit [by Syrian artillery], inflicting heavy
damage and numerous casualties."

At the Virginia Military Institute in Lexington, Virginia, "Bill the Bugler" (then 70 years old) stood in front of the old barracks, blowing "little toot," signaling two minutes to the next class. Cadets in black duty jackets and gray wool trousers filed out of the barracks into falling snow, headed for classes. The barracks had housed the Corps of Cadets since 1843, and the feel of the place had changed little since then—or since "Stonewall" Jackson taught there in the 1850s or since George Marshall graduated in 1901. The cadets moving through snow to class were part of an old tradition.

Robert Forrest sat in a corner classroom looking out through tall gothic windows at snow falling when Major Bowen, professor of history, entered the room. The Major was small and fit. There was a faint scar down the left side of his face, and his left eye was lifeless. The major leaned against the front of his desk, arms crossed, looking out at the snow with his good eye. The black, waxed floor reflected the shape of the windows and a clear upside-down image of the Major. The room was quiet.

The class was called "History of Warfare," a too-broad title for a class that focused only on the nitty-gritty ground level action that was not covered in standard texts. It was during the Cold War, and VMI required every cadet to take a commission upon graduation. The point of the class was to give the cadets a whiff of what to expect when the time came.

The Major began the class with an overview of the battle of Spotsylvania in 1864, soon after Grant took over command of all federal armies. He described the battle step-by-step until he got to the worst part, at a place in the Confederate lines later called the "Bloody Angle." He picked up a book and opened it to a marked page. Then he looked up. "One of the Union generals, Horace Porter, later described the fight that day at the Bloody Angle." The Major looked down at the book and started reading slowly. The passage explained that "rank after rank was riddled by shot and shell and bayonet thrusts, and finally sank, a mass of torn and mutilated corpses..." The major looked up and paused, scanning the room with his good eye. Then he looked down again and continued with Porter's descriptions. "Trees over a foot and a half in diameter were cut completely in two by the incessant musketry fire... we had not only shot down an army, but also a forest... skulls were crushed with clubbed muskets, and men were stabbed to death with swords and bayonet thrusts between the logs of the parapet. Even the darkness failed to stop the fierce contest, and the deadly strife did not cease 'till after midnight." The professor paused. He looked up and explained that Porter walked along the trench line the following morning, where he found "the dead were piled upon each other in some places four layers deep... below the mass of fast-decaying corpses, the convulsive twitching of limbs and the writhing of bodies showed that there were wounded men still alive and struggling to extricate themselves from their horrid entombment." The Major closed the book and leaned back on his desk.

Forrest glanced up through the window. It was still snowing.

The Major turned and walked back across the polished floor. "The Bloody Angle was real. It happened. It's not just ink on a page." He looked out the window. "The battlefield is just over those mountains. It was loud; the kind of loud that shakes windowpanes and vibrates the ground. It smelled of ruptured bowels. Thousands of men and boys played out a horrific reality—a drama with wounds and anger and screams and grunts and sweat and exhaustion. A place where hundreds of dirty, exhausted men and boys split open by bayonet or shot piled together in pain, groaning, calling, bleeding out. The blood of all mixed together in pools at the bottom of the muddy trenches. It really happened." He gestured out the window. "Just over that mountain."

Forrest looked down at his textbook. There on the page was a map of the battle movements. The units were depicted as perfect rectangles lined-up neatly on the crisp white page.

"Quite a few cadets who lived right here in the barracks across the street fought in that war. There were forty-eight boys in the VMI class of 1855. Eight of them got killed in the War."

The cadets sat silently.

"The soldiers in that war, and at the Angle, were like you." the Major continued. "Cadet Stapleton Crutchfield, class of 1855, matriculated from Mount Pleasant, Virginia. His signature is there in the new cadet registry—the same book you signed on matriculation day. Cadet Crutchfield signed the book on August 8, 1851, 130 years ago. He was killed on the retreat from Petersburg to Appomattox on April 5, 1865, four days before the surrender. Miles Cary Macon, Class of 1856, was killed at Appomattox on April 8, 1865. John Ashby was killed two hours before the surrender. Those boys lived in the same barracks you live in." The major paused. "That's what happens. In combat, many good boys, like you, get killed. Sometimes for a lost cause." The Major looked out the window again. "Walk down to the Memorial Garden sometime. Read the plaques."

Forrest looked down at the polished floor.

"It's peaceful out there in the snow," the Major continued. "But young men leave this serenity and go out there into the world. Young men who lived there in the barracks across the street fought at the Bloody Angle—and in France, and the Philippines, and Normandy, and Okinawa, the central highlands of Vietnam, and on and on and on," he turned his eye to the class, "and on. It's a continuum. You boys are part of it."

The room was silent.

"Major," a cadet asked, "you think some of us will see combat?"

"Oh, yes," the Major said without hesitation. "Some of you will. You will get shot at. You will return fire. You'll have a wonderful time." He made a half-smile.

None of the cadets smiled.

"Where, Major?" the cadet asked.

The major thought for a moment, then shrugged. "The Middle East."

Forrest focused on the long, faint scar down the left side of the Major's face and his lifeless eye.

The Major leaned against his desk with his arms crossed. His eye scanned across the classroom again. "You will find yourself in a third-world hell-hole of a country with dead men on the ground. And there ain't no po-lice-man to call"—his eye bulged with sarcasm. "No, just you and your weapon and your mates. Your team against theirs in a fight to the death, thousands of miles from home. Out on the outer rim of civilization where there are no referees, no police, no rules, no cause, just a savage bloody fight to the death.

"Ready yourselves."

"You won't be fighting the Russians in World War Three. The operations today are more ambiguous, like Vietnam and Korea. The purpose of the operation will be debatable and questioned. The use of force will be based on a judgment call made by a politician. The operation will be discretionary and only arguably important. But for you—on the ground—it's all or nothing, live or die. In Vietnam, we lost 58,000 of our people; and then Uncle Sam just walked away. The War was discretionary for Uncle Sam, but not for the 58,000. They're dead," his eye caught Forrest's, "*finito*."

The Major's eye contact startled Forrest. The warm classroom in the snowy valley seemed far removed from Middle East warfare. But the Major's comments, his scar, and the look in his good eye spoke truth. The Major's words, "you will get shot at, you will return fire," turned slowly inside Forrest's mind.

Forrest glanced down at the gleaming floor and thought back to his boyhood. To the 1960s news, flashing across the black & white TV screen night after night—his dad chain-smoking and yelling at "that goddamned Walter Cronkite." On the grainy screen, Marines in flak jackets ran with a man on a stretcher through saw grass waiving under the rotors of the medevac helicopter. A column of dirt-worn Marines behind an M-48 tank moved into Hue City. Every Friday night, the news showed the weekly death toll posted on a board by the North Vietnamese, Viet Cong, South Vietnamese, and American flags. It seemed there were always 300 or 400 dead VC or NVA to only 50 or 60 American and RVN dead—but somehow, the story line never hit an optimistic note.

Then the seventies spilled out of his TV. Gas lines and riots and hippies and mass demonstrations and the assassinations of Dr. King and Bobby Kennedy. And it all just piled up higher and higher—the TV kept it coming—millions of boat people after Vietnam fell, death camps in Cambodia, and the Iranians taking the U.S. Embassy staff in Tehran hostage. The Russian invasion of Afghanistan and communist operations in Angola and Central America. The pile of it accumulated without resolution, and it seemed there was nothing and nobody to carry any of it away.

Forrest raised his hand. "Sir," he said, "It's hard to imagine the United States using force. Iran *attacked* a US Embassy. We've done nothing about it. The Soviets invaded Afghanistan—we boycotted the Olympics. We just gave up Southeast Asia."

"Well," the Major answered, "history teaches that appeasement and retreat from aggression causes more vigorous aggression. So our enemies will push harder and closer until we act. So we will act, eventually. And one more thing, next month Ronald Reagan will take the oath of office. The world is about to change."

On his way back to barracks after class, Forrest stopped by the edge of the parade field. Flurries fell softly and silently over the Shenandoah Valley. Snow fell on small tree-covered foothills populated by white tail deer and turkey, fields of cows, and the mountain ridges of the Alleghenies to the west and the Blue Ridge to the east. The scene before him was painted in bold strokes—the smooth, yellow-white walls of barracks standing on the edge of the white field under a darkening sky. The bronze figure of "Stonewall" Jackson was on a concrete pedestal in front of the barracks overlooking the parade ground and distant mountains, just as the man had done overlooking battlefields. Forrest looked out across the snowfield and shivered as cold wind blew over his exposed ear lobes.

The professor's phrases turned in his head. "You will get shot at, you will return fire." Standing there in snow at twilight, he felt for the first time in his life the threat *to him*. There were dangerous enemies out there, thousands of miles away. Sooner or later, somebody had to deal with them—"*you* will be shot at, *you* will return fire." Everywhere he looked now, he noticed what had always been there—memorials to young graduates who never aged.

He walked by a bronze statue dedicated to cadets killed in the battle of New Market a hundred and seventeen years earlier. A figure of a woman slumped with grief, draped in Virginia's flag. Behind the statue, stones poking up through the snow marked the graves of cadets killed in the battle. Forrest stood in the snow, looking up at the monument—at the face of a grieving mother. Flakes drifted down, collecting on her head and slumped shoulders. He looked down at the gravestones behind the statue and pondered his professor's words. He turned in the snow and walked back out to the street and then down to the Memorial Garden, an open area bordered on one side by a wall covered by ivy and plaques. Forrest walked into the open, snow plowing around his knees, and stopped. He looked across the wall at dozens of bronze plaques that were hung like antelope heads.

It was quiet. White flakes sparkled against the gray sky.

Forrest realized that each plaque represented a person once young and warm who dreamed of adventure and love. For all of them, the warmth and the dreams and life itself were lost suddenly and violently; some thousands of miles from home. Forrest thought of Whitman's poem, from *Leaves of Grass*:

Look down fair moon and bathe this scene,
Pour softly down night's nimbus floods on faces ghastly,
Swollen, purple,
On the dead on their backs with arms toss'd wide,
Pour down your unstinted nimbus sacred moon…

On battlefields all over the world they had laid dead, some under moonlight, as in the poem. Some fell in dark jungles, others on sunny beaches, but all the same—dead.

Forrest walked slowly along the wall, looking at the names, and the places: France, New Guinea, Algeria, Korea, and Vietnam. He felt dim echoes of battles long over. He could hear faintly in the silence the fights that caused these plaques. In his mind, he smelled the sweat and felt the fear of former cadets in the Central Highlands of Vietnam and on the beach at Normandy. The Major was right, Forrest realized. The artillery and flying dirt and nervous sweaty hands gripping rifle stocks had gone on and on and on. He thought of the Major's words: *good boys, like you, get killed—sometimes for a lost cause.* He looked out across the wall at the flakes filtering down through the trees and thought about that old black and white TV and everything it had dumped into his boyhood. Forrest looked up and saw his professor standing in the window, watching him.

It was getting darker. Flakes sparkled in the light of a streetlamp on the edge of the garden. As the day faded, the parade field transformed from bright white to cold blue, and the far tree line bled into the darkening sky. In the dark, Forrest walked towards the barracks, snow crunching underfoot, still thinking about the professor's words.

Chapter Two

The New York Times
"The Sum of Beirut's Human Misery Goes Beyond the Massacre in the Camps."

September 20, 1982 – "Well over 200 people are known to have died violently in Beirut since Tuesday night, and more than 330 to have been wounded. Hundreds have been widowed, orphaned, or bereaved. Thousands have lost their homes. Hundreds of thousands are living without electricity, drinkable water, gasoline, or the right to travel freely. Countless others are living in fear .... The most widely reported casualties are the 106 bodies counted by a Western diplomat in the Sabra and Shatila refugee camps, most of

*them apparently murdered by right-wing Christian militiamen.
At least 300 refugees are believed to have been killed, according
to reports received by United States officials, but it is believed that
many bodies remain to be counted."*

The Washington Post
"Grenada Promises to Institute Reforms."

*November 19, 1982—"Grenada Prime Minister Maurice Bishop,
bowing to pressure from Caribbean leaders, vowed today to institute at least limited democratic reforms on his leftist island, sources
said."*

The USS BARNSTABLE COUNTY, an amphibious ship, pounded
through ten-foot waves, bound for West Onslo Beach at Camp Lejeune,
North Carolina. Down inside the tank deck, a large hangar space
inside the ship, ten amphibious assault tracked vehicles—LVTP7s or
"amtracs"—were staged with engines running. There were twenty or
more Marines loaded in the troop compartment of each amtrac. Red
tactical lights gave the area a sickening pallor. The ship would pass one
mile off the beach and then lower its stern gate; and one-by-one, the
amtracs would drive out into the ocean. When they were in the ocean
and on-line, they'd assault the beach. It was 04:15.

First Lieutenant Robert Forrest walked through the narrow space
between the amtracs and the tank deck bulkhead, headed for his vehicle,
positioned fourth in line to launch. The area hummed with the sounds
of idling diesel engines, ship fans sucking out exhaust fumes, and the
rattling of equipment as men filed into the troop compartments of the
amtracs. Every few steps, Forrest reached a hand out to steady himself
as the ship rolled. When he reached his amtrac, "Alpha Four-Zero," he
grabbed the built-in ladder hold and climbed up to the machinegun
turret. He stepped up on top and stood for a moment, taking in the
size of the vehicle—fourteen feet high at the turret, twenty-six feet long,

twenty-five tons, and well-muscled up front, like a boar hog. In fact, the Marines sometimes called them "hogs." Each one had a crew of three Marines, and twenty-five more combat loaded Marines fit in the troop compartment. In the ocean, it sat low, with about 90% of its mass underwater; and the diesel engine pushed the vehicle along with jet drives, like a swimming hog with his back above water. The vehicle was designed to ride in from the ship and then drive across the beach and fight as an armored personnel carrier. There was a .50 caliber machinegun mounted in the turret.

The amtrac crews worked through the pre-launch checklist—hull plugs in, pumps working, plenums dogged, stern drive buckets working. The platoon sergeant, Gunnery Sergeant John Coleman, known to all as the Gunny, worked his way from vehicle to vehicle confirming all systems were go. The crews issued gray inflatable life preservers to each Marine embarked on the amtrac, and each crew chief gave a safety briefing.

By the ship's stern ramp, a Navy lieutenant climbed a ladder up to the control room to direct the launch. As he climbed, the ship's movement swung him from side to side. In the control room, he stood behind Plexiglas, looking out over the amtracs staged in a column of twos. He pulled a cassette tape from his pocket and pushed it into a tape player. The sound of electric guitars blasted over speakers in the hangar-like tank deck, obscuring the hum of blowers and idling engines. It was the theme of the newest Rocky movie, "*Eye of the Tiger*." Forrest looked up at the Navy officer and smiled. He should have been a Marine, Forrest thought. He took off his helmet and listened to the music and looked over his ten amtracs. Forrest had been the amtrac platoon leader for over a year and had spent most of that time training in the ocean off Carolina and Virginia and in the pinewoods of Camp Lejeune. Earlier that year, they'd landed with Dutch Marines on Vieques, Puerto Rico, as part of "Ocean Venture 82," a large-scale NATO war game simulating an invasion of a Caribbean island. Forrest assumed the practice was for Cuba. He'd never heard of Grenada.

Forrest looked up at the ready light above the stern ramp of the ship. It was still red. As the ship pitched over a large wave, he felt a shudder work through the ship's hull. The ready light turned yellow—three minutes to launch. The ship's stern ramp slowly lowered, like the gate of a castle dropping over a moat. Forrest focused on the black sky and watched it grow bigger as the stern gate lowered. Sea air spilling into the tank deck was cold and salty. He put his comm helmet (tank and amtrac crews wore "cvc"—"crew vehicle communications"—helmets, but called them "comm helmets") on and stepped inside the turret hatch and lowered himself down inside. Once seated, he put on his wool-lined leather gloves and stretched out his fingers. He closed the hatch and twisted the handle to lock it. He flipped a switch on his control panel to turn off the red turret light. Sealed in darkness, Forrest leaned his head back, closed his eyes, and felt the amtrac's engine idling and his own weight shifting as the ship pitched and rolled.

Forrest pulled up on a handle under his spring-loaded turret seat, lowered down to the bottom of the turret, and stuck his head down inside the troop compartment below and behind the turret. The amtrac's third crewman, PFC Shields, was sitting on the jump seat at the stern, illuminated by a red tactical light. The dim red glow barely penetrated the pungent air. Twenty Marines were crammed-in, shoulder-to-shoulder in inflatable gray life jackets, flak jackets, and steel combat helmets. Each man held an M-16 rifle between his legs. The experienced men sat with eyes closed, as though sleeping. The boots' eyes darted nervously.

Out in the tank deck, the green ready light came on. A Navy officer posted by the stern ramp banged on four-one's hull with a ball peen hammer. Four-one's driver pushed the gas pedal to the floor and the vehicle surged forward and shot out onto the stern ramp, dropped to the ocean at a 45-degree angle, and then splashed nose-first into the ocean, its momentum taking it temporarily underwater before it popped up and motored away from the ship. Then each of the other amtracs rolled forward a spot. When Forrest's amtrac rolled forward, he swung back up into his turret and raised his seat. Through narrow slits of bulletproof glass, he could see the ship's bulkhead moving by slowly. In less than a minute, four-zero was at the top of the ramp. Forrest braced himself by holding his hands against the azimuth ring along the front of the turret. Goode, the driver, floored four-zero, and its 400-horse Detroit Diesel came to life. Forrest felt the vehicle accelerate and then drop, flume-like, to the ocean. He felt himself dropping, then braced himself against the splash. The amtrac dove into the ocean, its nose dipped underwater, and Forrest looked up and saw water running over the bulletproof glass around the top of the turret. After the water drained, he popped the hatch and stood up on his seat, head and shoulders out in morning air. It was still completely dark.

A wave broke over the top of the amtrac, soaking Forrest and piling up foam around the turret. He licked his lips and tasted salt and then looked up at the overcast sky. The vehicle surged over a large capping swell and then slid down in the trough between towering waves.

Down in the troop compartment, each man felt his center of gravity shifting, like a fly buzzing around inside his ribcage. Seawater pouring in from the open turret hatch collected at their feet and sloshed around with the surging and pitching movement of the amtrac. They heard the diesel engine straining and smelled its fumes. After the first man threw-up, the odor of vomit mixed with the diesel smell, and Marines leaned forward one or two at a time, making sure to spew into the water at their feet. Their vomit splashed down into water and was sucked eventually down through holes in the floorboards to bilge pumps. The third crewman, PFC Shields, put on his gas mask, which he plugged into the vehicle's filtered clean air supply.

Forrest spotted beach center, which was marked by a strobe light, and he saw they'd been dropped too far south. He turned in his turret and looked back at the ship, which was now just a black shape in the night. It started sleeting. Little ice specks bounced off the metal surface of the turret and along the top of the amtrac. Forrest dropped down in his turret for warmth; he heard a man down below belching.

The last vehicle to splash was the Gunny's, four-nine. He'd been with Forrest since his first day with the platoon fourteen months earlier, and now his raspy voice crackled into Forrest's earpiece—which was in the ear flap of his comm helmet—"Four-zero, nine's wet, over."

Forrest stood up in the turret. All ten amtracs were now in a column stretching out behind the ship. Forrest pulled his helmet-mounted microphone to his mouth and ordered a right flank. All ten amtracs turned in the ocean to face the beach with plumes of white foam boiled from the jet drives. The amtracs headed for the beach on line at full speed, which was about eight knots. Forrest looked to his left and saw in the dim light four amtracs on line, piling up water in front of square bows with foamy water boiling from their jet drives and sheets of sleet angling down. To his right, the other five amtracs were on line. Forrest pulled his microphone to his mouth and keyed the net. "This is four-zero. Make four degrees to the right for beach center, out." The amtrac noses all veered slightly to the right.

Everything went smoothly for the next four minutes. With the new course, four-zero's turret and driver's hatch were no longer sucking down seawater. Forrest keyed his internal vehicle intercom and pulled the microphone to his mouth. "How're the helmet-heads, Shields?"

Shields's voice crackled back clearly through the microphone affixed inside his gas mask. "I think they're done, sir. They still heaving, but they on empty."

Forrest relaxed a little. The sleet stopped.

Then, in his earpiece, he heard: "Four-zero, four-seven, over."

Forrest pulled his microphone to his mouth. "Go seven."

"We've lost power, over." Four-seven was powerless and drifting with its side to the waves. The Gunny's amtrac moved in to tow four-seven to the beach.

Closer to shore, the amtracs still in the assault closed on the beach. In the surf zone, wind-driven waves grew as they rolled over shallowing water. In the dim light of an overcast dawn, Forrest saw the foam-streaked backside of the waves with spray blowing off their crests and white explosions of seawater on the beach. He looked to his left and right.

The eight amtracs still in the assault were more or less on line just outside the surf zone.

Forrest dropped down inside his turret, closed and dogged the hatch, then braced himself. Four-zero rode up the back of a cresting wave, then slid back as the next wave pulled from behind. When the next wave caught the amtrac's buoyancy, four-zero lurched forward, accelerating nose down, like a 26-ton surfboard. The tracks hit sand, stopped, bounced, and then stopped again. The wave surged over and crashed on the beach. Forrest popped his hatch and stood up in the turret. The driver, Lance Corporal Goode, engaged the tracks and pushed the power pedal to the floor. As the wave's water fell back to the ocean, four-zero roared out of the surf zone and gathered speed as it pulled free of the ocean. Eight amtracs crossed the beach on line, stopped at the dune line, and dropped the troop ramps. The infantry piled out and moved into an assault on the pine thickets on the other side of the dunes. Forrest sat in his seat, wet and cold. He let out a long breath. Then he grabbed the turret handle grip and spun the turret 180 degrees. He stood in the turret and watched four-nine towing four-seven in through the surf.

The Gunny made it look easy. He got four-seven up on the edge of the beach and stopped before the rope broke. Between waves, two Marines from four-nine waded out and shackled a steel cable between the vehicles, careful not to get crushed when a wave pushed four-seven forward. Once the cable was in place, four-nine towed four-seven up onto the beach. Forrest took off his helmet and rubbed his hands over his face. He climbed down into the troop compartment, where PFC Shields was inspecting the floorboards for vomit.

"Looks pretty clean," Forrest said.

"Yes, sir," replied Shields, "ocean water scours pretty good."

Forrest paused and looked out the open back-end of four-zero. In dim morning light, the ocean was slate gray with white caps. It was sleeting again. Forrest breathed in the cool sea air and for a moment did not feel cold. Then he stepped outside into the wind and shivered. He walked over to the place in the dunes where the infantry company was staging for "cattle cars" (large trucks that carried troops) that would take them back to Camp Geiger. Forrest saluted the grunt captain, wished him a pleasant weekend, and then stood on the sand behind a high dune that blocked the wind as the infantry filed away.

Forrest walked out to the edge of surf. The Gunny walked up and spit a wad of brown juice onto the sand. The Gunny was "old school" Marine Corps. He had three combat tours in Vietnam, all with amtrac platoons. He was just less than six feet tall and weighed about 175 pounds. He was nearly bald, and his voice was scarred by a lifetime of yelling. His light-colored eyes were set evenly in his sunbaked face. In the field, he seemed always to have a wad of chew stuffed behind his right cheek. When "in the rear," he never chewed tobacco and wore starched utilities and highly shined boots.

"What's the story on four-seven, Gunny?"

"Generator again."

"Didn't we put a new one in last month?"

"Yessir."

Forrest and the Gunny turned and walked back along the edge of the surf.

"Happy's gonna be pissed," Forrest said.

"Yessir. He's always pissed."

"Must've been a bad generator," Forrest said as he watched a line of Scoters fly along the top edge of a wave building in the surf.

"Well, LT …could be."

"What else?

"Apricots."

Forrest looked back, smiled, and let out a muffled laughed.

"No shit LT. I caught Corporal Wood eating apricots on four-seven yesterday morning on the beach up in Virginia. I chewed his ass. Crew chief should know better."

Forrest stopped. "You believe what they say about apricots?"

"I believe in playing it safe."

"You shit'n me, Gunny?"

"No, sir." The Gunny studied Forrest's face for a second, wondering if he really didn't get it. Then the Gunny explained: "We had this First Sergeant in Vietnam, First Sergeant Adams. He was Old Corps, salty as hell. Served in China. First wave at Tarawa. Inchon. He was in his second tour in 'Nam in '69." The Gunny spit tobacco juice. "I had to go see him about something. Don't remember what. I walked into the CP tent. He's sitt'n there eat'n apricots out of a C-rat can. *Holy shit!* I says to myself. The First Sergeant, of all people, eating apricots." The Gunny looked over at Forrest. "Can you believe that, LT? Anyway, I said, 'First Sergeant, ain't that bad luck, eat'n apricots?' The First Sergeant looked at me, spoon full of apricots in his mouth and a nasty snarl, and he says, 'Coleman, you stupid motherfucker' — he was the graphic type—'I thought you could smell good enough to detect a steaming pile of horse shit heaped in front of your face.'" The Gunny chuckled. "The man was a poet. Anyway, the First Sergeant went back to eating those apricots."

The Gunny paused and spit again.

"Okay, Gunny," Forrest said, "so what?"

"That night, he got killed when a rocket hit his hooch."

Forrest paused, took off his combat helmet, and scratched his head. "You think the apricots gave him bad luck?"

"Don't know, LT. But there's such a thing as bad luck. Can't deny that. First Sergeant went through Tarawa and Inchon. He'd been in Vietnam for nearly two years. He never got a scratch in all that combat. Then he ate a can of apricots and got killed in his hooch."

"Well," Forrest said, "how do you know he hadn't been eating apricots for all those years? He probably ate apricots on Tarawa. He'd never have made it ashore at Inchon without a dose of apricots for good luck. Could be those apricots got him as far as he got."

"All I know is what I saw, LT. Sometimes a guy gets killed 'cause he's doing something stupid ... out alone where he shouldn't be, or not wearing his helmet, or being reckless. But sometimes a fella does everything right and still gets killed right off. Just bad luck. I don't know what causes bad luck. Do you, Lieutenant?" The Gunny looked up. Sleet specs bounced off his helmet like dancing albino gnats.

"Well…"

The Gunny interrupted. "What the hell, LT? I can live without apricots. I don't even know what a fucking apricot is. Now, if it was *apples* at issue, that'd be different. I love apples. I might live dangerously for an apple. But for apricots?" He spit again. "I figure if there is one chance in a zillion that apricots are bad luck, why fuck with 'em?"

Forrest nodded. "It's hard to argue with your logic, Gunny."

The Gunny studied Forrest's expression, gauging whether he understood.

"Okay, Gunny, let's go home."

Forrest smiled to himself as he turned away from the surf. He walked to four-zero, climbed into his turret and put on his comm helmet. Then he looked up and paused, scanning from the surf across the sloping beach to high dunes covered with sea oats against a slate colored sky. Sleet slanted down and collected in white piles along the lower edge of the dunes. The First Marine Division set up a tent camp there in September 1941 where they trained for Guadalcanal; and by 1983, the base covered 244 square miles. Forrest breathed the good-smelling air and thought how this cold and empty beach would never be on a Marine Corps Recruiting poster, but it was an inner sanctum of the Marine Corps.

Forrest nodded to his driver. Lance Corporal Goode backed four-zero away from the dune slowly so it wouldn't throw a track. Then Goode stopped, shifted into first gear, and pushed the accelerator pedal to the floor. The flapper on the exhaust stack just aft of the turret shot straight up, and black smoke plumed up. The engine screamed, and four-zero's 26 tons lurched forward. Goode drove four-zero down to the edge of the surf zone where the sand was hard-packed and fast. The other amtracs fell into a staggered column behind four-zero, weaving across the open beach down to the edge of the surf—except four-nine, which moved along at a steady pace with four-seven in tow.

The ground vibrated under two hundred tons of screaming steel and homogeneous aluminum on spinning tracks and wheels, throwing up sand, pounding the beach. Forrest sat up in his turret, fourteen feet up and looked ahead at miles of empty beach and dunes. The ocean was on his left and steep dunes to his right. Forrest looked back at the other amtracs of his platoon running the edge of the surf, the engines screaming and tracks pounding and throwing up water. Smiling, he leaned back in the turret and thought how fine it was to be an amtrac platoon leader in the United States Marine Corps.

Twenty minutes after the column turned off the beach, four-zero popped out of the tank trail on the far end of a field next to the concrete ramp. The ten amtracs slowed to a walk, and ground guides brought them onto the ramp, which was a slab of concrete about the size of a small airport. It was home to the 185 amtracs of the Second Assault Amphibian Battalion, Second Marine Division. When all ten amtracs, including the disabled four-seven, were lined up evenly in their assigned area, Forrest walked into the maintenance shed to see Chief Warrant Officer "Happy" Hernandez (warrant officers were called "Gunners")—one of the best (and meanest) maintenance officers in the Corps.

Forrest walked through the maintenance shed to the door that opened to the "A" Company maintenance office. He stepped in and immediately appreciated the heated space. Happy sat at his desk, looking down at forms, scribbling. The walls of the small office were covered with cheap brown paneling. By the door hung a framed black and white picture of Hernandez taken in 1967. It showed a twenty-year-old corporal with a high and tight and a narrow, neatly trimmed mustache in a green t-shirt, holding an M-16 and standing by the six-by-six supply truck he drove. There were two bullet holes in the hood of the truck, visible over his right shoulder. The photo showed that Happy's sneer dated back at least to Danang in '67.

"I hear you fucked-up one of *my* amtracs, Lieu-ten-ant." Forrest outranked the Gunner, at least technically; but Happy hated lieutenants, and for him, most military courtesies were reserved for captains and higher ranks.

"Lost a generator, Gunner."

Happy kept scribbling and said nothing for a long minute. Forrest stood in silence, hearing only the sound of Happy's pencil scratching. Then Happy slapped his pencil down and looked up. "You think I don't know that?" His eyes were squeezed down to slits, his top lip pulled tight over his teeth. Forrest had already learned that as far as Happy was concerned, breaking one of "his" amtracs was like shitting in his hat. "How the fuck did you blow a brand fucking new generator? You know what those fuck'n things cost?"

"No, Gunner."

"Two-thousand-five-hundred-fucking-dollars, Lieu-ten-ant."

"Must've been something wrong with it."

"Yeah, my ass, Lieutenant. My fucking ass!" Happy blamed the platoon leader for every breakdown, no matter the cause.

Happy looked back at his papers and started writing again.

"Well, there was one thing, Gunner," Forrest said.

Happy stopped writing, leaned back in his chair, and crossed his arms. "Yeeaaaah?"

"Crew chief ate some apricots," Forrest said seriously.

Happy's eyes widened. The wound-up rubber band that powered this little man was twisting tighter, knotting and double knotting. His pupils vibrated. His face reddened more. Then he seemed to double-up his grip on himself and calmed a hair. "Don't fuck with me, Lieutenant."

"Okay, Gunner," Forrest said.

"I'll get another generator in next week. 'Till then, four-seven's dead-lined." Happy turned back to his paperwork. "Gunner."

"Yeeaaaah." He answered without looking up.

"When was the last time you smiled?"

"Get the fuck out of my hooch, Lieutenant."

...

Forrest dismissed the platoon at 16:30. and headed for his truck. By that time, the sleet had turned to snow and was starting to stick. He walked across the ramp, passing rows of amtracs parked side-by-side. He thought about the breakdown that morning in the ocean, wondering if there was something to the Gunny's apricot phobia. He threw his pack in the back of his F-150 and climbed behind the wheel, still damp from the landing. He started the engine and then turned on the heat and the radio. Bonnie Tyler's "Total Eclipse of the Heart" was playing. As the truck warmed, he pulled out onto the road and headed for the back gate of Marine Corps Base, Camp Lejeune.

Forrest slowed as he passed through the gate. The Marine sentry stood at attention and delivered a crisp salute. Forrest returned the salute and then accelerated down the road towards the shrimp docks at Snead's Ferry. He crossed the Snead's Ferry Bridge, passing a wooden shrimp trawler tied to the dock off to his right, then drove down the long stretch of road through loblolly pines toward the bridge to Topsail Island.

Topsail, a barrier island, stretched along twenty miles of oceanfront south of Camp Lejeune. One-story flat-roofed cinderblock houses and trailers were clustered along the two-lane road. Between houses and trailer parks, there were stands of sea oats and scrub pine. Forrest and another amtrac lieutenant, Ed Kirby, lived in one of the cinderblock houses on the ocean side of the road. More a live-in garage than a house, the place had no insulation, was heated by space heaters, and the floors were covered with outdoor carpet. The furniture was junk.

Forrest pulled up in the snow-covered sand in front of the house and parked. He walked in the house, dropped his pack, and headed for the liquor cabinet. He filled a plastic cup with ice and added a slug of Jack Daniels. Then he turned up the space heater and sat on the sofa and propped his damp boots up on the flea-market coffee table. He took a sip and swished it around his mouth, savoring it. Clean, dry clothes would feel good, he thought. But he was tired, and the Jack Daniels burned good and he sat in his damp utilities sipping. A moment later, Kirby pulled up.

Ed Kirby grew up on a farm in Tennessee, spoke with a distinctive drawl, and had gone to Vanderbilt and double majored in biology and chemistry. He planned to go medical school after his three-year commitment to the Corps, and he hoped to get the Navy to pay for it. Forrest and Kirby met at Amtrac School in California, and they were platoon leaders in the same company.

The screen door screeched. Kirby walked in and stomped snow off his boots. Forrest looked by Kirby at the snow falling outside drifting down through street lamplight. The snowfall made even their little cinderblock hut seem warm and cozy.

"Robert, I hear your platoon fucked up in the ocean today."

Forrest rolled his eyes.

Kirby flopped on the sofa and put his boots up on the coffee table. "Your boys been eat'n apricots?"

"Where'd you hear that?"

Kirby shrugged. "I don't fuck with apricots. And I haven't had a breakdown in the ocean—*ever*."

Forrest took a sip.

"I'm just concerned about your safety, Robert," said Kirby. "You eat apricots in Beirut, and some raghead's gonna put a bullet in your head or cut your nuts off or some other nasty shit."

Forrest closed his eyes, smelled his whisky, and then took another sip.

"So stay away from the apricots," Kirby said as he stood and headed for the bottle. "By the way, the Atwells are meeting us at the Pirate's Den for dinner in about thirty minutes."

The Pirate's Den was a restaurant directly across the street in a one-story windowless blockhouse. Its beige paint harmonized with the color of the dunes and brown grasses sticking up through the snow around the restaurant. Inside, there were booths along one wall and tables in the middle covered with red and white-checkered plastic tablecloths.

A Pac-man video game sat in a dark corner. It was well heated.

When Forrest and Kirby walked in, Larry and Cathy Atwell were sitting at a candlelit table, halfway through their first beers. Cathy looked up with blue eyes. Her long auburn hair caught the candlelight. She wore blue jeans with a starched white blouse, unbuttoned just enough to be tasteful and tempting at the same time. Her husband, "Larry the Lifer," stood and shook hands with Forrest and Kirby. He gestured to two Jacks on ice at their respective places at the table.

Larry and Cathy were both from Wisconsin, and they'd met at the University of Wisconsin, where Larry was on a Marine Corps Scholarship and enrolled in the Naval ROTC program. Larry planned to make a career in the Marines, which is why Forrest and Kirby called him "Larry the Lifer."

Forrest took a seat. He wore khaki trousers, a white cotton shirt, and a black wool sweater. Feeling clean and warm and dry, he looked down at the cold, caramel-colored liquor in a glass of ice cubes, and he was happy. He picked up his glass, raised it, and smelled the liquor.

"Your boys been eat'n apricots, Robert?" asked Larry.

"Who told you that?"

"When a tread-head eats apricots, it throws the Universe out of balance," said Larry. "Every tread-head on Earth felt it. An amtracer in Okinawa probably fell out of his bunk or woke up babbling in a cold sweat. You know," Larry said, "there's an *Andy Griffith* episode on this point."

"What point?" Forrest asked.

"Bad luck. You know the episode where Barney has to qualify with his pistol, but his confidence is shot because of all the unlucky stuff that happened after he trashed a chain letter?"

"What's with you and *Andy Griffith*?" asked Kirby.

"You don't like *Andy*?" responded Larry.

"I like the show, but it's not a holy canon," said Kirby.

"Only the black and white episodes hold special wisdom; the color episodes are apocryphal, like the Gnostic gospels," said Larry.

"Physicist, mathematicians, and philosophers all search for one unifying principle—one principle that explains everything else." Larry sipped his beer and looked around the table, smiling. "I've found the one thing."

"*The Andy Griffith Show?*" asked Forrest.

Larry nodded, smiling. "Now, like all scientific theories, it can be tested. Give me a life situation, and I'll tell you which episode speaks to the point."

"How about my love life?" asked Forrest.

"Well," said Larry, "that's easy, any episode with Goober."

They all laughed.

"Larry, tell Robert and Ed your big news," Cathy said.

Larry held his hands around his beer glass on the table, focusing on the beer. "Lost my platoon today."

Forrest and Kirby said nothing. They'd already heard the news but acted like they were just hearing it for the first time.

"I've been assigned to the MAU (Marine Amphibious Unit) staff, headed for Beirut next October with two-eight (Second Battalion, Eighth Marines)."

"Congratulations, Larry," Kirby said. Kirby's platoon was slated to ship out for Beirut in April with First Battalion, Eighth Marines, and part of the 21st Marine Amphibious Unit. Forrest would ship out with Larry the following October.

"That's great, Larry. You'll be with me," said Forrest.

"I'd rather have a platoon," Larry said. "But better to be a staff weenie than not go at all, I guess."

Cathy Atwell perceived excitement in the all three Marine officers, mostly in their eyes and stupid grins. She was annoyed that her husband and the other two never acknowledged the danger posed by Beirut. She finally said, "I think it's going to be a shit–show over there. Marines are going to die, and nothing is going to be accomplished by it."

The three Marines stopped talking and just looked at Cathy.

Forrest thought she was probably right, but he'd never say that out loud. It was bad form for a Marine to complain about getting killed. When he was a kid, he'd sometimes talk too much; and his Old Man, a retired Marine, would say he sounded like a second lieutenant, which Forrest knew meant "nit-wit" (Forrest made of point of keeping his mouth shut as much as possible until he'd been promoted to First Lieutenant several months earlier, and he was still cautious with his mouth). Forrest thought that Cathy could not possibly expect them to engage in a serious discussion of the issue she raised. Forrest and the others spent hours together training on the tank trails and beaches of Camp Lejeune and on amphibious ships down from Little Creek, but they never talked about getting killed or whether their deaths would mean anything. That kind of talk just ruined everybody's fun. Talking about *The Andy Griffith Show* was much better.

"Well, Larry," said Forrest, "if I get sick or something, you can have the platoon."

Cathy looked down into her beer. After a moment, she looked up at Forrest. "You still getting out and going to law school?"

He nodded yes. Forrest's Beirut deployment would go from October 1983 to May 1984. His three-year commitment would expire a month later. He planned to take the LSAT and apply for admission for the fall of 1984.

"Where you applying?"

Forrest shrugged. "Virginia schools."

After dinner, the Atwells headed home, and Kirby and Forrest stepped out into the night and stood for a moment under a streetlight. The cold penetrated their faces, and they could see their breath. After making drinks, the two of them walked to a wood deck built atop the dunes that overlooked the ocean. As they sat on the cold wood bench sipping their drinks, freezing wind off the ocean hit their faces and made their eyes feel like snow balls.

"You sure about getting out?" asked Kirby.

Forrest took a sip and thought about his answer for several seconds. "Well, I love it here. I love the ocean and this beach and the pinewoods up along this coast and the troops and the amtracs and the ships and being outside all the time. I even like Happy."

Kirby hooted out a laugh. "Don't go too far, now."

Forrest continued. "My old man loved the Corps, too. While he was in Vietnam, Americans back here were flying commie flags and burning our flag. Jane Fonda went on a morale-building visit to the troops at the front ... but not *our* troops. You've seen the pictures of her posing with North Vietnamese gun crews. I read in the paper the other day that somebody did a survey that found that Jane Fonda is one of the most admired women in America.

"When we gave up and lost the War, that literally killed my father. He drank himself to death after that. One reason I'm here is that I wanted to make him proud. But he always thought that the country betrayed those Marines he knew and saw killed, and that disloyalty broke him. So even though I love the Corps, after Beirut, I'm getting out and going to law school. The longer you stick around, the more chance of getting killed. While I don't mind getting killed so much—we're all dying sometime—I hate the idea of getting killed for a country that admires Jane Fonda."

"Nobody in Tennessee admires Jane Fonda," said Kirby.

"How about you, Ed? Any chance you'll stay in?"

"Naahh. I love it here, too; but after three years, they'll ship me off to some non-fleet billet somewhere, recruiting officer or such. I'd go from leading a front-line combat platoon of United States Marines to a government bureaucrat doing the most boring job imaginable. I think I'll try to cure cancer instead."

Kirby called it a night and headed back to the house.

Forrest stayed in the cold alone and could not avoid thinking of his former girlfriend. As he sat sipping, the whisky amplified his loneliness. Within a couple weeks of his volunteering for Beirut, she'd ditched him. He still thought of her every day. He thought of her now as he sipped Jack Daniels and stared out at the frozen night. He thought of her smile and her smooth, fragrant warmth and the glow of her skin in summer light, the smell of her, the feel of her blond hair, and her smooth skin in the warm bed. The memory hurt. He had thought his feelings for her meant something. But he was wrong, he realized. It had all been just an arms' length transaction. She was looking for the best deal she could get. As soon as she found one that suited her better, she was done—with a cold snap of her fingers. He couldn't fault her, though, figuring he'd have done the same thing. There was no injustice in it. It was just tough shit, that's all. Forrest slipped into self-pity as Jack Daniels pumped through his veins. He spiraled down farther, thinking how she crushed him. He slurred out loud a poem popular in the Marines:

A yellow bird
With a yellow bill
Was sitting on my window sill
I lured him in
With a piece of bread
And then I crushed his fucking head.

He smiled with numb lips and looked up at the black sky. The poem captured the essence of his love life, he thought. Then his smile faded as he looked around, absorbing the fullness of his isolation in the empty night.

Chapter Three

New York Times

"Grenadians Anxious Over New Influence of Soviet and Cuba."

August 7, 1983—"Public support for the Government of Prime Minister Maurice Bishop, who seized power in a coup four years ago, is diminishing rapidly as Cuban and Soviet influence here grows, according to many Grenadians."

The island nation of Grenada is two thousand miles southeast of Camp Lejeune. Grenada was an English colony until granted independence in 1974. Five years later, armed communist militia of the New Jewel Movement took power, suspended the constitution, and established a People's Revolutionary Government, headed by Maurice Bishop, who declared himself Prime Minister.

On the morning of August 26, 1983, Members of the Central Committee of the New Jewel Movement gathered at Government House at St. George's, the capital city. The purpose of the meeting was to address the increasing split between hardline Marxist-Leninist who believed in stringent government control of every aspect of the economy and moderates who believed in limited economic freedom. By 07:50, eleven members were present. Only Phyllis Coard was missing, due to illness. At the meeting, one of the members reported the findings of an internal report addressing the nation's poor economic performance under communism. The report focused on "growing unrest in the Party and in the masses." The Central Committee itself had "reached a number of conclusions about our progress that are not correct." Some Central Committee comrades were "not functioning properly," and the Party was "in a state of rut or are performing in a weak manner." East German and Cuban advisors advised that the Grenadians' "state of work is bad." Foreshadowing events to come, the report indicated that the Peoples' Revolutionary Army thought "the level of party guidance" was inadequate. After this report, General Hudson Austin stated, "My concern is great. The lesson of Poland showed that when the revolution was in danger and there was chaos in the party and in society, it was only the armed forces that were able to rescue the situation."

...

At 01:00 the following morning, a Peoples' Revolutionary Army lieutenant walked alone up the hill to Fort Rupert. As he approached the fort, he looked up at the billboard, blue and silver in moonlight and inscribed with "POLITICS DISCIPLINE COMBAT READINESS EQUALS VICTORY." His black eyes fell away from the words, shifting to the front gate. He flashed his military ID card to the guard and entered the fort. The French had named it Fort Royal. When the Brits took over in 1763, they renamed it Fort George, for George III—the same King who lost America. In 1979, Maurice Bishop renamed the fort for his father, Rupert.

A man waited under a light by the blockhouse inside the fort. He wore khaki slacks and a brown polyester shirt, wet with sweat and matted to his well-developed chest and shoulders.

"Lieutenant."

"Yes. You are?"

"Dey call me Meat."

The lieutenant nodded.

"Follow me."

Meat opened a thick door and stepped into a dimly lit corridor. As they walked, the sound of their steps echoed off stone walls. A water hose ran along the floor, and little pools of water had formed at the hose section connections. The lieutenant stepped over a puddle and then came to an open doorway. Meat walked in first. The lieutenant stopped in the doorway and looked in.

In the middle of the room sat a man cuffed to a chair under a plume of light dropped from a tin-hat fixture above. White light fell across the man, highlighting his bold features. Light reflected off his sweaty bald head and there was a dollop of yellow-white on top of his head, directly under the light bulb. The upper ridge of his brow and the bridge of his wide nose were lit brownish-white. The recesses of his face, around the eyes under his brow and below his wide nose and chiseled lips, were dark brownish-black. The man's eyes were visible as blinking glints. A cloth gag pulled tight at the corners of his mouth stretched his lips tight. His muscled chest, caramel colored, cast a dark shadow across his stomach. Water mixed with blood dripped rhythmically from him onto the bare stone floor.

A fat white man in sweatpants and a t-shirt moved out to the edge of the light, a cigar between his teeth. The man's face was white as paper, zitty and translucent, and stood out like a clown's face. Cigar smoke rose in lazy curves in the light, mingling with floating lint and the smell of sweat. The white man held the squirt-handle of the hose. The lieutenant wondered if the white man was East German, but he'd never seen a fat East German before.

Back in the corner stood two figures in the dark.

The man cuffed to the chair looked up at the lieutenant. The two stared at each other for several seconds, until the fat man squirted the cuffed man in the face. Meat stood in front of the man cuffed to the chair and began slowly wrapping electrical tape around his hand and over his knuckles.

"What'd he do?" the lieutenant asked. "It not what he do, it what he is," Meat answered. "He booooggggwaaa. Own a farm. Big profit man. Big mouth, too."

The lieutenant looked over at the cuffed man. He seemed well composed, under the circumstances. "He's a farmer?"

"He might be something else, too," Meat answered. "Give heem another squirt, Heavy."

The fat man sprayed water into the cuffed man's face. The man lowered his chin and leaned into the water, trying to keep it out of his eyes and mouth.

The lieutenant noticed Meat's glee as he wrapped the black tape. He glanced at a blood stain on the stone wall under the light, smelled sweat and stale smoke, and heard the man in the chair breathing through his nose in long, heavy draws. A voice in him screamed – *get away. Run.* But he held his place on the stone floor. The lieutenant told himself over and over again – *be ruthless...be ruthless... be ruthless. Somebody must do this thing—for the good of the workers. Must be disciplined. Focused. Proletarian.*

Whack! Meat slapped him across the face. *Whack! Whack!*

The man in the chair grimaced through the gag and squeezed his eyes shut.

The lieutenant wanted to look away, but he didn't.

Another man stepped forward into the light and held out a pair of leather gloves. The lieutenant wanted to run but didn't show it.

He held his hands together, awkwardly, with his right forefinger and thumb gripping and twisting his wedding band on his left ring finger. He looked at Meat. Meat nodded. "All de comrades must share in dis. We all must have blood on our hands."

Meat hit the man in the nose. Blood gushed from his nose, soaking into the gag and oozing down over his chin in a gooey mix of blood and snot. The man's head was back now, his face tilted up to the light. The blood glistened over his black skin like wet paint. Meat giggled.

The lieutenant looked over at Meat. "Enjoying yourself?" Meat looked down at the bleeding man, and then answered. "Do'n good make me happy."

"Rooster, get the gun," Meat said.

"Lieutenant, I was told you gonna hep us," Meat said.

Panic and dread flashed through the lieutenant. He felt a surge of nausea.

The man in the chair was looking up now, his eyes like yellow saucers, his black pupils fixed on an empty corner. The lieutenant walked over and stood directly in front of the man. In his mind he replayed over and over Lenin's words – *be ruthless, be ruthless, be ruthless*. Meat walked up close to the lieutenant and said softly, "Nobody say dis easy. It haaaarrrd—take a disciplined focused man. A proletarian man. Unlike our boooogwaa friend here." He gestured to the man in the chair.

Rooster walked back into the room carrying an AK-47. The victim's eyes snatched into focus as the rifle was toted in front of him. There was a glimmer of fear, then he focused on floating dust in the light, and his eyes lapsed back to resignation.

"If you hit him hard on de high ridge of his left cheek bone, you'll make blood Lieutenant," Meat said. "Dat all. Draw blood. We do de rest."

The lieutenant put on the gloves. He pushed his left foot forward, balled his right fist tightly, then drew back and followed through with a right hook into the man's face. The man's head snapped back. The lieutenant stepped back, grimacing. He held out his right hand, palm down, and looked down at blood on his gloved knuckles.

Rooster stepped forward. Without hesitation, he hit the man hard in the ribs with the butt of the AK-47. The wood rifle stock hit solidly with a thud. The man's eyes bulged, and he opened his mouth wide, gasping but unable to breath. Then Rooster drew the rifle back again and hit the man in the same spot. The man screamed silently. Meat giggled.

Meat stepped forward and leaned into the bound man's face. "We know you part of de plot. We know you were in on de bombing. Who in dis wit you?"

The lieutenant was not aware of a bombing.

The fat white man stepped forward into the light. He was holding a device with a handle and a probe. There was an electrical cable running back into the darkness. The end of the probe glowed yellow-hot. The lieutenant's gut twisted another knot. Meat picked up the hose and squirted the man in the chair in the face, then all over. Then he stopped. All was quiet, except the sounds of the man trying to breath and drops plopping into the puddle below the chair. The man's eyes fixed on a tiny dust particle floating in the light.

Meat said, "Give me two names," and then slapped the man's face. "Look at me, dog!" The man looked up at Meat's eyes, refusing to glance at the yellow hot rod glowing off to his left.

"Two names. Dat all. Dis be over. Two names, or Heavy burn you." A broad yellow grin grew across Heavy's pasty face. In that light, Heavy's zits glowed like blue dots on his clown face.

Meat nodded. Heavy smiled, excitement glistening across his monster's face. He waddled over and laid the rod down on the man's exposed wet arm. The man trumpeted, a high-pitched scream through clinched teeth and the bloody gag. White, stinky smoke rose from the burn. After two long seconds—*one thousand one…one thousand two*—Meat reached out his left hand and pushed Heavy back. Heavy's smile faded to a scowl.

"Don't make 'm pass out," Meat said.

Heavy understood, nodded, then smiled again.

The lieutenant hadn't known that many white people. There were the Russians and East Germans, who'd been as humorless as they were colorless. The lieutenant could not remember ever seeing a white person smile. And here was this fat white man smiling through the smoke of burned flesh. Finally, the lieutenant thought, he knew what made white people smile. He looked down at Heavy's belly hanging below his t-shirt, white and hairy. Swaying in the soft light.

Meat spoke in a whisper. "See, Lieutenant, he like a caterpillar. We make him crawl out along the sharp edge of a razor blade—but slooow. We want heem cut, not split. Suffer, but awake." Meat snorted a laugh. "We push the pain 'till he almost pass, den back off. Dat way he suffer more. Dis an art." As he spoke, he kept his eyes on the man in the chair. Smoke rose from the man's arm.

"Where did you learn to torture people?" the lieutenant asked in whisper.

"We not thugs. We intelligence agents."

"Okay. Where did you learn your ...methods?"

"Fraternal brothers, dat all you need know."

There was a hiss of searing meat. A muffled, pathetic scream. Spit and blood spewed out into the light, droplets catching bulb-light as they arced out over the dirty floor and a sick putrid smell filled the room. Heavy pulled the smoking probe away from the man's right arm. The man lost consciousness, his head dropping to his chest. Meat picked up the hose and squirted the man in the head. The man woke. He lifted his head, grimacing. Smoke rose from both arms.

"Two names, comrade. Two names. Dat all."

The man closed his eyes.

"I don't get two names from you, I have Heavy here impale you wid dat rod."

The man's eye's opened wide.

"Two names?"

The man squeezed his eyes shut.

Meat was lean and sweaty. His pupils were lifeless as stones, and his face revealed an absence of feeling. He fixed the lieutenant in an inhuman stare. The room was silent except for heavy breathing from the man in the chair and water droplets plopping. Meat shifted his gaze to Rooster and nodded. Rooster walked over into the dark corner of the room and re-emerged holding a meat hook on the end of a chain. He walked up behind the chair and put the hook under the handcuff chain. Then he walked back into the darkness and all except the man in the chair stood quietly listening to the sound of the hand-crank clicking. The man's arms lifted behind him. He then lifted himself with his legs as best he could until he was standing on tiptoes with his burned arms bunched up behind him.

"I can't watch this," the lieutenant said.

Meat turned and looked at him. He nodded to the open doorway and led the lieutenant out into the hall. "Aren't you one of the comrades we sent to Moscow?"

"Yes."

"You can't leave. We need your help."

"No."

"Comrade, we all face tests in dis life. We fail de test, we go down. We pass de test, we go up. Understand?"

"I understand what you say."

"The American imperialists are pressuring us. Dat man in der is CIA."

"CIA?"

"Yes."

"You sure?"

"Yes."

"How do you know?"

"Can't say. The information is secret. But I swear to you he is CIA, and he is hurting the Revo. Will you come back?"

The lieutenant hesitated, buying time to compose himself. Finally, he nodded, and followed Meat back into the torture room.

When it was over, they left the man hanging unconscious in the cold and dank room that still smelled of burned human flesh. The lieutenant stepped back, starring, and then walked rapidly into the hallway, holding his stomach. He put his hands against the cold stone wall and hung his head. His stomach contracted as though electrocuted, causing him to heave again and again, spewing onto the floor. He put one hand on the stone wall and held his stomach with the other, spitting. Tasting vomit. He looked up as Heavy waddled out of the room with a smile on his pasty, fat face. Sweat glistened on his broad white forehead.

"How can you do this?" the lieutenant asked.

Heavy stopped and looked at the lieutenant but said nothing for several seconds. Heavy's wide, flat face seemed blue-tinted in the dim light; and the baby fat that rounded his jowls was zit-marked. He spoke in a deep, steady baritone voice that seemed better suited to a less flaccid man, and he sounded like an American. "It wasn't easy the first time, but it gets easy as you go. You get used to it. We do what we do for the workers. Anyway, he's CIA. I enjoyed what we did to him. He deserved it." Heavy turned and moved down the dim hallway, like a dirigible easing away, his girth blocking the light.

Chapter Four

August 30, 1983—"Two Marines were killed and 14 wounded to-day amid heavy shelling and fighting here that brought Lebanon to the brink of full-scale civil war. After their positions were barraged with rockets and mortars for more than five hours this morning, Marines responded with a salvo from their 155-mm artillery on Druse positions in the foothills of mountains overlooking the capital."

Forrest heard this news on his truck's radio while driving across the Sneads Ferry Bridge, on his way to the back gate at Camp Lejeune. Up to that point, no Marines had been killed or wounded in combat in Beirut.

That day, Forrest's platoon began three days on the machine-gun range with the tank platoon's five M60 tanks. The tanks and amtracs were armed with turret mounted M-85 .50 caliber machineguns that fired 500 rounds per minute. The work at the range would give the gunners valuable gun time but also help the platoon and section leaders to practice communicating across platoons and to coordinate their fire. He'd been a platoon leader for almost a year, but he was still amazed by the power and noise of the guns. As they fired, clouds of white smoke sifted up from the guns, and spent brass piled up on the ground under each turret's ejection port, and the streams of lead shot out at 2,800 feet per second with an effective range of two miles. As five guns split the air violently with their fire, Forrest felt the blasting in his chest; and for an instant, he felt invincible. And these guns were just a part of the Marine Corps symphony they would set up around the airport in Beirut that would include heavy and light mortars and TOW missiles and artillery and naval gunfire and air support from the carrier. Forrest was awed by the hitting power of their little battalion, and that made him feel safe. That feeling lasted for only a few seconds, though, until Forrest realized that their enemies had big, nasty guns, too, and he tried to imagine streams of lead and high explosive rounds shrieking in at him. He knew that when they faced off on the battle field, it would be bad for both sides.

After three days at the range, the platoon moved to the beach to practice landings. It was late September, and fall was settling over the

Carolina coast. Day after day, cool sea air drifted across the barrier islands. You could look out across the marsh and see clearly the tips of marsh grass sparkling in morning sunlight and the fine detail of pine branches in the sun against blue-shaded recesses in the stand of trees, and the sky was creamy blue. Flat creek water reflected the pastels of the early morning, and blue-winged teal flew the edge of the woods. Out on the beach, schools of bluefish blitzed the surf under knots of gulls, and their high-pitched chirps carried on the sea breeze. It was a good season for beach training.

They got out to the beach in the late afternoon and built fires among the dunes, and the battalion sent out a hot meal in green vats. The firelight flickered off sloping dunes and brought up from the blue night colors of sand and sea oats. The Marines sat around the fires, eating on paper plates, and they told stories and jokes. The sound of Marines talking and laughing drifted out from the warm circles of firelight over the dunes and across the beach to the ocean. The fourteen amtracs (the platoon was beefed up to fourteen for Beirut) were lined up along the beach side-to-side with their noses facing the ocean.

Forrest walked down the beach alone and stood at the edge of the surf. He looked up at the stars and thought of his former girlfriend and how she'd dumped him; but he'd loved being with her, and he missed her now. He figured that at that moment she was nestled in some cozy space, warm under lamplight, with her sweet smell and soft warmth nestled into *him*. Maybe they were watching TV together or reading; *if* he could read (Forrest imagined his replacement as an illiterate). She would not be thinking of Forrest, of course. She had her man and his warmth and whatever else he offered. Forrest looked down at his boots in the sand and tried to think of something else. He did not have her, but he did have the cool, moonless night and the smell of the ocean and the sounds of the surf and the troopers laughing in the firelight up the beach. Pretty soon, he would have a ship ride to Beirut.

Forrest took a deep breath of salt-air and then moved back to the amtracs. He finally walked into the light of one of the fires.

"Lieutenant," said Corporal Simpson, "I was just tell'n the boys here about the time we got into dolphins during that dog and pony show at Mile Hammock Bay."

Two new guys, PFCs, sat listening.

"You remember the time we did that dog and pony show for those Boy Scouts, Lieutenant?"

Forrest nodded. "Yep."

"Well," Simpson continued, "we strapped open the cargo hatches so the Boy Scouts could stand on the seats and look around while we went for a ride in the bay. Corporal Seaborne was in the back of four-four with a bunch of Boy Scouts. Well, there was this one kid who was handicapped—had some kind of problem. He's just sitting there in the back of the amtrac. All he could do down there was look at the radios and smell diesel fumes and maybe get sick and throw up. Well, we got into dolphins. Right there in the bay. Can you imagine? Remember that, Lieutenant?"

"It was something."

"These dolphins were swimming around the hogs. Backs coming out of the water. Close enough to touch. They'd come up and exhale from that little hole on their backs. You could hear their breath coming out. It was cool. Anyway, this messed-up kid was missing it, so Corporal Seaborne reached down with one hand and grabbed this crippled kid and stood him up on the seat so he could see the dolphins. Then he let go of the kid, figuring the kid could hold on. Well, the kid went flopping down on the floorboards. Seaborne figured the kid was missing out on the dolphins, so he grabbed the kid again and picked him up with one hand—the kid's arms were flailing around now and he was trying to say something, noises coming out. Seaborne put the kid up on the bench and let's go. Kid went ass over teakettle onto the floorboards again. Seaborne kept picking the kid up; kid kept falling. Finally, the kid figured out how to hold on."

"How many times did he fall?

Simpson shrugged.

"I'll tell you one thing," Sergeant Tabb added, "that kid loved Corporal Seaborne. After we came in, the kid hobbled over to Seaborne and looked up at him. I thought he was going to give Seaborne a kiss. He blurted out a thank you, sort of groaned it out. Seaborne grinned. I don't think I ever saw Seaborne smile any other time. That boy got some Marine Corps training that day."

"You see any of it, Lieutenant?"

"No. I was watching the dolphins." He stared down into the flames and felt the heat on his face. Light flickered off the bank of the dune. "I'll see y'all at 04:30," he said as he turned and walked into the cool darkness beyond the firelight.

Forrest walked over to a concrete bunker on the beach and sat on its flat roof. He stared out at the ocean again, thinking now of his grandparents' house in York County where he spent most summers and where his dad had retired from the Corps. It was a white clapboard house with black gum and white oak and loblolly pine trees in the yard, and the afternoon breeze would bring up from the river smells of saltwater and marsh mud. There was a tangy, almost putrid smell when it hadn't rained in a while, but he loved it. The heavy-trunked hardwood trees around the house melded into a pine forest, and then beyond the pines, the marsh reached out wide and flat to the river. After the move to York County, Forrest's boyhood had been calibrated by the seasons on the river. In the spring, he'd cast up in the marsh reeds on high tide and catch speckled trout and rockfish. In summer, he'd work crab pots on his small wooden boat, the *General Lee*. There'd be more rockfish and trout in the fall and then duck hunting in the winter. As the seasons folded from one to the other, his life had settled into predictable constancy defined by trout and rockfish and crabs and ducks. As he sat on the concrete edge of the bunker, looking out at the dark ocean, he felt the pull of it—the hard attachment to the things that made him. He loved that river, and he thought it loved him back.

Forrest's thoughts turned to his father. His father lived long enough to see Forrest graduate from VMI and then the old man beamed with pride as Forrest was sworn into the United States Marine Corps as a second lieutenant, which was surprising because the old man always said that second lieutenants were idiots. Smiling to himself, Forrest remembered the night that "Goddamned Walter Cronkite" announced on the CBS evening news that the Vietnam War was lost. His father was already drunk. With a cigarette in his mouth, he stumbled to his study and then came back with his .45 and a box of shells. He started loading the magazine, and it was obvious from his muttering that Cronkite was about to catch a .45 round through the TV screen. Fortunately for the TV, his momma intervened and took Pop's gun away. She was the only person who could pull that off.

Chapter Five

International Airport repeatedly came under rocket grenade and small-arms fire from nearby Shiite Moslem areas."

On the morning of October 17, the platoon was back on the beach, but not for training. Later that morning, the USS MANITOWOC, an amphibious ship, would arrive offshore and the Marines would drive the amtracs out into the ocean to meet and board the ship. Early that morning, Forrest rolled out of his sleeping bag on top of the concrete bunker. He put on a clean set of utilities and then filled the steel shell of his helmet with cold water for a shave. Then he climbed a high dune and sat among sea oats and stared up at the stars and smelled the cool sea breeze and enjoyed the quiet of that calmest hour of the day. Just as the first dim hints of light spilled over the horizon, the Gunny walked along the beach, yelling reveille.

The Gunny climbed up the dune and tossed Forrest a C-rat meal in a cardboard box. "Thanks, Gunny."

"Don't know what you got there, LT. I grabbed the last box for you."

Forrest opened his box. He pulled out a green can and held it up, squinting to read the black letters. "Oh, shit. Ham and eggs."

"You don't like ham and eggs, LT?" The Gunny chuckled.

"I like ham and eggs that look and smell like ham and eggs. Not this shit. If we fed it to POWs, we'd be up for war crimes."

"Yessir, LT, but it makes shitting in the woods a whole lot better. I don't know what they put in here—cardboard or something. But it makes a nice, hard shit. You ever notice that, LT?"

Forrest nodded. He opened the can with the tiny opener (called a "P-38" or a "John Wayne") that came with the meal. He peeled back the can top and looked down on a waxy yellow-white layer of congealed fat spread across the mouth of the can. He pulled a plastic spoon out of the box and stirred the fat down into the colorless mixture. As his spoon broke through the fat, he whiffed a soapy smell.

Streaks of mandarin orange and brilliant yellow were forming low in the sky out over the ocean. The colors were pure, like oil paint straight from the tube.

The Gunny had baked beans with bite-sized pieces of hot dog mixed in—a meal he called "doggy dicks." He put a spoonful in his mouth and talked as he chewed.

"I ever tell you about eating C-rats with the South Korean Marines in Vietnam?"

"Don't think so, Gunny."

"We killed two zipper-heads in the wire one night. Next morning, these two Korean Marines drug the bodies in. I was sitting on top of my amtrac, eating C-rats."

"Ham and eggs?" Forrest asked.

"Don't remember, LT … could've been." The Gunny put another spoonful in his mouth and kept talking. "One of the Koreans pulled out a John Wayne. He took that little thing and started opening up one of the dead gooks. He poked that thing in the gook's neck and started working it down, like gutting a fish. He pulled out the heart and sat it on top." The Gunny was eating earnestly now. "Then he pulled out the lungs and placed them and the heart on top of the body—dude set the organs in place just so, like they were still inside. He cut off fingers with his knife. Them was some sick fuckers, LT."

Sea gulls hovered overhead, crying for food.

The Gunny chewed silently for a moment. "Thing is, they wasn't giggling or joking or making fun like you'd expect. They was …what's the right word?"

Forrest had no idea.

The Gunny repeated, "What's the right word? Like a doctor, you know, all business-like."

"Clinical?"

"Yes sir, LT, 'clinical'—that's the right word. Those Koreans were *clinical* when they cut up those dead gooks. It was weird."

The Gunny spooned in cold beans and dog pieces and chewed silently.

Forrest looked down at his ham and egg mixture and lowered his nose to it. The soapy smell overpowered the smell of the ocean. He looked up at the Gunny. "So did it mess up your breakfast, Gunny?"

"Smelled like shit, that's for damn sure." The Gunny snorted out a chuckle. "But I've always had a pretty strong stomach." The Gunny scraped the last cold morsels from the can and then started opening a can of peaches. "Fifteen years in the Corps has dulled my vocabulary," he said. "I use the F-word now for just about everything when I talk to the troops. It's a good word, though—universal donor of the English language. It can fit any sentence and can mean damn near anything. See, the word doesn't really mean anything; it's the way you say it that carries meaning. No other word has such utility. I figure the F-word was the first word ever, and all language evolved from that one word. I picture these cave men sitting around their cave just saying 'fuck' all the time, but with different inflection and combined with sign language to mean different things. Of course, there's always a risk of misunderstanding when one word means so many different things. I can see a Neanderthal with a big, hairy brow and his eyes set way back in his head and all hairy and grunting. He hands his old lady a roasted hunk of Mammoth meat, and she looks at him with a smile and a little glint in her eye and says 'fuck' real soft and nice-like. She means 'thanks,' but he thinks she means something else. Next thing you know, there's a hairy little cave baby running around." The Gunny hooted out a laugh.

The Gunny stood. "There's the ship, LT." The ship's running lights were visible far out at sea. By then, yellow light creased the low sky out over the ocean; and above the yellow, the sky had lightened to a bluish-pink. The western sky remained dark. The Gunny stared out at the ocean and said, as though speaking to himself, "Sky is beautiful this early."

Forrest nodded.

The Gunny looked over at Forrest and said, "No matter where you are or what kind of shit mess you're in, you can always look up and see the same sky we see right here at home. In my first tour in Vietnam, we were running those old P5 amtracs with gasoline engines. We hadn't learned yet what an anti-tank mine would do. Our lead tractor, loaded with 15 or 20 grunts inside, ran over a big mine rigged out of an artillery shell. Blew the shit out of that amtrac and blew the gas and killed everybody on board. I was a Lance Corporal, and I was driving the next amtrac in line. Saw the whole goddamned thing. That was the first time I saw dead people—and these were badly mutilated and burned. The crewmen on that tractor were close friends of mine. I'd gone through boot camp with one of them. It was a shitty day. Anyway, later that evening, around sunset, I think I noticed the sky for the first time in my life. I looked up at the colors, and I realized it was the same sky I'd been looking at from home my whole life. Everything else about Vietnam was foreign, but not the sky. So now I always take some time for the sky. Anyway, we started sandbagging the tractors and riding on top. And now we have P7s with diesel engines."

Forrest descended the dune and then climbed up to his turret, and the Marines mounted their amtracs. The drivers started the engines, and the fourteen vehicles sat idling along the dunes with their noses facing the ocean. The ship came in parallel to the beach a mile out and confirmed by radio readiness to board. Forrest gave four-nine the word, and its driver pushed its pedal to the floor. Four-nine's engine screamed, and it sped down across the beach and powered over a small curling wave and then settled into the calm ocean. With its jet drives engaged, four-nine pushed ahead. Then four-eight splashed. One by one, the amtracs screamed into the surf; and finally, four-zero cruised across the hard-packed sand to the ocean. As four-zero churned out towards the ship, Forrest turned in his turret and looked back at the beach. In the clear October dawn, morning sunlight fell across the sand and glistened on dew-moistened pines farther inland. The sea oats along the dune line picked up the light and wisps of wild grasses added color along the tops of the dunes. Forrest smelled the air and looked up the long empty beach under the pale sky. He loved this beach and he hoped to see it again.

Chapter Six

The Washington Post

"Prime Minister of Grenada Dies in Military Coup."

October 20, 1983—"The military seized power on the Caribbean island of Grenada today in a bloody confrontation that killed Prime Minister Maurice Bishop and several of his Cabinet members, the official Radio Free Grenada announced."

General Hudson Austin and Bernard Coard, the leaders of the more radical wing of the revolution, placed Maurice Bishop under arrest and held him at his home on the mountaintop. On the morning of October 19, "the masses," 10,000 of them, assembled in the market square in the capital city of St. George's. They carried banners that read, "Coard means oppression," and, "No Bishop, No Work, No Revo." As the crowd chanted support for Bishop, a large group of uniformed school children broke away from the crowd and headed up the mountain road towards Bishop's house. The crowd then fell in behind the children, and the mob moved up the narrow streets into the mountain foliage, chanting all the way. The troops guarding Bishop refused to fire on unarmed civilians, and Bishop was rescued.

Bishop and his crowd then came back to Market Square. As the crowd gathered around him, Bishop stood on an elevated platform, waving, so all could see he was free. Bishop stepped down from the platform and worked through the crowd, headed towards Fort Rupert at the head of a mob.

Bishop was out front, walking up the road to the fort. He stopped in front of the fort's gate, and the people stopped behind him. The crowd became quiet. Thousands stood under a bright blue sky, staring at the fort. Three Peoples' Revolutionary Army ("PRA") guards stood in front of the gate with loaded AK-47 rifles. The three were nervous, their eyes darting. Bishop stood there, tired, unsteady, but powerful.

Bishop ordered the guards to drop their weapons.

They did.

Then Bishop walked forward calmly and swung open the gate. He entered the lower courtyard of Fort Rupert and headed for the metal stairway to the communications room on the second floor of a barracks building overlooking a stone courtyard. As the crowd moved into the courtyard, three women soldiers confronted the mob's vanguard. They held up their AK-47 rifles, screaming for the people to stop. The mob overwhelmed the women and seized their weapons. A large man from the crowd slapped a crouching female soldier with his open hand, and the woman screamed and started crying. Four other soldiers in the courtyard dropped their weapons and raised their hands.

Hundreds packed the courtyard, all chanting, "Bishop, Bishop, Bishop!" Outside the gate, in the small open area in front of the fort's thick walls, thousands more chanted. On the periphery of the crowd, children played and danced. The mood was festive. Bishop walked out onto the balcony outside the communications room, overlooking the courtyard, which by now was packed with people. The crowd fell silent, and Bishop looked out over a sea of color—the pink and white and blue of islander clothing dotted with many black faces. Bishop had not eaten in twenty-four hours, and he had spent the previous night on the floor of his bedroom cuffed to the foot of his bed. Bishop paused on the shaded balcony, looked down briefly at the surging crowd, then held his head with his right hand, holding the railing of the balcony with his other hand. He turned to the crowd and held up both hands and shouted, "Austin is fired as General of the PRA!"

The crowd cheered.

Then Bishop yelled, "I have appointed Einstein Louison to take his place." The crowd cheered again.

Drained from the walk and from speaking loudly, Bishop rubbed his forehead and steadied himself with the rail. He walked back into the communications room, followed by several government officials and his companion, Jacqueline Creft, who was visibly pregnant. Bishop picked up the telephone and tried to get a line. One of Bishop's ministers walked back onto the balcony and shouted for volunteers with militia training. He and Louison worked their way down to the armory and distributed weapons. The crowd hovered in and around the fort. Bishop and his closest supporters stayed in the communications room. The heat in the room was thick and wet, and the air stunk of body odor.

Bishop finally got an outside line and spent his time talking on the phone. Between calls, Bishop paced and smoked. Creft sat on a hard chair in the corner, fanning herself with a manila folder. She looked at Bishop and said they had to keep the crowd around them because the PRA would never fire on the people.

Two hours passed.

At 12:48, three BTR-60s (Soviet-made wheeled armored vehicles armed with 14.5 mm heavy machineguns) moved through St. Georges with soldiers riding on top. The crowd around the fort on the edge of town was not alarmed. They still celebrated and danced. A group of small children dressed in light-colored shorts and t-shirts stopped and saluted as the vehicles moved up the neck of the Peninsula to the fort. The BTR-60s stopped in front of the fort, and the troops deployed, rushing out into a battle formation with AK-47s held at port arms. The soldiers wore pea-green fatigues and web belts fixed with magazine pouches and little round canteens in cloth holders and goofy-looking East German steel helmets, and each man held an AK-47 with a fixed bayonet. The sun blasted them with light and carved in the hard sun-bleached ground dark angular shadows. The soldiers' grim, sweat-soaked faces were mostly shaded by the lips of their helmets, but their tightly held mouths were visible and scary-looking. As people realized what was happening, many raised their hands and started walking down towards Market Square. Many others stood bravely in front of the gate, between the BTR-60s and Bishop.

The two sides faced each other now across a few yards of sun-hardened dirt and gravel. Heat radiated visibly up from the ground. Seconds ticked by. Tension grew. It was like a gas leak slowly building up. Once the mixture was pumped up enough—the tension pulled tight—the tiniest spark would trigger an explosion. Bishop stood silently in the communications room with the phone receiver in his right hand and a burning cigarette in the other.

The PRA men were visibly nervous. They stood in the heat with sweat dripping down their black faces and into their eyes and they gripped their rifles with wet hands. The last peaceful moment hung in the hot air. Both sides held back until the weight and strain of it was too much to bear.

The shooting started all at once. Bishop's people on the rampart shot down on the PRA troops. Brass shells were pouring out of the weapons and clinking on the stone surface at their feet. The lead BTR-60 fired its machinegun into the crowd of men, women, and children standing outside the fort and people ran screaming in all directions. The PRA soldiers fired at the men on the rampart and picked off running civilians. The air was filled with high-pitched screams of hundreds of women and small children and screeching wounded men and the sounds of automatic weapons firing in short bursts and long loud bursts from the heavy machineguns. Smoke rose in a white cloud in front of the fort and drifted out over the bay. Bodies now lay about on the hot ground in front of the fort.

Bishop yelled, "My God! They've turned their guns on the masses!"

One of his government ministers ran out on the balcony yelling, "No compromise! No compromise!" A stream of heavy machinegun bullets cut the man in half. The man's upper torso fell over the railing to the stone courtyard. His legs dropped on the balcony, twitching. The BTR-60 then sprayed the top edge of the rampart, killing one of the three men fighting there. His body dropped alongside his rifle. The other two men hunkered down behind the wall.

Having disbursed the crowd outside the fort, the PRA troops entered the courtyard and opened fire on the crowd there. As they shot, the people, who were mostly unarmed, retreated to the upper courtyard, pursued by a PRA squad. The people retreated farther to the rampart along the back wall of the fort—women, children, and unarmed men pushed together in a mass along the wall. The PRA troops kept the pressure on by firing steadily into the crowd even as the people screamed and pleaded. With bodies at their feet, people started jumping over the stone wall to the tangle of bushes ninety feet down. Most were trying not to jump but were pushed by the crowd. Men and women—eyes wide with fear and screaming and some crying—all with dark black skin and dressed in white or pastel colors as they fell over the wall, screamed louder. And as they crunched down on top of others at the bottom of the wall, the sounds of broken people created a steady groan from the broken mass of humanity heaped on the rocks.

Bishop screamed for his own people to stop firing. The men holding the communications building dropped their weapons and walked out onto the balcony with their hands raised.

The sound of gunfire died away. The smell of burned cordite and white smoke hung over the fort. Scores of wounded civilians worked their way down the narrow peninsula towards Market Square, leaving trails of blood. Dead bodies lay about in clumps in front of the fort and in the courtyard. Several PRA soldiers also lay dead in front of the fort. In the communications room, Bishop leaned against a table, holding a lit cigarette in one hand and his head in the other. The others waited silently, burned out by adrenaline and almost too tired for fear. A man in a green PRA uniform walked up the stairs with a 9mm Beretta in his right hand.

The PRA man's mouth was frozen in a puckered-up frown, his mouth squeezed down to about two centimeters across. Sweat poured down the side of his face. He was breathing fast through his nose, either winded or two worked up to stay calm. Across the bay at Fort Frederick, up on the ridge above St. George's, Coard and Austin were directing the military take-over.

In the communications room at Fort Rupert, the soldier walked in and stared directly at Bishop. "Outside."

Bishop looked up with sad eyes and took a puff from his cigarette. He looked over at Creft and then glanced down at her pregnant belly. She gazed back at him with tears in her eyes and sweat streams down the side of her face. Bishop walked slowly across the room and passed by the soldier without looking at him. The others followed. The last person out was Creft. She held her rounded tummy with both hands as she walked by the soldier with her head down. The prisoners were lead to the courtyard by a basketball hoop near a slogan painted on the wall: "Towards a Higher Discipline in the PRA."

A team of six soldiers stood now facing the prisoners across fifteen feet. From the rampart of Fort Rupert, the soldiers could see Fort Frederick on the side of the mountain south of St. George's, where General Austin made his headquarters. A red flare shot up from Fort Frederick and then arched over and fell to the sea.

"Bishop, over here," the soldier said.

Bishop shuffled over and stood in direct sunlight in front of the soldier. The sun was high now, almost directly overhead, so Bishop stood in the glare without casting a shadow. He stared calmly into his executioner's eyes.

"Today your last, Maurice Bishop," the soldier said. Then he nodded to his man.

Bishop sighed and crossed his arms. One of the soldiers raised his pistol and pointed it at Bishop's face. Then he paused. After three long seconds, the pistol went off with a slight kick upward and a brass casing ejected into the hot mid-day air. The shot knocked Bishop's head back in a misty pink cloud. His body collapsed to the ground, twitching and kicking, the faceless head turning from side to side as though looking for something. Then the body settled into a lifeless lump.

The others stood gasping in the heat, their eyes wide with terror and their mouths twisted with fear.

The soldier looked up at his squad and nodded. The first man looked down and pulled the bolt back on his AK-47 and chambered a round. The other five men chambered rounds. The victims stepped back towards the wall, looking from side to side for a way out. The metal on metal clicking of the bolts going home obscured the muffled moans from the people still heaped in a pile over the wall and lying about in the stone courtyard. The moment should have weighed tons, but the tension from earlier was gone, and the executions had the feel of clean up after a tense athletic event. It was too easy.

Creft stepped forward, pleading tearfully. "Comrades! Comrades! You mean you're going to shoot us? To kill us?"

The soldier stepped towards the crying woman, anger flashing in his eyes, and screamed: "You fucking bitch! Who you call'n comrades?"

Her tears mingled with sweat on her cheeks.

The soldier continued, "You're one of dose who was gonna let de imperialists in."

The squad opened fire together, spraying bullets into the people. The victims' screaming lasted only a few seconds. As bullets pumped onto them, blood sprayed, and fleshy pieces splattered against the slogan on the wall. The rifles clacked as their bolts opened and shut over and over again, with brass flying out and clinking on the ground. Powder smoke filled the air. Then it was over.

Chapter Seven

The Washington Post

"U.S. Says Situation Still Unclear as Naval Force Nears Grenada."

October 23, 1983—"U.S. officials on Friday directed two separate naval task forces towards Grenada, a five-ship amphibious landing force with 1,800 Marines aboard and a 16-ship battle group led by the carrier USS INDEPENDENCE.*"*

Forrest sat at the wardroom table with three other lieutenants. A dozen black dominoes laid flat on the table, white dots up, and rows of dominoes stood on end in front of each lieutenant. They waited for Lieutenant Stanard to play.

Forrest glanced around the wardroom and fixed his look on the black portholes. He thought about their warm little wardroom game of dominoes in the middle of the dark and cold ocean. As he pondered the contrast, Stanard looked up from his dominoes and smiled. He pushed his chair back from the table slowly. He stood, stepped back from the table, and then swung his right arm overhead and slammed a domino down hard on the table with a loud plastic clap. "Twenty!" Stanard pulled his chair back and sat down, still grinning.

Lieutenant Jones's turn was next. Unable to play, he drew a domino from the pile. Then he drew another. And another.

"Looks like I put your sorry ass in the bone yard, Henry," Stanard said, still smiling.

Jones kept drawing.

"Henry is in the bone yard," Forrest said flatly.

Jones kept drawing. He finally played a non-scoring domino.

In the other section of the wardroom, the captain and two Navy officers were watching *Poltergeist* on the Beta-Max. From the dominos table, the movie sounded like muffled talking with occasional screams. As Jones laid down his domino, there was another scream.

"I bet Beirut's haunted," said Stanard.

Forrest looked up from his dominoes. After a pause, he said, "Don't think it has been ghosts killing our people over there, Jack."

Lieutenant Cabell laid down a non-scoring domino.

"Killing kids has to leave a mark on the place," Stanard said.

"You serious?" asked Cabell.

More screams from the movie.

"That would be a shitty deal," added Forrest.

"What?" asked Stanard.

"Haunting Beirut," Forrest said. "If you've got to be a ghost, you want to haunt a nice mansion—a bed and breakfast in the Shenandoah Valley. You could hang out on the front porch on summer evenings watching fire flies." Forrest slapped down a domino. "Five. But I guess you can't enjoy a cocktail if you're dead. So not much point in watching fire flies."

Stanard and the others nodded.

"But Beirut is a shit hole," Forrest continued. "Think how crowded it'd be. As soon as you get killed, you'd be standing in line with all the other poor bastards who got killed there. That's a lot of pissed off spirits. All those dead Arabs would hate you. You'd have to find some Phalange or Israelis just to have somebody to talk to, but I guess there'd be plenty of them, too. And there would be nothing you could do about it. You can't kill the bastards 'cause they're already dead."

Stanard nodded thoughtfully. "What would we be standing in line for?"

Forrest shrugged.

"Well," Stanard said finally, "if there's such a thing as ghosts, that'd be the place to find one. All those women and children massacred in those refugee camps."

There were more screams from the Beta-Max, mixed with the sound of the ship creaking, like an old man's bones popping.

Stanard played a domino.

More screaming from the movie—high-pitched, desperate screaming.

"Kill'n kids is bound to fuck a place up," Stanard continued. "Bad things are gonna happen there."

"Bad things been happening there for a long time already," Forrest said, as he stood to slam a twenty-five-point score.

"Yeah. And it probably all started a couple thousand years ago when somebody killed a kid."

"I guess," replied Forrest, smiling over his score.

"When I saw those pictures from the refugee killings—mama corpses holding baby corpses—all bloody, gave me the creeps. I read a newspaper story about the Red Cross finding a whole Druse village wiped out. They found tables set for breakfast with rotten jam and English muffins and decayed people sitting around the table for family breakfast. Those are some cold-hearted bastards that did that," said Stanard.

"Yeah, and the ones who did that are the cold-hearted bastards on our side," said Cabell, as he played another non-scoring domino.

"I figure everybody over there must be a cold-hearted bastard by now. Bad Karma." Stanard played a domino. "Five."

A Navy runner knocked then entered. He handed a stack of papers to the Marine company commander, Captain Henry Wise (known as the Captain, or "Skipper"), who was sitting by the reading lamp in front of the movie.

Twenty minutes later, the game ended and the lieutenants moved over to the living room area. The movie was over, and the Navy officers had left. The Marine captain was sitting alone in lamplight, reading the message traffic.

"Any word from Beirut, Skipper?" Forrest asked.

"More casualties. They've had firefights three days in a row. One Marine killed today. Three wounded."

"Got any names, Captain?" asked Forrest.

"No. Who won the game?"

"I beat their asses sir," said Stanard.

"You were lucky," said Cabell.

"Well," said Stanard, "That's 'cause you're disrespectful to the bones. I respect the bones. Respect the bones, and they'll take care of you."

The Captain stood to leave.

"Oh, one other thing in the traffic," the Captain said. "There was a coup attempt earlier today in a little island down in the Carib. Place called Gren-ah-da. There's an American medical school there."

"Gren-ah-da? Like the car," asked Forrest.

"I don't know how you pronounce it. I never heard of the place."

The following morning, Forrest walked out on the flight deck at 06:50, ten minutes before morning formation. He stood at the edge of the flight deck, looking out over the indigo-blue ocean. Right away, he noticed something was different, but he couldn't figure out what it was.

The Gunny walked up beside Forrest.

"Morn'n, sir."

"Morn'n, Gunny."

"LT, you notice something different?"

Forrest nodded.

"We've turned south."

Forrest looked over at the Gunny, said nothing.

"Yessir. Lebanon is that way." He pointed to the sun, low in the sky off the port side of the ship. "Every other morning, we've been headed more-or-less into the sun. I figured yesterday that something was up because they had flight ops to load us up with more ammunition. We got fourteen crates of .50 cal. and a shit-load of 5.56."

At 07:00, Golf Company and the amtrac platoon fell into formation on the flight deck. The men stood in four ranks. Forrest stood in front of his platoon. The Gunny was to his right, two paced back. The platoons stood in a horseshoe-shaped formation around the edge of the flight deck. The Captain and the company first sergeant stood at attention in the center of the flight deck.

The First Sergeant yelled, "Fall in!" All the men snapped to attention in neat well-aligned ranks.

The Captain barked out, "Report!"

Each platoon reported, "All present or accounted for, sir!"

The Captain returned the salute. "At ease."

The men relaxed but stayed in formation.

"We received orders this morning to turn south. We're headed for an island in the Caribbean called Gren-ah-da." He pronounced the name like the car, rhyming with sonata. "The communists there executed their prime minister and others yesterday and killed civilians. They've established a twenty-four-hour-a-day shoot-to-kill curfew. There is an American medical school on the island with a few hundred students, mostly citizens of the United States. We understand there is a Cuban force on the island and a Grenadian army, called the Peoples' Revolutionary Army. The Marine Amphibious Task Force and the entire USS INDEPENDENCE Battle Group has been directed to proceed to Gren-ah-da at best speed. We'll be there in a few days."

As the Captain spoke, Forrest felt through his feet the low hum of the ship's engines far below the flight deck and heard the spray from the ship's bow slicing through the calm ocean surface.

"We do not have a mission yet," the Captain explained. "Could be invasion. Could be evacuation of United States citizens." The captain called the Marine detachment to attention and dismissed the formation.

The Marines talked quietly as they milled around after the formation.

The Gunny walked over to Forrest. His dark tan brought out the blue in his eyes. "If it's an evac, they won't use us, LT. They'll use helicopters."

"Yeah, I figured that."

"You ever heard of Gren-ah-da, LT?"

"No. You?"

"No, sir."

Chapter Eight

Reuter News Service
"40 Marines Said Killed in Blast."

October 23, 1984—"Buildings housing large units of U.S. Marines and French soldiers were devastated by a bomb blast early today. [A Lebanese radio station reported that] 'moans and pleas for help were heard from beneath the rubble of the three-story Marine command center.' [The structure] 'collapsed into one story.' Slabs of concrete were folded down over the edges of the smoking rubble."

Beirut was once called "the Paris of the Middle East." The city sits astride the Mediterranean Sea, and there is a wide French-style boulevard along the sea wall that is lined with palm trees; and behind the city stands snow-covered mountains. There is good skiing in the mountains, and there are several European-style ski resorts. From classrooms at the American University of Beirut, students can see green lawns, ivy-covered stone buildings, and they can smell the fresh sea air. Five-story condominium buildings stand along the boulevard, with balconies that look out over the cool, vast sea and blue mountain ranges north of the city. From a distance, the city looks like Manhattan.

After the 1948 Arab-Israeli War, 110,000 Palestinians ended-up in refugee camps in Lebanon. Over the years, the Palestine Liberation Organization, led by Yasser Arafat, staged terrorist attacks against Israel from southern Lebanon. In 1982, the Israelis decided to wipe out the PLO and Syrian forces in southern Lebanon. On June 6, 1982, the Israelis attacked with one reinforced division, amounting to 78,000 men, 1,240 tanks and 1,500 armored personnel carriers, all backed by U.S.-made Sky Hawks and Cobra helicopters. The Israeli attack pushed to the outskirts of Beirut and drove all PLO and Syrian forces out of southern Lebanon. In a U.S.-brokered deal, the U.S. Navy and Marine Corps evacuated the PLO fighters and terrorists to Tripoli. These people left their families behind in the refugee camps.

On September 14th, 1982, a Syrian communist assassinated the newly-elected President of Lebanon, Bachir Gemayel. The Israeli army then occupied West Beirut. A few days later, the Phalange entered the Sabra and the Shatila refugee camps and killed between 460 and 3,500 civilians (depending on who you ask)—mostly Palestinians and Lebanese Shiites. In the United States, *Time* magazine featured a black and white photo of a dead woman down on the street, her corpse clutching a dead child. In response to this tragedy, the United States, Italy, and France sent an International Peacekeeping Force to Beirut. The Italian Marines and French Foreign Legion were assigned sectors in the city. The United States sent in a Battalion Landing Team ("BLT"), comprised of one Marine battalion reinforced with tanks, amtracs, artillery, and helicopters backed by a carrier battle group. The Marines took up positions at the Beirut International Airport (the "BIA").

The BIA sat on the coastal plain of Lebanon between the Mediterranean Sea and the Chouf Mountains, just south of the city. Shiite slums were clumped around the northern section of the airport, and to the east were run-down suburbs and farther south some open, hilly country interspersed with concrete and cinderblock buildings. Back closer to the mountain, at Tahwitat Al Ghadir, there was a campus of the Lebanese and Arab University, complete with soccer fields and swimming pools. To the south of the airport, there was some open country and then a small town called Khaldah. A modern highway ran along the Med, linking the city with southern Lebanon. The Israeli border was a hundred miles to the south.

The Israeli Defense Forces withdrew closer to Israel in August 1983, and civil war immediately flared up—the Lebanese Army and Phalange against the Amal (Shiite) and Druse militia, with dozens of other militia groups mixed in. By October 23rd, the three infantry companies of First Battalion, Eighth Marines, were stretched along a front east of the BIA runway that covered about 3,000 yards and also held positions north and south of the main runway. The Amal killed two Marines in a firefight in late August 1983. By mid-October, six Marines had been killed in gunfights with militia.

The BLT headquarters was set-up in a building inside the terminal complex. This building served as barracks for the headquarters company, the recon platoon, medical teams, men on work details, and miscellaneous other units. In all, about 350 Marines and sailors lived in the building.

On Sunday, October 23rd, at 05:45, most of the Marines on the line and in the BLT barracks were still sleeping. It was dark and dead calm. Out on the line, Marines on watch sat in fighting bunkers in total silence. It was cool, and the air smelled clean and sweet. In the positions north of the runway, Marines could smell Canadian bacon cooking in the Shiite slum. In the makeshift barracks rooms in the BLT headquarters building, sea air circulated through open windows. The Marines slept in green sleeping bags on green cots, and by each sleeping Marine, there was a pack and a "war belt" (web belt with suspenders) fitted with canteens, a first aid pouch, and two pouches that held three M-16 magazines each. M-16 rifles and LAW rockets leaned against the walls. It was quiet because teenagers don't snore. In a few minutes, 241 of them would be dead.

By 06:22, the sky was getting light in the east over the mountains. A lone nineteen-ton yellow Mercedes stake-bed truck with headlights on drove down the access road in front of the BLT headquarters building. The truck drove through and over a barbed wire fence and then between two sandbagged guard posts, where Marine sentries were not allowed to keep their M-16s loaded and ready to fire. As the truck passed the sentries, the suicide bomber, a man with black hair and a black beard, looked directly at a Marine sentry and smiled. By the time the sentry slapped a magazine into his M16 and chambered a round, the truck was closing on the barracks. The truck swerved between concrete sewer pipe barriers and crashed into the building's lobby. After two seconds, the truck erupted in a massive explosion—so powerful that it lifted the building off its concrete foundation and then caused the building to implode. Marines in bunkers a mile away felt the energy of the blast. The plume of black smoke that snaked high into the air looked like a nuclear blast plume. The blast was the equivalent of six tons of TNT, and it woke up every man in the building, just an instant before most of them were crushed to death. It was the worst single-day death toll for the Marines since Iwo Jima.

When it was over, the four-story building was a pile of concrete and glass within a cloud of gray dust. Debris, including dead bodies and parts of bodies were scattered about. Crushed body parts stuck out from between concrete shards, and there was the smell of dust and that awful, sickening, gaseous smell that leaks from ruptured bodies.

Within a few minutes, another truck bomb attacked the French barracks a few miles north in the city. The target was a nine-story building housing the 3rd Company of France's 1st Parachute Chasseur Regiment. Sentries shot the driver, and the truck stopped fifteen yards from the building, but the terrorist detonated the bomb. The building collapsed, killing 58 French paratroopers. After the attack, the Marines worked for days to recover the dead and wounded, all under Amal sniper fire. The following day, a C130 loaded with replacement troops landed at the BIA.

On the 4th of November, the Israeli Military Governor's headquarters in Tyre was destroyed by a truck bomb, killing 46.

Chapter Nine

The New York Times
"Grenada Radio Warns of Attack."

October 24, 1983—"'An invasion of our country is expected to-night,' the radio said, 'The revolutionary council has made it clear that the people of Grenada are prepared to fight to the last man to defend our homeland.'"

One day out from Grenada, the ship pushed south through a cold front. In a hard rain, the ship rose over large cresting waves, then rode down into long deep troughs. As the ship dropped down into a huge trough, Forrest was almost weightless in his bunk. The trashcan by the sink lifted off the floor, bounced off the sink, slammed against the wall, and then rolled in an arc across the moving floor and banged the wall again. As the ship bottomed out in the trough, he felt his weight settle into the bed. The trashcan rolled across the room and banged into the metal bulkhead again. For the next hour, Forrest laid there, his weight shifting back and forth with the rolling ship. The trashcan rolled to one wall, banged, then rolled back. At 04:30, he'd had enough. He rose and turned on the light. He put on his pressed camouflaged utility trousers, clean green boot socks, and combat boots. Holding onto a pipe by the sink, he shaved. The light of the sink highlighted his well-developed chest and shoulders. His dog tags hung in his chest hair, swaying as the ship pitched. He put on a clean green t-shirt and his utility top. Then he worked his way down the passageway to the wardroom. Every few steps, he reached up a hand to steady himself.

He stepped into the wardroom and closed the door carefully. The lights were on. Coffee was brewing. Navy cooks were working in the kitchen. At the end of one of the tables sat the Marine captain. He held a white sheet of paper in one hand, a Styrofoam cup in the other. The three portholes along the wall were black.

The captain looked up.

"Trouble sleeping, Robert?"

"Yes, sir. Can't sleep in this weather. I'd never make it as a squid."

"Yep. Same here." He sipped his black coffee.

Forrest poured a half-cup and sat.

"What's up, Skipper?"

The captain handed Forrest the piece of paper.

Forrest read:

TO: CMDR BLT 2/8
FROM: CINCLANTFLT
MSSG URGENT
SECRET

0345Z
SITREP
BEIRUT
0659 LOCAL TIME BLT 1/8 HQ HIT BY TRUCK BOMB.
74 CONF DEAD
TOTAL CAS UNK

Forrest looked up from the paper. Up to that point, 1/8 had lost six men in firefights. Service in Beirut had been more dangerous than driving a car; less dangerous than mountain climbing. But the numbers, and the odds, had just changed.

"What were they using for headquarters?" Forrest asked.

"A building. Four stories, I think. I'm not sure."

"You must know some guys in 1/8."

The captain nodded. "Lots. You?"

"Don't know. Never worked with them."

The Navy man walked out of the kitchen in a white smock. "Good morning, gentlemen."

Forrest and the captain nodded.

"What would you like for breakfast?" the Navy man asked cheerfully.

"Nothing for me," said the captain.

"Orange juice," said Forrest.

After drinking his juice, Forrest made his way down dark passageways and stairwells to the troop compartments well below the waterline where the Marines slept in bunks stacked five high. On one end of the berthing space, there was a small sitting area with a TV that ran off a ship-wide system. He found the Gunny inspecting the area while the men were on the mess deck getting breakfast.

"How we looking, Gunny?"

"Real good, LT."

Forrest nodded.

"What's up, LT?"

"1/8 HQ got hit by a truck bomb."

The Gunny looked down for a moment.

"What happened?"

"Don't know. Got some message traffic on it. Seventy-four confirmed dead, so far.

The ship creaked and shuddered as it rode over a wave. Forrest and the Gunny both held onto a bunk to keep from falling over.

"That's a motherfucker, Lieutenant."

"Yep."

In the late afternoon, Navy orderlies posted the first lists of the dead. Marines gathered around bulletin boards on the mess deck and in the troop spaces, checking for names of friends in 1/8. The officers gathered around the board in the dark passageway outside the wardroom. A small light mounted atop the board lit the four pages of typewritten names. The names covered the pages, single-spaced, in two columns. Forrest stood back, waiting and wondering if Kirby was on the list.

"Ohhh. Damn," uttered Stanard. "Crockett."

"He's got a one year-old," said Sisk.

Forrest stayed back, waiting, listening to the recognition of names.

When the board cleared, Forrest stepped up and scanned directly to the Ks. Ed's name wasn't there. Forrest exhaled, relieved. Then he ran his finger down the list. His finger stopped on a name he recognized. Lance Corporal Oliver Evans. Evans had been one of Forrest's crew chiefs. When the amtrac battalion got a request for men to join the reconnaissance battalion, Evans volunteered. Forrest saw him only once more after that.

It was a hot August day in North Carolina. Waves of humidity radiated up from white sand on the tank trail, and Forrest felt like his head was stuck in an oven with flames burning in his ears. The only sound was Forrest's breathing and the incessant clicking of insects. Forrest's amtracs were all pulled into the thick bushes along the edge of the trail while he waited for an order to attack Combat Town, about a mile down the tank trail. He stepped out of the brush onto the edge of the tank trail, pulled out his canteen and drank hot water. Then a squad of recon Marines jogged by, wearing packs loaded with sand, and there was Evans, chugging along in the heat, sweat bleeding from his red face. Forrest let out an *oohhhrraaah!* Evans had looked over with a painful smile and returned the gesture with a breathless grunt. Now he was dead.

Forrest looked down at the list and shook his head. He stepped out on deck and leaned on the railing and looked out on the sun setting in the west. The sky was orange and yellow with shades of blue, and the colors reflected on the ocean and made a beautiful painting. The mounting death toll gave him a sick feeling deep down in his chest. He became a Marine to make his father proud and for thrills, and he'd always loved running the amtracs in the ocean and along beaches and tank trails and shooting the heavy machine guns at the range, but this was no longer a game.

As Forrest contemplated his situation, a Huey helicopter landed on the small flight deck and the skipper boarded for a ride over to the USS *GUAM* to receive a briefing and orders for the operation. Forrest stayed on the deck, deep in thought for two hours before he heard the helicopter returning. The sound of the helicopter blades hacking the air got louder until the black silhouette of a Huey framed by running lights emerged from the dark sky off the stern of the ship. The Huey descended slowly and landed. A lone figure hopped out, ducking as he walked away from the helicopter. When he was clear, the helicopter lifted off the pad, rotated to the left, then dipped its nose and moved rapidly away into the night. The sound of the chopper receded gradually until he could once again hear the bow spray. Forrest headed for the captain's stateroom. All of the Golf Company lieutenants were there huddled around the skipper. The skipper sat in a chair by his bed with a dip under his lip and a spit-cup in hand. He looked around the quiet room, drawing out the suspense.

"Gentlemen," he said, "our mission is to seize and occupy the island nation of Grenada, to neutralize the Peoples' Revolutionary Army and Cuban forces, to disarm the population, and to defuse the political situation." He smiled with tobacco-stained teeth. The skipper then gave the standard "five-paragraph order" outlining the detail of the operation. "We've got one map here. I've got photocopies of the area around Pearls Airport and Grenville." He handed them out. The lieutenants copied down on their maps the checkpoints, objectives, and phase lines. Then they filed out of the room, headed for their platoon areas below. As Forrest stood to leave, the skipper stopped him.

"Robert, we're going to have a rough ride to the beach. Weather report forecasts waves in the surf zone at seven or eight feet. There's a coral reef." The skipper gave Forrest an aerial photograph of the beach at Pearls Airport and laid it out on his bed. The photograph showed the reef, but there was no way to tell how deep the water was over the reef. Forrest said, "Don't worry, Skipper, amtracs can handle that." Forrest stood and walked towards the door. He stopped and looked back. "I never thought I'd get to do something like this."

The skipper nodded. "The world is going to wake up tomorrow and find out the Marines have landed." He smiled with his mouth closed, a bulge of snuff under his lower lip.

One of the Navy lieutenants stuck his head in and handed Forrest a pile of launch schedules. Forrest took five and handed the rest to the captain. Then he headed down to his platoon area four decks down. It was almost 20:00 when Forrest opened the watertight hatch and stepped into the brightly lit tank deck. He stepped out onto the asphalt-covered deck and worked his way through the narrow passage between the amtracs and the port bulkhead. He found the Gunny and section leaders waiting for him in the open area by the ship's stern ramp in front of four-one. The air smelled of diesel fuel and lube oil. They were all wearing pressed camouflaged utilities with an American flag sewn on the left sleeve and an eagle globe and anchor stenciled over the left breast pocket below initials, "USMC." Forrest looked up at the nose of four-one and patted it like a horse. Then he looked back at the Gunny.

"What's the word, LT?" asked the Gunny.

"Invasion." Forrest cracked a half-smile.

"Holy crap!" said the Gunny. "I didn't think we'd do it."

"Well, there's a new sheriff in town," Forrest said flatly.

Forrest laid out the five-paragraph order using the photocopied map. Then he handed out the launch schedule.

Forrest started packing for the invasion when he got back to his stateroom. He packed socks and drawers, t-shirts, shaving gear, toothbrush, toothpaste, and soap in a plastic container, a hand towel, one box of C-Rations, and a poncho. He laid out a clean uniform, his flak jacket, and his combat helmet. Then he sat on the edge of his bed and pulled off his VMI ring. He held it in his hand. It was gold with a blue sapphire stone and the image of the statue on post called *Virginia Mourning Her Dead* molded into its side. He imagined his ring hanging on a chain around a Cuban's neck and decided to leave it in his stateroom with his sea bag. He raised his dog tag chain over his head and removed one of the tags. He unlaced his right boot and threaded one of his dog tags onto his bootlace and retied his boot so there'd be a better chance of identifying him if his head got blown off.

At 01:30, Forrest walked into the wardroom. He poured coffee in a white Styrofoam cup and sat. The other lieutenants were already there, drinking coffee. The skipper came in, poured coffee, and sat without saying anything. It seemed like another routine dawn landing. Because Forrest had been on dozens of these landings while training, the morning seemed routine. But as Forrest sat sipping his coffee, he felt his nerves. The little fear spider was inside his chest, spinning a web around his courage. He looked around the table and appreciated the outward calm of the others. Forrest knew this was the worst time. Once the stern ramp dropped and they were in the ocean, there'd be enough work to keep him from thinking about the various dreadful contingencies.

A Navy man walked out of the kitchen with a serving dish covered with steaks. Then he brought out a large bowl of scrambled eggs, a bowl of hash browns, and a basket of fresh, hot toast and biscuits. Forrest put a strip steak on his plate with eggs, hash browns, and toast. He looked down at his plate and basked in the homey aroma. As he took his first bite of steak, he hoped he would be keeping his innards intact throughout the day—didn't want to spill any steak and eggs out on the beach. They ate in silence. Forrest looked up at the black portholes and held onto the table as the ship slid sideways over a huge swell, shuddering and creaking as its huge steel frame bent and twisted. It would be a rough landing.

When Forrest stepped into the tank deck, the blowers were running. He walked through the center of the tank deck, between parallel rows of amtracs. At four-eight, he found Lance Corporal Walton feeding a belt of .50 caliber machinegun rounds up to Corporal Turner in the turret. Turner was carefully layering the belt into the magazine. Forrest stood on the ramp, watching. The section leader, Staff Sergeant Jefferson, stepped up on the ramp beside him.

"Morn'n, sir."

"Morn'n, Staff Sergeant."

"You think those people will fight us, sir?'

Forrest shrugged. "I guess we'll find out here in a couple of hours."

Forrest worked his way down the line. He poked his head in four-zero. Garnett was stacking small cardboard boxes of M-16 ammunition into a recess behind the radios. The driver, Lance Corporal Goode, was sitting on the third crewman's jump seat by the stern ramp, loading rounds into an M-16 magazine. The sounds of metal banging and men talking echoed off the steel walls in the big, empty space of the tank deck, and it smelled of grease and oil and diesel fumes.

"You going to give us a good ride today, Goode?"

Goode looked up, and a white, toothy smile crossed his black face. "Yessir."

The Gunny and Forrest got coffee and moved to the back of the tank deck in front of four-one, just inside the ship's closed stern ramp. To keep steady, Forrest held onto a ladder rung welded to the side of the bulkhead—the one the Navy man would stand on with his ball peen hammer.

"Gunny, I've been thinking about that day four-seven crapped out in the ocean."

The Gunny nodded.

"That happens today, you do the tow with no back-up. We've got to get everybody on the beach as fast as possible."

The Gunny nodded. "Don't worry, LT. We've done this a hundred times, and nobody has eaten any apricots, I made damn sure of that." He smiled slightly.

Forrest looked at his watch. It was 03:20. "Let's undog."

"Roger that, sir." The Gunny turned away and started working his way down the narrow space between the two lines of amtracs. As he passed the word down the line, the crews started unshackling the cables holding the amtracs to the deck.

Forrest stood by the ship's stern ramp, sipping coffee and studying his photocopy of the map showing their objectives and phase lines. Forrest looked up from the map to the turret of four-one and focused on the thick barrel of the M85. It was smeared with purple grease to protect it from ocean salt.

The landing still seemed routine. After all, Forrest and his platoon were doing exactly what they had done over and over again—ungripe the amtracs, load the grunts, radio check, splash, and then run to the beach. They could do all these things in their sleep. But down inside, Forrest felt fear in the idle moment. Fear of partially digested steak and eggs on cool pink sand in the sun ...drying, flies gathering. Of never again seeing his mother and brothers. The fear spiders inside his chest cavity were spinning away—crawling through his heart, tiny legs tickling his cardiac membranes, spinning a web around his heart. Forrest patted four-one's nose and thought of the landing. He took a sip of coffee and moved down through the amtracs, talking to the troops. He walked by four-nine, the last amtrac in line, and leaned against a jeep dogged down several feet behind it. The Gunny walked over, nodded with a slight grin, and stood by Forrest. Silently, they watched the grunts filing out through the watertight hatchway into the tank deck, moving in single file to their designated amtracs. Their faces were painted with yellow-green, brown, and black shapes and stripes—war paint.

When the grunts were loaded, Forrest stood away from the Jeep and looked at the Gunny. "See you on the beach, Gunny." The Gunny nodded. Forrest walked along the starboard bulkhead to four-zero. He looked up to the turret and patted its side, over the "A40" painted there. Then he climbed up to the top. It was 03:53. Forrest listened to the rumble of the diesel engine and noticed the exhaust flapper popping up. He looked forward and then back. All the amtracs were running with ramps up. Although everything in the tank deck was still and seemed visually to be sitting on a flat platform, Forrest felt the pull of gravity on him, shifting from left to right as the ship heaved over ocean waves.

Forrest climbed down into his turret and flipped on his red tactical light. He wedged his photocopied map between hydraulic pipes. Then he double-checked his preset radio frequencies. The skipper had already climbed into the troop commander's hatch and put on the amtrac's comm helmet, so he could talk on the vehicle intercom and access the amtrac's radios that were preset to the company's assigned frequency and the battalion tactical frequency. Forrest had a separate frequency for the amtracs, and he could change channels with a switch on the turret control panel.

The white lights in the tank deck went off, red tactical lights came on, and a red glow settled over the amtracs. The ship's stern ramp lowered slowly, letting in warm sea air. Forrest did a radio check on his platoon frequency, and then he lowered his turret seat and reached up and closed and dogged the hatch. He switched off his turret light and then leaned forward with his comm helmet against hydraulic pipes. He closed his eyes and waited. Minutes passed. Nothing happened. He looked at his watch. It was 04:12. Something was wrong.

A Navy SEAL team had reconned the beach and concluded that the surf conditions were too rough for amtracs to land. So the two hundred and thirty Marines of Golf Company and the amtrac crews stood close by. Forrest lay down on the top of four-zero by his turret and using his helmet as a pillow went to sleep. About 10:00, Goode woke up Forrest and passed along the message that Forrest was wanted on the bridge.

A few minutes later, after walking up six levels, Forrest stepped onto the bridge and squinted at the blistering brightness. The windows all around were bright with green and blue light. It was like walking out of a cave into midday sunshine. He walked over to the chart table where the skipper stood with the ship's captain, a Navy lieutenant commander. Off the right side of the ship, about a mile away, was Grenada. There was a beach of white sand and a thick grove of palms. The sky was deep blue, and the ocean was the deep indigo you see in super deep water beyond the Continental Shelf.

"Lieutenant," the ship's captain said, "we haven't gotten clear word from the SEALS about the beach, but we know the waves in the surf zone are up to about eight feet. We're not sure you can make it over the reef." He paused, gauging Forrest's reaction.

Forrest nodded.

"We're sending you ashore with one amtrac to see if you make it."

That seemed dramatic, but Forrest knew he would make it—he wondered why nobody had asked him about the capabilities of the LVTP7A1. "Sir," Forrest said, "our battalion SOP says we should never put an amtrac in the ocean alone, in case a tow is needed. Can I take two?"

"No, can't afford to lose two. We'll have a SEAL gunboat ride with you to the surf zone. If you need help, the gunboat will be there."

Forrest nodded. "Aye-aye, sir." Forrest looked over at the skipper. "Any scoop on the situation ashore?"

The Navy officer answered. "Two companies ashore. There's been some mortar fire. No casualties, as far as we know."

"When do we splash?"

"Soon as you're ready."

Chapter Ten

The New York Times
"1,900 U.S. Troops … Invade Grenada and Fight…"

October 26, 1983—"An Assault force spearheaded by United
States troops invaded before dawn today and soon seized both of
the island's airfields. But the advance of the invaders, who included contingents from seven Caribbean nations, was reportedly
slowed in the afternoon by heavy fire in the capital."

Forrest descended the dark stairwells to the tank deck, where two
hundred thirty Marines sat on, in, and around the amtracs. Some slept.
Some played cards. Others just lay there, staring up at the top of the

tank deck. Forrest made his way through the crowd to the stern gate. Two Navy officers were standing in the launch tower, looking down at him as he approached. One of the officers nodded to him.

Forrest met with the Gunny, the first section leader, Staff Sergeant Clark, and the crew of four-one—the amtrac first in line to splash. The men stood in a semi-circle around Forrest in front of the ship's closed stern ramp. They were all dressed in flame-retardant Nomex suits and inflatable life jackets. "The squids aren't sure we can cross the reef," Forrest said, "so we're taking four-one in alone to find out. A SEAL gunboat will run to the surf zone with us, and then we'll be on our own. After we get in, the rest of you will make the landing."

The men stood silently, looking back at Forrest.

"You taking just one amtrac in the ocean?" asked the Gunny.

Forrest nodded. "Any questions?"

"No, sir," answered Corporal Allen, four-one's crew chief.

The crew turned back and climbed onto four-one. The Marine infantry was not expendable, so they had already filed out of the amtrac.

Forrest walked over to the turret side of four-one. The Gunny followed.

"Lieutenant…"

Forrest stopped and turned.

"Sir, shouldn't I do this? You get killed, I'll get blamed." The Gunny smiled.

Forrest smiled back. "No, Gunny. You're married. Anyway, it'll be alright. We've done this a million times."

"Not over a reef in seas like this."

"We'll make it."

Forrest pulled his magazine out of the pouch on his .45 holsters. It was empty.

"You got any .45 rounds?"

The Gunny reached in his cargo pocket and pulled out a box. He handed it to Forrest.

Forrest dumped seven bullets in his left hand and then pushed the bullets one-by-one into the magazine. As he did, he turned away so the Gunny would not see his hand shaking.

"You know what this means?" Forrest asked, holding up the magazine loaded with seven .45 rounds.

"What's that, sir?"

"Means I'm six times more lethal than Barney Fife." Forrest laughed. He thought of Atwell and his *Andy Griffith* obsession.

The Gunny smiled politely and told Forrest to keep the box.

Forrest reached up and grabbed the handhold and looked over at the Gunny. "Semper Fi."

The Gunny nodded. "Semper Fi, LT."

Forrest stepped up on top, behind the turret, and looked back at the other thirteen amtracs staged in the tank deck and the Marines crowded on their tops. As he settled into the moment, he was suddenly conscious of all the things that made him he who he was. There was the love of his mother and father and brothers, the marsh down by the house, and the woods by the river. Childhood Christmases and duck hunts and pulling crab pots. There were inherited memories of a long line of granddaddies that fought at places like Yorktown (twice), Sharpsburg, Normandy, and the Chosin Reservoir. It was all there, all at once. In that moment, he looked back over the generations. Then it was all gone, and there was only the heat, the sound of the four-one's engine idling, and the smell of diesel fumes, and the ship's movement.

The ship's stern ramp lowered, forming a crack at the top. Bright sunlight beamed into the tank deck. As the ramp lowered, the colors of sea and sky and the smell of salt water engulfed him. Forrest stepped down inside the turret and stood on the seat and picked up the comm helmet from on top of the periscope sight. He slipped it on his head and checked the connection into the junction box inside the turret and then got a radio check. He sat down inside the turret and checked the ammunition magazine. It was full—750 rounds of .50 caliber machine-gun bullets linked together in a long belt of ammo folded neatly into the magazine. Forrest checked the end of the ammunition belt in the feed tray leading to the gun. It was loose and ready to slide into the gun. He sat back and looked up through the open turret hatch above him. He felt his weight shift with the movement of the ship. He lowered the hatch and dogged it. Then he keyed the microphone on the ship's frequency. "Alfa Foxtrot seven, Romeo five November, over." His earpieces transmitted the clear, incoming radio-modulated voice of some Navy officer. "Five Romeo, Foxtrot seven, go."

"Ready to splash, over."

"Roger, out."

One long minute later, the hammer pinged the pontoon and four-one surged forward. Inside the turret, Forrest held his hands on the forward part of the azimuth ring to steady himself as four-one angled down off the ramp. He felt the vehicle dropping, his weight pressing back in the seat. Then four-one's nose dug into the ocean. The amtrac's pontoons swam under clear water, and their buoyancy quickly brought four-one's nose to the surface. The amtrac leveled off and moved away from the ship, its jet drives pushing white foam. Forrest popped his hatch open and stood up in the Caribbean sunshine.

Four-one rode up a large swell and hovered for a moment at the top. Forrest saw the SEAL gunboat for the first time. It was a gray fast-mover. He scanned the beach and the thick grove of palm trees and thought how beautiful the place was. To his right, Pearls Island rose out of the ocean—a rock cylinder rising hundreds of feet from the sea surface, topped with trees. It gave the scene an exotic *James Bond* quality that Forrest had not expected. He wondered if anyone had ever climbed to the top of the thing. He loaded and cocked the machine gun and then flipped a switch to "safe."

When close to the surf zone, the gunboat peeled off to the right. Forrest watched the boat drop over a large swell and disappear. He ducked down in his turret and locked the hatch. Closed in, Forrest looked up at the back plate of the M-85 machine gun and then out the small thick rectangular window. He held himself steady in the turret as four-one surged forward. A wave broke over four-one, and the amtrac eased back. Forrest felt the tracks hit the bottom, then lift again as the next wave surged up from behind. The vehicle lifted with the wave and surfed forward until the tracks hit bottom again. The wave crashed over, engulfing the amtrac in white water. Forrest popped the hatch and stood up just as another waved crashed over them, lifting the amtrac sideways in the surf zone. The driver, Corporal Allen, flipped the vehicle to land mode and drove four-one onto the beach. Forrest sat in his turret and sighed. He keyed his intercom. "Put her in the palm grove."

"Roger that, sir," answered Allen.

Allen pushed the fuel pedal to the floor, and four-one surged forward. He drove across the white beach and parked in the shade of the palm trees and then lowered the ramp. Forrest lowered his turret seat to the bottom and took off his comm helmet. He stepped out into the troop compartment, took off his life jacket, put on his combat helmet, and stepped out onto a soft bed of palm fronds. There was no sign of people. No Marines. No PRA. No civilians. Thirty feet behind four-one, there was a fighting hole with a palm log laid in front. Three RPGs and six Russian hand-grenades lay on the ground by the hole.

Allen and the crew fanned out around the amtrac and took positions covering the approaches to their position. Forrest stepped into the troop compartment and plugged a handset into the radio. He keyed the handset. "Alfa Foxtrot seven, Romeo five November, over."

"Five Romeo, Foxtrot seven, go."

"We're on the beach. Conditions okay, over."

"Roger, Romeo five November, copy, out."

Forrest walked out to the beach and watched the USS *Manitowoc* making its run parallel to the beach to launch the rest of the amtracs and Golf Company. He walked out to the beach and looked in both directions—palm trees hanging out over white sand, waves building to translucent blue walls that curled and crashed in piles of foam. Down the coast, there were green mountains that faded to blue in the distance.

The ship passed along the beach at four knots about a mile out. Standing now in the shade of a palm tree, Forrest focused binoculars on the stern of the ship. The ramp was down, but no amtracs popped out. The ship passed by the beach—still no amtracs. The ship turned away from the beach and headed for the horizon. Forrest saw through his binoculars that the ship's stern ramp was rising. "Holy shit," he said out loud to himself. He looked around the deserted grove. They were alone.

Forrest walked into the troop compartment and picked up his handset. He keyed the net and spoke. "Alfa Foxtrot seven, Romeo five November, over."

"Romeo five, Alfa Foxtrot, go."

"You leaving? Over."

Static.

Forrest stood on the ramp, watching the ship getting smaller, listening to static on the speaker. The response finally came back through the speaker. "X-ray, Tango, seventeen, Bravo, Cat, Zulu, House, over." Forrest looked back out at the ship sailing away, unable to decipher the explanation he'd just received because he did not have a shackle sheet to decode it. He paused for a moment in the midday heat, wondering what to do next. Then he keyed his handset again. "Roger, out." He stepped back onto the ramp and looked at Corporal Allen. "I think we're on our own."

Allen looked around. "What are we gonna do, sir?"

Forrest stepped out under the palms. He looked around the empty grove, then over at Allen. He couldn't believe the Navy abandoned him with three men on an enemy beach. In fifteen minutes, he could have re-boarded the ship. "Well, Corporal," he said finally, "we're going to seize and occupy this island and disarm the PRA and defuse the political situation." Then he hooted out a laugh. "Don't worry," Forrest said. "The commies have run off. Echo Company is down in Grenville. Fox Company should be on that little mountain there," Forrest gestured to the high green hill north of the airport. He pulled out his map and oriented himself on the ground. As he looked down the runway, he was looking almost due west. The map showed that one click (1000 meters) to his left, there was a "Racecourse (disused)," Echo's LZ that morning.

"Allen," Forrest said, "I'm gonna link up with Fox up on the mountain there. You stay here with your crew and keep four-one safe."

The airport was a typical "Banana Republic" style facility cut out of seaside palm groves. There was a short runway that could handle small private aircraft and a metal Quonset hut for an office that sat on the far edge of the runway, away from the ocean. There was one twin-engine prop plane sitting on the grass off to the left of the runway.

Forrest started off down the edge of the tree line by the open area adjacent to the runway. Other than insects clicking in the heat, there was no sign of life. At the end of the runway, Forrest turned into the jungle. The shade was less hot, and there was an aroma of jungle so acute he could taste it. He worked his way through a loose web of wide leaves and giant ferns that was like a setting for a dinosaur movie. As he moved away from the edge of the forest, the area opened up enough to see forty or fifty feet, and the ground changed from a soft mat of rotting organic refuse to an uneven, rocky climb. As he worked, heat rose under his steel helmet and flak jacket. Sweat dripped down the side of his face, stinging his eyes.

Halfway up the hill, an invisible voice stopped him. "Hold up there."

Forrest stopped dead. "Amtracs," Forrest said.

"The sky is blue," said the voice.

Forrest answered, "I love the Catskill mountains," – the challenge and pass words were "blue" and "Catskill."

The unseen Marine stepped out in the open. "Come on up."

Forrest followed the Marine up the hillside. Off to his right, he noticed a spot of color amidst the dark blue-green of the jungle shade. Forrest stopped and looked down on a lone orchid. He noticed the shape of the flower, its curves and color, pastel pink. Then he stepped forward towards bright yellow-greens of a clearing in the sunlight. There, in the sunlight, was a scorched 23mm anti-aircraft gun and three dead PRA soldiers laid out on the edge of the small clearing. All three had been hit by 20mm cannon fire from a Marine Cobra, which left the bodies badly mutilated. Just under the crest of the hill, Forrest found the battalion commander, a lieutenant colonel (the "Colonel") in the middle of his CP, talking on the radio. The Colonel finally looked up. "Lieutenant Forrest, I'm glad to see you." His smile reassured Forrest. "You know what's going on?"

"No, sir."

"We had to send Golf Company over to St. George's to reinforce a SEAL team that's hemmed-in at the Governor General's house. The battalion staff is flying over to meet them in an about an hour, you're coming with us. But just you. Your guys stay here with Echo."

"Yes, sir." Forrest nodded. "I'll pass the word to my guys." He excused himself and then walked down to four-one. It was afternoon now. The sky had mellowed to a deep blue, and sunshine angled down through the palms, spackling light on the amtrac. As a kid, Forrest had fantasized about going to a Caribbean island for a vacation some day, and he had a full set of images and an idea about what that would be like—umbrella drinks and pretty girls in bikinis. He saw his first palm tree on a family trip to Disney World when he was sixteen and always associated the tree with exotic vacations. Now, walking alone along the edge of the palm grove, he was amused by the reality of this particular Caribbean getaway.

Back at the CP, Forrest found a soft place in the jungle and sat. He took his helmet off, leaned against a tree, and relaxed. He thought how the operation looked like Vietnam, or at least his idea of Vietnam. Here was the Colonel, winner of the Navy Cross for heroism fighting in Vietnam, on a combat mission in another jungle. Much of their gear dated to Vietnam. The command post in the jungle matched images imprinted in Forrest's mind from hundreds of evening news broadcasts he watched as a kid during the War. Now, the scene was alive before him in vivid color with the smells of the jungle and heat and the feel of sweat-soaked uniform against his skin and smelly dead bodies off to the side.

At dusk, a CH-46 helicopter flew in and landed on the runway. The Colonel and his staff, now including Forrest, boarded and took off. After a stop for several hours on the USS RALEIGH, they flew to the USS GUAM.

As they approached, the pilot pulled the nose of the CH-46 up and eased the helicopter down towards the flight deck. The helicopter vibrated as it slowed, waking Forrest. The CH-46 settled down on the deck, and the ramp dropped. Forrest and the others walked out onto the Caribbean night, and as soon as he cleared the fumes of the chopper, he caught a warm sea scented breeze and thought of summer nights at the beach. Then he followed the others down a stairwell into the gray innards of the ship, where the sea salt smell was overtaken by the smell of fresh paint. A Navy officer led them down another stairwell into a small passageway near the command center. Forrest and several other officers stood by in this passageway while the Colonel and his senior people went into the command center for a briefing. After a few minutes, Forrest sat on the floor and took off his steel helmet.He leaned back against the wall and tried to go back to sleep. It was well after midnight.

At 03:00, the Colonel walked out of the command center into the passageway.

"Let's go," he said.

Forrest stood, put on his helmet, and followed the staff officers into a small room below the flight deck to wait for the helicopter. While they waited, the Colonel walked over to Forrest and lifted his map. "Lieutenant Forrest, we're going to land here at Grand Mal. Golf Company and your platoon and the tanks are there waiting for us. At 04:30, we're going to attack down this road." He pointed his finger down the coast road to Queen's Park Racecourse, just north of St. Georges. "Intelligence reports there is a PRA battalion defending this hill here on the far side of the racecourse." The Colonel pointed to a large hill sandwiched between the racecourse and St. Georges. The small village of Gretna Green was spread out along the lower portions of the hill. "Intelligence also reports a small force of Cubans, maybe a company, north of Grand Mal. We're going to leave three amtracs with an infantry platoon as a blocking force at Grand Mal. The rest of your tracs and Golf Company are going to attack down this road and across the racecourse. The tanks will follow."

Forrest looked surprised. Tanks usually lead an attack.

The Colonel paused, interpreting the look. "Can't afford to lose a tank. Tank gets hit, we'll be stuck on that road, bottled up. Amtrac gets hit, we'll just push it aside and keep on going. Then," the Colonel continued, "Golf Company is going to push up into the hills above St. George's and secure the Governor General's house." His finger traced on the map up mountain ridges to a small black dot labeled "Governor General Residence."

"You and the tanks will deal with the PRA battalion on that hill."

The hatch opened, and a Navy man gave the signal to climb up to the flight deck. The Colonel went first, with the staff following along. The CH-46 helicopter was waiting for them, engines running, rotors chopping at the night air. As it sat, the nose of the helicopter was higher than its rear, back on its haunches like a stalking lion. Forrest bent slightly as he walked into the helicopter and then found a seat on the canvas bench. The engines powered up, and the rotors beat the air harder until the chopper lifted off and gained altitude. The nose dipped down and the helicopter gathered speed. After the pilot turned off the red cabin light, it was dark, and the round portholes were filled with the color of the night. The helicopter hummed along in the dark, gradually getting lower, heading into the black mountains silhouetted against the night sky. Two hundred yards out, the chopper banked to the left and flew along the dark coastline.

The helicopter finally slowed to a hover, dropped down, and the Marine crewman signaled the passengers to jump from the chopper's opened stern ramp. Forrest stood and worked his way to the stern ramp and jumped blindly into the darkness, dropping into about two feet of water. He waded to shore with the others and stepped up on dry land. The helicopter pulled up, pitched, and headed out. Forrest walked up into a small clearing. All around, amtracs and tanks loomed in the darkness. He was home again.

At 03:30, the officers gathered by a dead tree lying on the ground near the beach. The Colonel sat on the tree. Several of the officers sat or knelt on the ground. Forrest stood. In a calm voice, the Colonel laid out the attack order. As he explained the tactical situation, a rooster crowed nearby. Then it crowed again. Ignoring the screeching bird, the Colonel clicked through his order. As he spoke in the darkness, Forrest looked over towards the sound of the rooster. Then, to the south, a C-130 "Spectre" gunship fired its 40mm Gatling gun—pouring down 1,800 rounds per minute. It sounded like a buzz saw in the sky. The Colonel stopped his order and looked up, waiting for the long burst to end. After the firing stopped, he explained that an infantry platoon and three amtracs would stay at the beach area to block reinforcements from a Cuban unit thought to be north of the position. Two infantry platoons, ten amtracs, and five tanks would attack south and assault the ridge just north of St. George's that was held by a PRA battalion. The column would head south on the coast road that ran along a steep ridge and then break into an open field called Queen's Park Raceway before hitting the wooded ridge and the little village of Gretna Green on the far side of a stream.

There was no moon, and it was so dark that Forrest had trouble finding four-zero. He finally did and then stepped up on the ramp and looked into the tar-black troop compartment. "Anybody home?"

"Yessir."

"That you, Garnett?"

"Yessir. Welcome back." Garnett walked out of the troop compartment, rubbing his eyes.

The rooster crowed again.

After the Gunny and the section leaders gathered by four-zero, Forrest gave them the attack order, and the men dispersed to explain the plan to their men. All around them in the dark, the plan was filtering down through the chain of command. Within twenty minutes, every Marine knew what to do.

Forrest stood now out in the open on grass and looked up at the palm trees silhouetted against the moonless sky. A gentle breeze drifted in from the Caribbean Sea. The Gunny walked up and stood beside him.

"You think the platoon is ready for this, Gunny?"

"Yes, sir. These are good Marines."

"You know, Gunny, every Marine everywhere is wishing he was here right now."

The Gunny nodded.

"We've been eat'n shit since Vietnam. I'm sick of Vietnam—no offense," said Forrest.

"I'm sick of it, too, LT."

"Russians invaded Afghanistan. Iranians took American hostages. Cubans in Angola and all over Central America. And we've been acting like a neutered cat. Just eating buckets and buckets of shit from the worst low-life sons of bitches on the planet. And now we get to attack somebody." Forrest's old cynicism about the country's loyalty to its allies and its military had no place on the beach that morning. This was exactly the kind of mission that inspired Forrest. Though he'd found his patriotic footing, at least for the moment, he was still scared. If there really was a PRA battalion at Gretna Green, they'd be in trouble because the Marine attack force was so small.

The C-130 gunship opened fire again, far off. The buzz-saw sound sent a chill up Forrest's spine.

Forrest walked quietly among the amtracs. Around each vehicle, Marines were lining up to board. His crews were checking systems and getting ready. The idling engines made a low rumbling sound.

Forrest found Sergeant Tabb by four-four. He would lead the column down to Queen's Park. The road along the coast was carved into the steep side of D'Arbeau Hill. For part of the way, there would be a steep cliff down to their right and a steep hill up to their left. This road fed into open ground at Queen's Park. For a few seconds, four-four would be the only amtrac exposed to whatever fire the PRA would muster. If the PRA soldiers were competent, they'd concentrate all their fire on one amtrac at a time as each one popped out into the open, knocking out the first one, then the second, until the attack was blunted.

Forrest wondered if Tabb would still be alive when the sun came up. He assumed Tabb was wondering the same thing. "I know you'll be hauling ass when you break into the open. Stay to the right so we can get in echelon on your left," Forrest said.

"Don't worry, sir. I've got it."

Forrest wanted to say more. He wanted to tell Tabb he was a great Marine and a good man. But that was too sappy. Doing what had to be done, *no matter what,* was expected. Forrest looked around in the dark at the amtracs and the tanks and the infantry preparing to load and felt a shot of adrenaline.

He patted Tabb on the shoulder. "See you down there."

"Yes, sir."

Forrest walked over to four-zero and climbed up to the turret. The engine was humming. The troops were loaded. The skipper was in the troop leader's hatch, checking his radio connection. Before lowering himself into the turret, Forrest paused and looked back again at the palms against the sky and breathed in salty sea air. Newspapers all over the world would report what was about to happen, he thought. And here he was, among two hundred fifty Marines in this dark tropical cove at center stage. The Rooster crowed again.

Forrest lowered himself down inside. He clicked on the red tactical light, then put on his comm helmet and tested his intercom with the skipper. A red light on the control panel showed that the M-85 was locked and cocked.

At 04:15, the column rolled forward. One by one the amtracs fell into the column behind four-four. Four-zero moved forward into the column as the fifth vehicle in line. As four-zero moved forward, Forrest felt the fear spiders crawling inside and the flutter of panic and dread swelling up through all the excitement and adrenaline. His heartbeat quickened. He gripped the front lip of the turret hatchway and held steady. As four-zero rolled easily from the grass onto the hard surface road, Forrest dropped down in his turret, gave himself the sign of the cross, and prayed silently: *Please, God, be with us today.* But the prayer wasn't really a prayer. Forrest had ignored God, and he did not approach the subject at that moment with anything close to humility or love or sincere belief ... he was just a scared guy alone in his turret who was trying to cope.

The amtracs, all running dark, moved along the edge of the ridgeline with a steep rise to the left and a cliff to the right. The column increased speed as the lead amtracs got out on the road and built up speed. From his turret, Forrest looked out through the palm trees on his right at the dark Caribbean below and up at stars overhead through the canopy of tropical foliage. To his left, there were small wooden houses on the steep hillside. The houses were all dark, save for blue glints of starlight reflecting off black window glass.

As four-four reached the last turn before breaking out into the open field at Queen's Park, two illumination rounds popped high above. The lights floated across the sky, lighting the field. Forrest looked up through the palm foliage at the drifting lights and made out the silhouettes of tree trunks ahead against the lit-up area of the open field. Four-four made the turn and started the downhill run into the open. Then four-three, four-five, and four-six followed. As they rolled out over open ground, they spread out in echelon so they could all shoot ahead into the far tree line. Four-zero rounded the curve, and Goode floored the fuel pedal. The engine screamed, and the stack-flapper shot straight up and the vehicle accelerated downhill, into the open. The illumination rounds had drifted down range, casting their flickering light on green hills far to the left. Down in front, four-four was on the far right, nearly halfway across the field with three amtracs staggered to its left. Goode drove four-zero to the left of four-six and swung around to face the tree line.

With his head up out of the turret, Forrest reached down inside and flipped the safety switch to "off." Then he twisted the control handled forward. The barrel of the M-85 lowered down, pointing at the lower edge of the black tree line ahead. Forrest glanced over as four-six's M-85 barrel lowered down. The amtracs were all hitting forty miles per hour in a staggered line, engines screaming, transmissions whining, rocking forward and back with the bumpy terrain, their guns on the far tree line, all surging forward together. Forrest felt the momentum of the attack—two hundred tons of armor hurdling across the field. It was a charge across open ground, and it was grand. In the past, there had been cavalry charges, horses on line, galloping, pounding the ground as they surged forward, sabers flashing in the sunlight. And great infantry charges, like Stonewall Jackson's at Chancellorsville—lean men in long ranks running forward, bayonets gleaming, high-pitched Rebel yells ringing across the battlefield. But this attack was something different. It was T-Rexes on line, bellowing a throaty, mechanical scream as they came on.

The PRA defenders fired RPGs, and sparkling explosions impacted across the field in front of the attacking amtracs. Standing in his turret with his head out in the open, Forrest watched the explosions, but he could not hear them over the noise of the engines.

Another illumination round lit the field.

The amtracs moved through the area where the RPGs had hit and made the edge of the tree line by a small stream bank, where they stopped and dropped ramps. The grunts fanned out in front of the amtracs, crossed over the stream, and took defensive positions on the far stream bank. Five tanks rumbled into Queen's Park and took positions covering the approach from St. George's and the road down from Mount Helicon. The PRA had withdrawn. The park belonged to the United States Marine Corps. The amtracs sat along the tree line with engines rumbling, like winded beasts.

A Marine patrol headed up the hill towards the Governor General's house. Forrest told Garnett to move four-zero to the edge of a steep hill on the south side of the park. Then Forrest called in the Gunny and his section leaders, Sergeant Tabb and Staff Sergeants Crockett and Jefferson. It was 05:15 and just starting to get light.

As the sun rose, Garnett boiled a pot of water on a portable gas stove. Forrest broke out a package of instant coffee from his C-rat box. He dumped the brown powder in the bottom of his metal canteen cup, then poured in steaming water. He sat on a dead tree trunk in the shade of a palm tree and sipped his coffee as he waited for his leaders. He looked out across open ground, at light green grass sparkling with dew in the morning light. The sun, low in the sky, cast yellow light on the green mountain, highlighting its eastern slopes. He felt remnants of an adrenaline buzz, but all the stress and tension was gone.

The Gunny walked up first. "You got any more coffee, sir?'

"C-rat coffee."

Sergeant Tabb and Staff Sergeants Crockett and Jefferson walked up together.

"Morning," Forrest said, nodding to Tabb.

"Morn'n, sir," Tabb said with a relieved smile.

"That was fun," Crockett said.

Gunny walked over to the dead tree and sat by Forrest. He sipped from his tin cup.

"What did they shoot at us?" Forrest wondered out loud.

Crockett shrugged.

"Mortars? RPGs? I don't know," said Tabb.

"You see it, Gunny?"

"No, sir, LT. They must've shot before we broke out."

Forrest sipped his coffee. "We need security patrols, especially over by you, Staff Sergeant Jefferson. It looks pretty thick over there, and you have that high ground overlooking your position. Take out a security patrol, but don't go too far."

Chapter Eleven

The New York Times
"Transcript of Address by President on Lebanon and Grenada."

October 28, 1983—"My fellow Americans, some two months ago we were shocked by the brutal massacre of 269 men, women and children, in the shooting down of a Korean airliner. Now, in these past several days, violence has erupted again, in Lebanon and Grenada. ...."

In early evening, after eating a C-rat dinner and walking the line, Forrest walked back to four-zero. The ramp was down and rested on two five-gallon oil cans so it was level, like a stage. He sat on the ramp and looked out at the Caribbean Sea and the pale evening sky and smelled food cooking in the little shanties on the edge of the park. He sipped bad coffee and watched the colors in the sky fade to a cool, breezy darkness. The full weight of his exhaustion settled over him, and he wanted to sleep.

After dark, Garnett brought a portable radio out onto the ramp and tried to pick-up a news broadcast. He sat on the jump seat by the ramp and slowly moved the AM dial. The channels dialed in and out, staggered with static. He finally settled on a British voice.

"Listen to this, sir," Garnett said. "They're introducing President Reagan."

Forrest stood and turned around. Shields and Goode appeared. Just before the speech, the Gunny walked up, too.

"What's up, LT?"

"President Reagan."

The Gunny nodded in the dark, turned and put one foot up on the ramp and leaned in to listen. The dark shapes of men gathered around the ramp. Above them, black silhouettes of palms moved gently against the evening sky.

"This is live BBC coverage of President Reagan's address concerning the situations in Lebanon and Grenada," the English voice said through static.

"Where is this coming from, Garnett?"

"Barbados, sir."

Then the unmistakable voice and rhythm of President Ronald Reagan radiated smoothly through the static. "This past Sunday, at twenty-two minutes after six, Beirut time, with dawn just breaking, a truck looking like a lot of other vehicles in the city approached the airport on a busy main road. There was nothing in its appearance to suggest that it was any different than the trucks or cars that were normally seen on and around the airport. But this one was different.

"At the wheel was a young man on a suicide mission. The truck carried some 2000 pounds of explosives, but there was no way our

Marine guards could know this." The President faded in static. Corporal Garnett picked up the radio and held it at different angles to pick up the signal. He tuned and tinkered until the President's voice came through the static again. He was still talking about the bombing. "The truck smashed through the doors of the headquarters building in which our Marines were sleeping and instantly exploded. The four-story concrete building collapsed in a pile of rubble. More than two hundred of our sleeping men were killed in that one hideous and insane attack."

President Reagan's smooth delivery resonated out from the darkness. He explained the background of the Beirut deployment and then turned to steps taken to increase security. Forrest listened closer.

"We ordered the battleship USS *NEW JERSEY* to join our naval forces offshore." Corporal Garnett let out a Marine grunt – "ooorraahh!"

"Without even firing them," the President continued, "the threat of its sixteen-inch guns silenced those who once fired down on our Marines from the hills. And there is a good reason we suddenly had a cease fire." The static picked up again and obscured the President's words. Forrest took a long drink of warm canteen water and then looked around Queen's Park. He could see several amtracs and two tanks.

"Brave young men have been taken from us. Many others have been grievously wounded. Are we to tell them their sacrifice was wasted ..." static obscured the voice. Then the voice came back, strong through the static: "We must not strip every ounce of meaning and purpose from their courageous sacrifice. Now, I know that another part of the world in very much on our minds..."

The dark figures standing around the ramp leaned in and strained to pick up every word.

"...a place much closer to our shores. Grenada." This was the first time they heard the name pronounced properly, not like the car, but like "grenade." The president continued, "The Island is only twice the size of the District of Columbia, with a population of about 110,000 people." Forrest glanced around at the handful of men with him in the dark, under palms in the delicate breeze, listening to the president of the United States talk about them.

"In 1979, trouble came to Grenada. Maurice Bishop, a protégé of Fidel Castro, staged a military coup and overthrew the government, which had been elected under the constitution left to the people by the British. He sought the help of Cuba in building an airport, which he claimed was for tourist trade, but looked suspiciously suitable for military aircraft, including Soviet-built long-range bombers." Static again obscured the president's words. Corporal Garnett picked up the radio again and repositioned it until the words came through. "...alarmed as Bishop built an army greater than all of theirs combined.

"Obviously, it was not purely for defense. In this last year or so, Prime Minister Bishop gave indications that he might like better relations with the United States. He even made a trip to our country and met with senior officials at the White House and the State Department. Whether he was serious or not, we will never know.

"On October 12, a small group in his militia seized him and put him under arrest. They were, if anything, even more radical and more devoted to Castro's Cuba than he had been. Several days later, a crowd of citizens appeared before Bishop's home, freed him, and escorted him toward the headquarters of the Military Counsel. They were fired upon. A number, including some children, were killed, and Bishop was seized. He and several members of his Cabinet were subsequently executed, and a twenty-four-hour shoot-to-kill curfew was put in effect. Grenada was without a government, its only authority exercised by a self-proclaimed band of military men.

"There were then about 1000 of our citizens on Grenada, 800 of them students at St. George's University Medical School. Concerned that they'd be harmed or held as hostages, I ordered a flotilla of ships then on its way to Lebanon with Marines—part of our regular rotation program—to circle south on a course that would put them somewhere in the vicinity of Grenada in case there should be a need to evacuate our people.

"Last weekend, I was awakened in the early morning hours and told that six members of the Organization of Eastern Caribbean States joined by Jamaica and Barbados had sent an urgent request that we join them in a military operation to restore order and democracy to Grenada."

The static thickened again. Forrest stepped away from four-zero and stretched. He had been up for more than twenty-four hours. He was thinking about getting some sleep on a bed of palm fronds under one the big palm trees. Then the static cleared again. "...the first photos from Grenada. They included pictures of a warehouse of military equipment, one of three we've uncovered so far. This warehouse contained weapons and ammunition stacked almost to the ceiling, enough to supply thousands of terrorists. Grenada, we were told, was a friendly island paradise for tourism. Well, it wasn't. It was a Soviet-Cuban colony being readied as a major military bastion to export terror and undermine democracy. We got there just in time."

The President talked about the progress of the operation and the Soviet roles in both Grenada and Lebanon. He talked about the need to endure hardship and sacrifices to defend strategic interests worldwide. Then he closed the speech with a story.

"May I share something with you that I think you would like to know? It's something that happened to the commandant of our Marine Corps, General Paul Kelley, while he was visiting our critically injured Marines in an Air Force hospital. It says more than any of us could ever hope to say about the gallantry and heroism of these young men." The Marines in the dark gathered closer to the radio in complete silence. "...young men who served so willingly so that others might have a chance at peace and freedom in their own lives and in the life of their country.

"I'll let General Kelley's words describe the incident. He spoke of a 'young Marine with more tubes going in and out of his body than I have ever seen in one body. He couldn't see very well. He reached up and grabbed my four stars just to make sure I was who I said I was. He held my hand with a firm grip. He was making signals and we realized he wanted to tell me something. We put a pad of paper in his hand and he wrote: *Semper Fi.*'"

It was silent around the ramp, except for the rustling of palms fronds in the sea breeze.

"Well," President Reagan continued, "if you've been a Marine; or if, like myself, you're an admirer of the Marines, you know those words are a battle cry, a greeting and a legend in the Marine Corps. They're Marine shorthand for the motto of the Corps: Semper Fidelis, Always Faithful." The speech was over. Garnett turned off the radio.

The men around the ramp were silent. Then the Gunny yelled out, "You girls better not be crying!" The Marines broke into laughter, then moved off in the darkness to their positions.

Chapter Twelve

The New York Times
"On the Island, Timid Waves for Invaders."

October 29, 1983—"Along the road into town, Grenadian civilians waved timidly today as truckloads of American and Caribbean soldiers headed into this capital. The soldiers came from Queen's Park, a soccer field where the United States Marines have their command post. At 3 P.M. 250 men from the Caribbean contingent of the multinational invasion force had landed by helicopter at the field."

The following morning, Forrest was summoned to the command post. It was early and cool. He could smell bacon cooking in Gretna

Green. As he walked, he looked over to his left at one of the tanks and noticed Marines moving in the palm trees near the bank of the stream. He passed a dead Marine covered by a white sheet with his lower legs and boots sticking out and thought it strange that they did not have any body bags. The sight shocked him—this was the first dead Marine he'd seen. Forrest looked down at his own combat boots, exactly like the boots sticking out from under the sheet. The observation made him queasy.

The command post was set up in the two LVTC7s—the amtrac command vehicles equipped with banks of radios. Forrest found the Colonel sitting on the stern jump seat by the open stern ramp of one of the C7s. The Colonel sat with no helmet, his flak jacket open, eating an apple. Yellow morning light fell on the side of his face.

"Morning, sir."

The Colonel nodded and explained that all of his infantry platoons were occupied in and around St. Georges. "Lieutenant Forrest. I need you to take out a patrol. We've got a guide for you." The Colonel gestured over to a native Grenadian standing by the other C7. "He says he knows where some PRA bad guys are hiding in the interior. On the map he was holding he pointed to a small town called Snug's Corner. Take three amtracs and fifteen or sixteen of your men and the guide and clear that area of PRA or Cubans. Capture them if you can, kill them if you have to. Give us a sitrep every hour. If you need help, let us know, and we'll send up one of Golf Company's platoons. Oh, and Forrest, don't do anything stupid."

"Yessir."

Forrest walked with the guide back towards four-zero. As they walked by the dead Marine, Forrest experienced an instant of self-reflection. In a flash, he saw himself truly as a collection of appetites—for praise and ambition and food and bourbon and fun and sex. He saw no actual purpose to his life beyond satisfying his appetites, and he realized he'd been living like a monkey and that he was nowhere near ready to die. He needed time to figure things out ... but that poor fellow under the sheet had run out of time. He felt a lump of panic trapped down inside his gut, the weight of the responsibility of getting the job done without any needless casualties, the need to suppress what he was feeling about that poor dead Marine laid out on the grass under a borrowed bed sheet, and his own sudden realization that he'd been leading an aimless life.

He looked over at the man walking beside him, a middle-aged black man with the dark skin of a pure African. The man had tinges of gray in his short hair and wrinkles around his eyes. He wore a plain, short-sleeved polyester red shirt and cotton khaki trousers and sandals.

"What's your name?" Forrest asked.

"Richard Smith."

"That your real name?"

"Yes, sir."

Forrest nodded. "You'll be guiding me this morning?"

"Yes, Captain."

"I'm a lieutenant."

The man nodded. "Yes, Lieutenant."

Back at four-zero, Forrest spread a map out on the ramp. "So, Mr. Smith, where are we going; and what are we going to find?" The guide said he knew where a PRA machine gunner was, and he pointed to the small village in the island's interior. Forrest's patrol would be the first American move into that area. Wondering if the man could be trusted, Forrest looked him in the eyes for several seconds. The man looked back steadily and smiled. "Don't worry, Lieutenant. I'm for you."

Forrest stood in his turret as four-zero rolled into St. George's slowly along the harbor road at the head of a three-amtrac column. A group of reporters stood along the stone seawall. Forrest hated reporters. As far as he could tell, the whole Marine Corps hated reporters. Reporters got no access and were widely regarded as a particularly virulent form of fungus—especially by Vietnam vets, many of whom thought the press lost the war. Forrest's old man had hated Walter Cronkite, and some of that had rubbed-off on Forrest. As the amtracs passed the reporters,

Forrest smiled when he noticed that they were all bunched together and escorted by Marines in full combat gear. It spoke volumes, he thought, that they were taking men off the line to keep these journalists contained.

They rolled slowly by redbrick houses that faced the harbor—Georgian houses dating to days of human slavery. The faces of the houses looked out into the yellow sky over the harbor and the distant horizon. The bricks were all dark burgundy in the morning shadow. The window glass was thick and wavy and reflected pastel colors of the morning sky. On the far side of the harbor, a green hill jutted out into the sea. The guide, sitting on top of the amtrac by the turret, signaled to turn left. Goode pushed the fuel pedal down and twisted the wheel. Four-zero revved and pivoted and moved up the road towards the purple shadows of the jungle on the mountain above St. George's.

The road ran along the edge of the ridge with houses above to the left and below to the right. Forrest looked back over his right shoulder at St. George's and the harbor and was surprised how fast the town and harbor had become small with distance. The road crossed over the ridge and then dropped into a hollow that was heavily shaded by jungle-covered ridges. Forrest took a last look at the town as Goode drove four-zero over the crest of the ridge and down into the hollow. At the bottom of the ridge, they came to a narrow bridge over a stream. On the other side of the bridge, the road flattened out through an open area where several stucco type ranch houses sat in bright sunlight on the right side of the road. Four-zero stopped. Forrest studied the houses through binoculars. There was no sign of any people. The windows were all dark, and sunlight glinted off the tin roofs.

Forrest took off his comm helmet, grabbed his combat helmet, and climbed up out of the turret and down to the street. Standing in dappled sunlight, he put on his helmet and walked out onto the short concrete bridge. When he stepped into sunlight, he felt the intensity of the hot sun. There was still no movement around the houses or along the roadside. On the far side of the bridge, there was a row of parked cars on the right side of the road. The car closest to the bridge was a tan Mercedes.

Forrest turned and walked back into the dappled shade by four-zero. The Gunny was standing on the road by four-zero now, stuffing a wad of tobacco into his mouth.

"You ought not go strolling out there like that, Lieutenant."

"I haven't eaten any apricots, so I figured it was okay."

"Somethin happens to you, they gonna blame me, you know." The Gunny spit tobacco juice.

Forrest nodded.

"Just making sure you don't forget, LT."

"Gunny, we can get over the bridge; but those cars don't leave us room to get by."

"Run the fuckers over." The Gunny was smiling with the thought of it.

Forrest studied the cars. He looked at the Mercedes. "Nice cars."

The Gunny nodded. "A little odd, though, LT. These houses probably belong to commie hotshots. We'd better be extra careful."

Forrest climbed back up to the turret. He looked over at Goode and nodded. A wide grin sparkled across Goode's face. He looked forward, and the exhaust-stack flapper popped up as the engine revved and four-zero surged ahead. Four-zero moved into sunshine and then across the bridge. Forrest lowered down in the turret with only his head sticking up in the air. He spun the turret to the right and pointed the M85 at the houses. Four-zero hit the Mercedes and heeled up on the right as it crossed over, with metal crinkling and glass popping. The guide looked back, his eyes wide, and he said something Forrest could not hear over the sound of the engine and the crunching and popping under the treads. After passing over the car, Forrest elevated himself in his turret and leaned out and looking back. The side of the car was squished down. It looked like half the car had been beaten with sledgehammers at the county fair and pounded down to less than three feet high.

Four-zero ran over the next car and the next. The other two amtracs followed in the same path, mashing down the cars even more. Four-zero crunched over the last car and eased out onto the clear road. Goode pushed the power pedal, and four-zero moved smoothly up the road. Just past the row of houses, Forrest noticed what looked like a dead body under a cloud of flies in the ditch on the right side of the road. They stopped. By the time the Gunny walked up, Forrest was down on the road. Up ahead, they saw a black arm rising up from the grass. The hand was drawn into a desiccated knot. "He probably ate some apricots," said the Gunny. It smelled awful, and Forrest clinched his teeth to hold his vomit and held his hand over his nose and mouth as he and the Gunny stood over the body. The body was black and bloated, and there were burn marks on the arms. The eyes were open and dried like a hardening film at the top of a bowl of vanilla pudding. Flies alighted in crowded bunches on the eyes and fluid around the nostrils and mouth. The Gunny leaned over the corpse and then looked over at Forrest. "Looks like he caught the blunt end of a riot."

"That's the smell of gooks nearby," said the Gunny.

Forrest looked over with a quizzical expression.

The Gunny shrugged. "Old habit. I don't know what else to call these fuckers."

"I'm sure we'll think of something," answered Forrest. Forrest looked up at the guide sitting on top of four-zero. "You think we can trust him, Gunny?"

"Lieutenant, we can't trust anybody."

Forrest looked up the road and noted how the thick jungle edged up to the roadside. It would be easy for a resolute enemy to hammer them with RPGs.

They remounted and headed up the road, rolling by the dead man in the ditch and moving up out of the valley. As the road took them high onto the ridgeline, he could see the ocean again, through palm trees by the roadside. The road crossed the ridge and dropped into another valley, and the column sank back into purple shade and then came to the edge of open ground on the valley floor and stopped. Two hundred meters out, there stood the village of small pastel-colored houses. A brook ran behind the village on the right and along the edge of the ridgeline to the bridge in front of four-zero. There was thick grass on the stream bank. From his distance, Forrest saw that the village was well-groomed—grass trimmed, white picket fences, and no garbage. White sheets hung on a line behind a house on the near edge of the village. A kid's bike was leaning against a white fence. But there were no people.

The men dismounted and gathered in a loose line in the shade near the open ground. They looked out on the little houses sitting quietly out in the heat, and no one spoke. Forrest stood quietly looking out into the sunlight and thought the day and the place was better suited for a summer party. He imagined himself sitting by the stream with his feet in the clear water, drinking cold beer and listening to "Free Bird," telling funny stories with his friends, and there'd be girls. He'd drink long, dreamy gulps of icy beer and look up at the blue sky and smell the jungle flowers, and it would be good. He looked back at his young Marines—good boys wearing old-fashioned American combat helmets and flak jackets and war belts and M-16s with faces tanned or black and their eyes fixed on the little village.

Forrest called the nervous guide over from four-zero. "Where we going?"

The guide pointed to the right of the road. There was a small one-story wood-framed house on the far side of a brown field about a hundred yards out. The house looked like a little playhouse off in the distance. It was white in the sun. The windows were dark.

"That house?" Forrest asked, pointing.

"Dere a big PRA man in dere."

The Gunny walked up. "We could use the creek bed. It'll give us pretty good cover to move around back."

Forrest looked over at the bank, then back at the house. He nodded slowly. "I see."

They stood for a moment. Forrest said, "These people are pretty good at shooting civilians and executing people, but I don't think they're going to fight us. I don't want to dignify them by trying to sneak up on them; that implies that we respect them. I'm just gonna walk up to the front door."

The Gunny nodded. "You're gonna get me in trouble."

"Leave Sergeant T here with four men."

The Gunny nodded again. "Yes, sir." He walked over to Sergeant Tabb.

Forrest stepped out in the sunlight and headed up the road. The men fell in behind him in a loose column. Thirty yards down, just before reaching the houses along the main road, Forrest stepped off the road to his right and walked into the field. It was hot under his helmet, and streams of sweat dripped down the side of his face, and he was wet under his flak jacket. The ground was covered with played-on grass and sunbaked, bald patches that were as hard and white as concrete. Forrest walked by a soccer ball, its top half glaring white in the sun, and then moved up behind a palm tree in front of the house and took a knee. The men moved forward quietly into a semi-circle around the front of the house. As they moved into position, all was quiet except the soft sounds of gear jiggling.

The house sat in a patch of palm shade. Back behind the house, the ground rose to the side of the jungle-covered mountain. Forrest dropped the magazine from his M-16 and ejected the round from the chamber—he didn't want an accidental firing when he butt-stroked the door of the house. He reinserted the magazine, stood, and ran across open ground to the front door. He slammed up against the front of the house and stood with his back to the wall beside the front door. He looked back at his men, all kneeling now in a wide arc, their faces shaded by the lips of their helmets. He heard women crying in the house. Forrest's heart was beating hard, but he was so focused that he did not notice the heat or his fatigue. He spun around and drove the butt of his rifle into the dry-rotted door. His rifle butt broke through the door, like breaking through a pane of glass. The women screamed. Forrest pulled the rifle back and then drove the rifle butt into the doorknob. The door flew open. Forrest chambered a round, flipped off the safety, and stepped inside with the rifle raised to fire. He quickly shifted to his left to avoid being backlit by the open door and then he stood for a moment, blinking to adjust his vision to the dark room. It was empty. The women were in a back room. Their screaming trailed off to sobs.

Forrest stood for a few seconds to let his eyes adjust to the darkness. The room was about twelve feet by fifteen feet. There was a brown wool rug on the floor and a straight-backed chair by the window. To his right, there was a closed door. To his front, there was an open entryway to a kitchen, where the women were huddled. He turned to his right and kicked the door open. Forrest poked the M-16 barrel in and then leaned forward. His eyes narrowed quizzically. Then he smiled.

Forrest was still in the doorway when the Gunny walked in. He looked down and hooted out a laugh and said, "Holy shit, LT!" There was a bed under the window on the right side of the room. A man's legs stuck out from under the bed. "A real gook would never hide under a bed," said the Gunny.

Forrest and the Gunny each grabbed a foot and pulled the man into the middle of the floor and dropped his feet. The man rolled over, looking embarrassed. "Tie him up, Gunny, and put him in four-zero." The Gunny kicked the man's bare leg. "Get up." The man climbed up slowly. He was wearing dark shorts and a white T-shirt with the words "Spice Island" printed across the front. He was tall and thin. He was light-skinned, his hair cut close to his head, and he had eyes that were too big for his head and half-covered by drooping lids. The Gunny gestured, and the man limped towards the doorway. Forrest watched the man's lanky frame move into the front doorway, his shape dark against brightness outside. Then Forrest turned and walked to the back of the house and stuck his head in the kitchen. There was a sink with a hand pump, a wood stove, and a little table. Thick glass in the window portrayed the back hill in smears of green. Three women huddled under the table, still sobbing, their faces hidden behind hands, their black skin contrasting with white cotton dresses. Forrest turned and walked out the front door.

Out in front of the house, the man stood straight now, with the sun on his face and his hands tied behind him. Forrest looked him in the eyes. The man's stare back lacked any hint of emotion. Forrest put a wad of chew behind his right cheek, spit on the ground in front of the prisoner, and then looked up into those dead eyes again. "What kind of asshole hides under a bed?"

The man stared back.

The Gunny and Shields led the prisoner away.

Forrest walked out behind the other men walking across the field to the road. People were out now, standing together in front of their houses. Within minutes, there were at least a hundred people outside, all dressed in light-colored cotton. People stared and pointed, smiles flashed here and there. As the Gunny and Shields led the man away, the crowd's excitement grew.

Forrest walked back to four-zero and checked his map. He circled a spot on the map with a grease pencil. After a few minutes, he walked back to four-nine. The prisoner was in the troop compartment sitting on the floorboards. The Gunny had wrapped him in towrope. The man had his head cocked forward, and he stared with his lifeless black eyes that seemed as cold as polished black stones. Forrest stared back. "I know you're a bad motherfucker, because this town came alive the minute we drug your sorry ass from under your bed."

The man kept silent.

"Gunny, you find any ID on him?"

"No, sir. Nothing."

"Take Shields and go back. Search the house. Find some ID and anything else you think might be useful to intelligence. Maybe those women will help you." Forrest snorted out a laugh. The Gunny took Shields and headed back to the house.

The guide walked up to Forrest with another man from the village. Both men refused to look at the man tied up in four-nine.

"Either of you know this man's name?"

"No, Chief," the guide said.

The other man shook his head.

"You're not afraid of a man who hides under his bed?"

Both men looked down.

Forrest nodded for the two Grenadians to follow as he turned and headed for the shade of a palm tree. Forrest took off his combat helmet and rubbed a hand across the top of his sweaty head. He glanced around at high green ridges all around, then at the two locals.

"What do you have for me?"

The man from the village said, "Dey is anodder one up de way dere."

The man seemed terrified. "Another man with no name?"

The man looked down.

"Anodder bad one. Bernard Coard stay up dere. Odder side of town. His mudda-in-law."

"You say Coard's mother-in-law lives up there?"

The man nodded.

"Is Coard up there now?"

The man shrugged.

"Will you show us the house?"

The man nodded affirmative.

Forrest walked back up to four-zero, "Sergeant T, I'm taking Garnett, Goode, Harris, Johnson, Kaufman, and Lewis up to check-out a house on the far side of town. You hear shooting, bring the amtracs up."

Sergeant Tabb looked at the two Grenadians standing by the road, then back at Forrest. "Yes, sir. I'll tell the Gunny when he gets back from that little house."

The guides led the patrol to a well-worn path into the jungle along the side of the hill behind the village. They headed up the hill, with jungle on the left and the backs of Easter-egg-colored houses on the right. Forrest walked in the lead, with the guide close behind. Weighed down by his flak jacket and steel helmet, Forrest panted for air as he chugged up the path. His helmet was a hot box, and sweat filled his eyes. He tasted salt around the corners of his mouth. He tried to take his mind off the heat and focus on the surrounding woods and houses. The path leveled. The guide pointed to a small, pink house under two palm trees on the edge of the jungle. A hot bead of sweat ran down Forrest's face and into his right eye. He blinked and rubbed his eye with a soggy sleeve.

Forrest dropped his magazine and ejected the round in the chamber of his M-16. Then he slid the magazine back in with a click. He stood and ran hard to the door of the house and rammed the butt of his rifle into the doorknob, popping the door open. Immediately, an old man ran to the door shouting:

"We're for you! …We're for you!"

Forrest grabbed the man's shirt under his neck and pulled him into sunlight and then passed him off to Lance Corporal Garnett. Forrest chambered a round and entered the house. In the living room, an old woman sat in a rocking chair, gripping its arms. She stared through Forrest with multi-colored jellybean eyes, mouth toothless, and jaw jutting.

Forrest stood in front of her in full combat gear, holding an M-16.

"Outside," he said, gesturing.

She rocked harder and stuck her chin out farther.

"Outside." Forrest gestured with his expression to the front door.

No response.

Forrest looked over at Goode, who was standing behind him. "You-all carry Mrs. Whistler here outside."

"Mrs. Whistler, sir?"

"Yea. Like the painting."

Goode shrugged.

"You never heard of *Whistler's Mother*?"

"*Whistler's Mother*?"

"It's a painting."

"Oh. No, sir. Who painted it?"

"Whistler."

"He sure had an ugly momma," Goode said with a laugh.

The woman bound up her toothless mouth in a soft knot and kept rocking.

Forrest held back a smile. "Well …anyway, take this old lady outside."

"Yessir."

Goode grabbed one arm of the chair and Harris the other. They lifted her, chair and all, and worked their way out sideways through the front door and put her down out on the dirt in front of the house. The direct sunlight beamed down on her, fully revealing deep lines in her face. She closed her multi-colored eyes and kept rocking.

"Garnett," Forrest said, "let's search the house."

They walked back inside.

"Good thing Gunny's not up here, sir," Garnett said.

"Why's that?"

"You know how he hates old people."

"Really? Why?"

"Ask him about social security sometime. He'll go off. No shit, Lieutenant."

"Really?"

Garnett nodded. "Says it's welfare for rich people."

They worked through each room of the little house, looking through drawers and under cushions and anywhere they might find notes or documents or weapons. Garnett came out of the bedroom with a sack full of EC (Eastern Caribbean Currency). "Look here, Lieutenant; there must be thousands of dollars?"

"I guess they don't trust the bank," said Forrest. "That's just like a commie, isn't it? Hording cash like that so the commie government doesn't know about it and can't confiscate it. These people are probably all for confiscating *other* peoples' property." He picked up a handful of bills, looked at them, and then dropped the money back into the sack. "Put it back. It's got no intelligence value."

Forrest then opened a door that led down a dark stairway to a basement. He felt for a light switch and found nothing. "You've got to be shitting me," Forrest said in a low voice to himself. He froze and listened for any sound from the basement. Silence. He sniffed and smelled cool emptiness. All he knew to do was to move down into the darkness. He stepped down, feeling his way with his feet, aiming his M-16 into the blackness. Each step creaked. Finally, he stepped down on concrete and inched out away from the stairs. He swung his arm out, felt a string, and pulled. Click. A naked light bulb created a dim light.

There was a chest-type refrigerator against the wall. Forrest walked over and lifted the lid. Garnett moved in beside him. White light lit their sweaty faces. Cold air drifted up, cooling them as they looked down on thirty bottles of frosted Banks Beer. "Aaahhh," said Forrest, feeling his dry tongue, swollen in his mouth. A gulp of ice-cold beer would be one of those little snippets of pleasure noteworthy enough to be remembered afresh on a deathbed fifty years later—an eternal moment. He and Garnett looked at each other with pained expressions.

Forrest shook his head. "Can't do it."

Garnett winced with regret and closed the fridge door. Forrest pulled his canteen and slugged down a gulp of hot water.

Forrest and Garnett stepped out of the house into sunlight. The old man and women were sitting—he on the ground, she in her chair—on the far side of a grassy ditch, guarded by Goode and Kaufman. Forrest put in a chew of tobacco to take his mind off the beer down in the freezer. He spit on the ground. Then he told the old man to stand up. "What's your story?"

"We're for you! We're for you!" the old man said.

"You told me that already." Forrest spit. "Well, sir," Forrest said, "we understand you and Mr. Coard are close friends. That true?"

"He's not here!"

Forrest spit again and looked into the man's eyes. "That's not what I asked you." The man looked down.

"Lance Corporal Garnett, let's take him with us." Forrest said.

"What about the old lady?" Garnett asked. "She seems mean as shit."

Forrest looked at her again. She had closed her big yellow-and-brown-spotted eyes but was still rocking. "No. Leave her here. Seems undignified to capture an old lady. She's probably the mastermind of this whole fucked-up situation, but we're not taking her." Forrest spit again. "She's not going anywhere. Somebody wants to talk to her, we can come up here and get her." Holding his M-16 in his right hand, Forrest walked over to the old man. "Hands on your head." The old man complied. "Let's go."

The patrol circled around the house and down to the main street and moved through the town. Forrest walked down the center of the road, followed by the old man with his hands on his head. Goode and Kaufman were on either side of the prisoner, their M-16's pointed at him. The other men followed along in a staggered column.

For the first time, Forrest saw the people up close. Hundreds stood along the edge of the street and in their yards, smiling and cheering and waving as the Marines walked by. An old woman stepped into the street and walked towards Forrest. She held her arms out. Tears ran down her cheeks. Forrest stopped. The woman dropped to her knees on the hot pavement. Her sweaty forehead reflected sunshine, and her shape cast a dark round shadow against the blinding brightness of the street. She grabbed Forrest's hand and kissed it. "T'ank you, t'ank you. God bless you," she said with toothless exuberance. She cried out, full of emotion, "God bless Ronald Reagan!"

Forrest nodded to her, speechless. Finally, he said, "It's okay. Please...please... stand-up, ma'am." The women stood and backed off the street, bowing as she went. Then she gave the old man from up the hill a vicious glance and turned back to her people. Forrest watched her blend into the crowd, then turned and looked up the long main street of the village. The people were on both sides of the street to see the United States Marines in their small valley. On the far end of the street, in the shadow of the mountain, four-zero sat quietly, looking back at him like an old friend. He moved up now behind his patrol and walked along in the rear, happy in the bright light of the blue day in this forgotten spot in the heart of Grenada.

Back at four-zero, Forrest found the Gunny sitting in the shade of a palm tree by the side of the road. The Gunny had found a PRA identification card belonging to the under-bed hider. They'd turn that in with the prisoner down at the POW camp set up at Queen's Park.

"Gunny, let's tie up grandpa here and put him in four-three."

The Gunny nodded. "Roger that, LT." He gestured to Corporal Pierce, who came over and escorted the old man away to the troop compartment of four-three.

Forrest climbed up to his turret and looked back at the village. The people had closed in now, filling the street. He slipped down inside and dropped his combat helmet into the bottom of the turret and put on his comm helmet. As the three amtracs pulled out of town, the crowd cheered.

The amtracs left the mountain the same way they'd come up— down the winding road by the dead man in the ditch, over the smashed cars, across the bridge, then down the last ridgelines to St. Georges and Queen's Park. On the last stretch, Forrest relaxed in his turret as he looked out on the sea and along the coast where jungle-covered fingers of island jutted out into the sea, the closer ridges green and, in the distance, blue. Four-zero rolled along easily on the hard surface road and crossed through swaths of late afternoon light interspersed with blue shadows.

The amtracs rolled into Queen's Park and pulled up to the make-shift POW camp set up in a storage building surrounded by a fence. The men pulled the two prisoners out and walked them into the camp. Forrest walked to the office, where intelligence officers interrogated prisoners. He explained where they'd picked up the prisoners and the circumstances and handed over the ID card. He also asked the guide to stick around and tell the intelligence people what he knew. Then Forrest checked in with the command post and walked back to four-zero.

Forrest dropped his flak jacket and helmet on the lowered ramp of four-zero, then sat on the edge of the ramp and rubbed his eyes. He unbuttoned his top to let air in. Then he sat on soft grass in the shade of a palm tree and pulled off his boots. He peeled off his damp socks and propped his bare feet up on a log to dry. He closed his eyes and drank in the pleasure of the breeze across his feet. He pulled his canteen out of its pouch and took a long drink. Then he pulled a clean pair of socks from his pack and put them on his feet. The cool, clean, and dry feel of the socks was as delightful as a cold shower on a hot day. He put his boots back on and buttoned up his top. Then he lay down on the troop bench in four-zero and rested his head on his pack. He felt the breeze drifting over him, smelled seawater in it, and fell asleep.

It was black and moonless when Forrest opened his eyes and sat up, feeling refreshed. He held his watch up and squinted in the dark to see the time. It was 04:37. He sat for a moment, orienting himself, remembering where he was. Then he walked out on the ramp. There was no one in sight. It was quiet. He looked up at the stars and stretched. Garnett emerged from the dark.

"Morn'n, sir."

"Morn'n, Garnett."

"I'm fix'n to put on a pot of coffee, sir."

"Wonderful."

Chapter Thirteen

The New York Times
"Invasion Troops Trained to Make Surprise Raids."

October 26, 1983—"The Marine amphibious unit that is fighting
in Grenada had been scheduled to go to Lebanon and relieve the
Marine unit in Beirut. An amphibious unit has five tanks, five
155-millimeter howitzers, eight 81-millimeter mortars, and four
Cobra helicopter gunships. The infantry companies are also equipped
with amphibious armored personnel carriers."

At 06:30, Forrest attended the Colonel's staff meeting held around the
ramp of one of the C7s. The entire staff was there, including intelligence,

operations, and logistics officers. The Colonel gave an overview of the operation, and each staff officer spoke briefly on his area of responsibility. When it was the intelligence officer's turn, Gunner Johnson stepped up closer to the ramp. He was tall and thin and old. He wore thick glasses that made him look goggle-eyed, and he had crow's feet around the eyes, a dark tan, white hair, and yellow teeth. "The PRA is collapsing," he reported. "We have Richmond Hill, St. Georges, Grenville, Pearl's Airport. The Army has the southern end of the island secured, including Point Salinas Airfield and the two medical school campuses. We think there are small bands of hard-core PRA still operating, looking for sniper or ambush opportunities. Bernard Coard and Hudson Austin are still out there somewhere. We have information that they have been using a house up in the mountains. We have an informant to guide us up there."

Three hours later, Forrest's three-amtrac patrol sat on a hard surface road near the top of the mountain behind St. Georges. The guide, who was sitting on top of four-zero to the left of the turret, pointed to a dirt driveway that wound up the ridge through the jungle. Forrest picked up his M-16 and walked out into the street. He took a deep breath of cool mountain air and thought how it reminded him of mornings in May when he and his father would head out onto the bay at dawn searching for schooling bluefish. It was a delicious smell.

Forrest stood facing the driveway. The guide walked up beside him.

"Dat it." The guide pointed up the driveway. "Dat der is de way to de big man's house."

"Ever been up there before?"

"I'm de pool man."

Forrest laughed. "You a pool man?"

"Dat right, Chief. What so funny?"

"Nothing." Forrest smiled at the shriveled looking man. "Why you help'n us?"

"'Cause what he did to Maurice."

Forrest nodded. "What's the layout up there?"

The man looked confused. "What dat you say?"

"Where is the house, the pool, how far up?"

"House up der about so far, couple of bends. House on de right. Pool behind de house."

"Anybody up there now?"

The guide shrugged. "Don't know, Chief."

The Gunny walked up. "What's the plan, LT?"

"Any ideas, Gunny?"

"I'd say leave the hogs here in the street. It's too cramped and hard to see up there. One ballsy fucker with a pile of RPGs could fuck us up pretty good."

Forrest looked at the thick foliage on the hillside, then turned and looked out at the sea.

"Gunny, let's leave six men with the amtracs." Looking over at Harris, he said, "put a man in each driver seat on the radios. The other three, set up on the ground, one down there." He gestured down the road they had taken to this high spot. "One here, and put another one on the hillside in the woods there." Then Forrest looked back over to the Gunny. "We'll go up with the other eight."

Forrest put two loaded magazines in his cargo pouch over his left thigh. Then he pressed the magazine release button on the M-16 and slid the full magazine out of his rifle. He felt its weight, then tapped the metal magazine on his helmet to make sure the rounds were properly seated. He slid the magazine back into the M-16 with a click.

Forrest walked up the driveway with the guide on his right. Behind him, Garnett and Shields followed a few paces back. The Gunny followed with five men. The driveway of compacted dirt and small pockets of gravel angled upward at about a five-degree angle. They reached a bend in the driveway, and Forrest raised his right hand. The men stepped quietly to the sides of the driveway and knelt. Forrest leaned forward and peeked around the corner. The road curved to the right and then about a hundred yards up curved back to the left. He studied the foliage on either side of the driveway. Everything was still. No sound.

No movement. He waited for almost half a minute, with his heart rate increasing with anticipation. Forrest finally stood up and stepped out into the open. A half-minute later, he gave the signal to move on. He walked around the bend and saw a truck parked back in the jungle on the left of the driveway. He stopped and held up his hand again. The patrol knelt. The Gunny walked up.

"Holy shit, LT."

"You can say that again."

"Holy shit, LT." The Gunny smiled.

Forrest and the Gunny walked into the jungle on the left. The first of ten trucks was parked back in the foliage on the edge of the driveway. The Gunny opened the driver's door and looked inside.

"Keys left in this one."

Forrest walked around behind the truck. A brown canvas tarp covered the cargo. Forrest studied the tarp and the back end of the truck, looking for trip wires or explosives. He grabbed the tarp and flung it over to the side. There were long wooden crates stacked in the back of the truck. The crates were covered with Asian writing. The Gunny walked around.

"Gunny, can you tell what kind of writing that is? North Korea, maybe?

"It's all gook to me, LT."

Forrest resumed the lead and headed up the driveway, passing several trucks. He rounded a bend and glimpsed the house. It was on top of the hill, about fifty yards ahead. He knelt. Garnett moved up on the right side of the driveway and knelt near the next bend. Forrest waited a full minute and then signaled Shields to move up, as well. After telling the guide to stay put, Forrest stood and walked up to the next bend in the road and knelt beside Garnett and Shields. From this spot, he had a clear view of the basement level door on the side of the house. He turned back and nodded to the Gunny.

The Gunny moved up, walking with a slight crouch. The other five men of the patrol followed the Gunny.

The house was a Frank Lloyd Wright knock-off, with a glass front under a flat roof and a commanding view of the Caribbean far below. It was quiet and still by the house, but something didn't feel right. His heart paced upwards. He finally stood and walked out into the middle of the driveway. With his left thumb, he flipped the selector switch on the M-16 from safe to semi-automatic.

Automatic weapons fire erupted from positions to the left of the house. Bullets zipped by Forrest's head with a sound so subtle that he felt more than heard them. With the first burst, Forrest's body moved on its own, falling face first as fast as gravity could pull him down. He seemed to hang in the air as he fell in slow motion. His peripheral vision perceived muzzle flashes from the top of the driveway. Bullets snapped though the foliage above and hit the dirt near Forrest as he rolled into a depression on the side of the driveway. He found himself on his back, looking up through tree foliage to a stippled sky, heart pumping. Leaf pieces fluttered down like green confetti. In the excitement, he was no longer hot or tired, but he was breathing hard.

Forrest looked over for Garnett and Shields but could not see them. "Garnett!"

"Yes, sir," said Garnett from the ditch on the far side of the driveway.

"Y'all alright?"

"Yes, sir."

The Gunny crawled up to Forrest.

"Looks like we found 'em," said the Gunny with a grin.

"I guess."

"I don't think we can just walk up there now," said the Gunny.

Forrest raised his head and looked over at the Gunny. He resisted the temptation to say, "No shit." Instead he said, "I'll take Garnett and Shields and run around below the house and set up on the back side. If we get contact over there, we'll break it off and come back, figure out another plan. If we don't get contact, you attack in exactly fifteen minutes. How many 203s do we have?"

"Two."

"Okay. Good. Shoot grenades up there, and then attack. Shake 'em loose. We'll hose 'em when they fall back, if I can find an opening back there."

"Roger that, LT."

The plan was a simple single envelopment that Forrest's platoon had practiced dozens of times. Forrest crawled back down the driveway until he was out of the enemy's line of sight. Then he ran across the road into the jungle below the house front. Forrest, Garnett, and Shields moved away from the thick foliage along the edge of the driveway into the open forest below the house. The three Marines moved across the spongy loam of the forest floor under a solid canopy of jungle. They jogged slowly through the forest, being careful not to make any noise. Forrest looked up at the glass wall of the house and realized they could be seen if anyone was looking.

After moving about a hundred yards, they stopped and took a knee, listening for movement and scanning for any sign of an enemy presence. Nothing. They jogged uphill on the far side of the house. Hyped on adrenaline, Forrest barely noticed the weight of his flak jacket and steel helmet or the loaded magazines he was carrying. They worked back to a spot in the jungle overlooking the pool behind the house. The three Marines knelt in a thicket of huge ferns on a small rise overlooking the swimming pool and the backside of the house. To their left were two Adirondack chairs sitting in a patch of lawn. The poolside concrete was painfully white in the sun. Around the pool, there were two tables with pastel-colored umbrellas and several chairs. The poolside appeared well kept, but the water was cloudy. The back of the house was mostly glass, like the front. Forrest could not see the shooters, but he knew they were down to his left, overlooking the driveway.

Everything was quiet now except for the sound of their breathing. Forrest caught a glimpse of a man walking inside the house. A rear door slid open, and the man walked out. Forrest whispered, "Hold fire." A black man in a pea-green uniform wearing an Eastern European helmet walked out and pulled the bolt back on his AK-47. The man crouched and moved into the foliage on the far side of the pool.

Forrest looked down at his watch. One minute to go. As the last seconds passed, Forrest looked to his left and right. The setup reminded him of duck hunting—gunners in a blind waiting for targets to fly by. Then they heard a plunking sound as the Gunny's team fired M-203 grenade launchers. Three seconds later, there was a series of blasts in the middle of the PRA position. The Gunny's patrol pumped ten high-explosive grenades onto the area where the fire had come from. Smoke drifted over the pool. Forrest heard a man grunting through clenched teeth. The Gunny's team fired several more grenades into the PRA position and then assaulted, yelling as they charged, up through the jungle cover to the left of the driveway.

Four PRA soldiers exploded from the foliage in full retreat and ran across the poolside concrete, their leather soles clapping. Then a fat white man moved up out of the woods, his belly swaying as he pushed himself along on rhino ankles. He wore a green t-shirt, sweatpants, and sneakers that were not tied. He carried an RPG over his soft shoulder. As the PRA soldiers ran across the concrete, Forrest lost himself in the scene. He felt only his trigger finger and the moment unfolding slowly around him. A memory of duck hunting flashed again—an image of ducks with curled wings pitching over the decoys, hunters rising in the blind, barrels swinging with the birds, shooting, shells ejecting. He sensed their barrels swinging together with the running men, and he fell in with the momentum of his target, like a duck gliding, then squeezed slowly. The M-16 popped with a tender toy-like recoil, and the first man's body rolled to the concrete.

Just as Forrest shot the first man, Corporal Garnett shot the fat man in his right shoulder. The fat man stopped and turned towards the Marines across the pool. He stood for a moment, swaying a bit, looking confused, but still holding the RPG. Garnett aimed at the man's head—his target like a peanut atop a watermelon—and shot the man in the face. The man's head snapped back, and a red and pink mist sprayed out the back of his head. The big man's legs buckled, and the huge torso sank down to the concrete and rolled over into a flaccid heap. The RPG clapped onto the concrete.

In the meantime, Shields had popped off four shots but missed.

As the moment passed, Forrest again felt the weight of his flak jacket and the wetness of his sweat-soaked utility top. He wiped his eyes with his fingers and stepped out of the foliage onto the poolside concrete. Forrest fired three shots into the foliage the PRA men had run into. There was no return fire, and Forrest assumed they were still running. Forrest, Garnett, and Shields walked out onto the concrete.

Forrest looked over at Shields. "Didn't the Marine Corps teach you how to shoot that thing?"

Shields shrugged, embarrassed. "Yes, sir. I qualified expert, but I never shot moving targets before."

"You should hunt birds."

Shields nodded. "Yes, sir."

They walked around the pool to the spot where the two bodies lay about four feet from each other. There was a thick aroma of organs exposed to the air for the first time and gasses leaking out. Forrest was nauseated but held his stomach. The first man was still alive, crawling slowly, trailing blood and colorless globs like slug slime. His funny-shaped East-German helmet had fallen off and was floating upside-down in the pool. The man was grunting with exertion and moaning with pain at the same time. Forrest walked up on the dying man, feeling awkward at meeting a man he had killed. The man stopped crawling and lay face down on the concrete in a growing puddle of his own burgundy-colored blood. Forrest stuck his left boot under the man and flipped him onto his back. He saw the entry wound under the man's right arm. The bullet had entered the man's chest cavity and apparently severed arteries. Very dark blood was seeping out of his mouth. The man blinked slowly. His eyes were still moist, but his pupils appeared not to focus. Forrest noticed the blank look and wondered if his eyes had already shut down, as the man's many life-supporting systems were shutting down, and he thought the man had drifted off to his final death dream where he would say goodbye to his family before he turned cold. After about a half minute, the blinking stopped, and the eyes started to dry out in the heat of the afternoon. Forrest put his left boot on the man's upturned shoulder and moved it. The joint was fluid and limp. Forrest noticed the blood-coated wedding ring on the man's still-twitching finger. There was a Berretta 9mm lying in the pool of blood where the man had been lying. Forrest kicked the pistol across the concrete.

The Gunny's team had followed the running PRA soldiers into the jungle behind the house and then set up a security position guarding the trail. The Gunny walked back to the pool and then up to the dead bodies.

"Everybody okay, Gunny?

"Yes, sir. We're Okay. One of those fuckers is down over there, though, crying like a baby. Price is seeing to him." Gesturing to the first man's body splayed in front of Forrest, the Gunny said, "You shoot this one, LT?"

Forrest nodded.

"On the run?"

Forrest nodded again.

"Good shot, Lieutenant."

"Lucky, I guess."

"Lucky for *you*." The Gunny snorted out a chuckle.

He looked over at the big man's body. "Who killed fatty?"

Forrest looked to his left, at Corporal Garnett.

"That'd be me, Gunny," said Garnett.

"You got a license for hippo, Garnett?" The Gunny hooted out another laugh.

The big man's body was like a fuel bladder. The Gunny put his left boot on the dead man's immense belly. He cocked his head one way, then the other, as he looked down on the enormity of it.

"Look," Garnett said, "the little one bled like a pig, but fatty hardly bled at all."

"That's 'cause of the head shot," the Gunny said. "Stop the heart, and they don't leak so much." The Gunny stood over the huge corpse for a long, silent moment. "You know what, Lieutenant?"

"What's that, Gunny?"

"We drag big boy here down to the butcher shop, all we'll get is bacon and hot dogs." He bent forward and sank his boot down into the blubber. "Nope, Lieutenant, not a steak in him. I didn't know they had white people down here. And how did he get so fat, anyway? I haven't seen any fat people on this island."

"He must like cheeseburgers," offered Forrest.

"Cheeseburgers? Do these people eat cheeseburgers? I haven't seen any cows, no Burger King," said the Gunny.

"Maybe they import cheeseburgers," said Forrest.

"I thought they ate fish," said Garnett. "Can't get fat like that on fish, though."

Forrest shrugged.

"Could be pasta, Gunny," said Shields. "You can get fat as shit on pasta."

"Well," the Gunny said as he poked his foot into the man's massive belly, "he sure is fat." The Gunny knelt down by the immense corpse and pulled a wallet out of the man's pocket. He opened it, looked inside. There were several bills of EC. He pulled out a five and looked down on the portrait of a young Queen Elizabeth. Then he pulled out the man's driver's license. "I'll be damned!"

"What's that, Gunny?" asked Forrest.

"This fat fucker's from California." The Gunny laughed.

"What's his name?"

The Gunny looked up at Forrest, squinting against the glare of the sun. "You really want to know, Lieutenant?"

Forrest looked down into the man's open head and shrugged. "I guess it doesn't matter."

The Gunny looked down at the body again. "What's he doing here?" the Gunny asked of no one in particular. "I know why we're here. And I know why that fellow there is laying there dead," the Gunny said as he gestured to the other body. "But this fat man's out of place in every conceivable way. He's white. He's fat. And he's an American." The Gunny pondered the situation for a long minute, then shrugged. He walked over to the man Forrest had killed and pulled out his wallet. The Gunny pulled out a photograph and then moved to slide it back.

"What's that, Gunny?"

"Nothing, sir. You don't need to see it."

Forrest held out his hand, and the Gunny reluctantly handed the photo to Forrest. It was a black and white picture of a black woman, smiling broadly with a little boy on her lap. The image of the boy's face was smudged with blood. Forrest reached down and slipped the photo into the man's left breast pocket, over his dead heart.

The four Marines who had followed the PRA into the jungle came out of the jungle and stood on the edge of the concrete.

Forrest walked over to a knoll where he could look down on the harbor far below and the green ridges that jutted out into the sea. He stood there, holding the M-16 in his right hand and let the tension of the day go. He'd been tense all morning as the column moved out beyond the Marine lines and then up the curvy road where he had to be ready to fire at any moment and an enemy armored vehicle or patrol could be around every bend. The tension had built as they walked up the drive way and then spiked when the shooting started. The more tense the situation became, the less he had noticed it—but it was there, pulling tighter all the time. As his tension and fear and worry grew, he had shut down the parts of himself that were attuned to those emotions and was conscious only of the immediate situation and the need to shoot clean and get the job done. As he stood on the grass, he looked up at the swaying palm fronds against the blue sky and felt himself coming down off adrenaline. As his nervous system slowly rebooted he felt his weight and wetness and he felt the sun on his face and relief that the hard part of the patrol was over. He looked down through an opening in the trees at St. Georges far below and the sailboats in the harbor, little more than white smudges in the blue distance, and the broad reach of the Caribbean. It was a scene for a postcard, except for the dead bodies and the butcher shop smells.

After five quiet minutes, Forrest walked into the house through the patio door. Garnett and Shields followed. They walked into the bright, open living room. The floor was highly polished blond hardwood. In the corner sat a jet-black baby grand piano. Forrest heard a shower running back towards the rear of the house near the pool. He crept gingerly toward the sound with his M-16 up. The door to the bathroom was half-open. He poked his boot against the door and pushed it all the way open. The shower stall was empty. He turned the water off, and then walked out of the bathroom. Garnett and Shields stood there in full combat gear, web belts, flak jackets, combat helmets, and M-16s.

"They're all gone," Forrest said.

"Except for them two out by the pool and the wounded one, sir," said Garnett.

Forrest looked through the open dining room and glass doors to the pool and the two dark lumps on the concrete. "Garnett, you and Shields check the other rooms."

"Yes, sir," answered Garnett. He and Shields worked their way down the hallway to check the bedrooms.

Forrest walked back into the big room. The polished hardwood floor glistened in the afternoon sunlight. There was a pile of paper in the middle of the floor. He stood there alone in the empty room, gazing through the tinted glass wall over the jungle foliage to the sea. He changed his focus to his own reflection in the blue glass—a Marine in war gear. He clunked his M-16 on top of the piano by a brown book. Then he took off his combat helmet and laid it on top of the piano by the rifle and sat on the piano bench.

He picked up the book. On the cover was Lenin's profile in faded gold relief. The title, *Lenin, Collected Works* also in faded gold. He opened the cover. On the first page was printed the following: "The Russian Edition was printed in accordance with a decision of the Ninth Congress of the R.C.P. (B.) and the Second Congress of the Soviets of the U.S.S.R." Forrest wasn't sure what that meant, but figured the Soviet Communist Party approved the book. He thumbed through the pages and found underlining and annotations in a chapter titled "'Left-Wing' Childishness and the Petty-Bourgeois Mentality." He read an underlined passage:

> On the one hand, we must ruthlessly suppress the uncultured capitalists who refuse to have anything to do with 'state capitalism' or to consider any form of compromise, and who continue by means of profiteering, by bribing the poor peasants, etc. to hinder the realization of the measures taken by the Soviets.

On the same page, "We still have too little of that ruthlessness which is indispensable for the success of socialism." Forrest turned the page. Written in the left margin in blue ink was a time and date, "8:34 a.m. 4th August 1983." He wondered why anybody would write such a precise time in the margins of a book and then dropped the book on the floor.

Forrest reached down and grabbed a pile of memoranda from the floor and dropped them on the piano top. He picked up a memo. The heading read "Minutes of Emergency Meeting of the N.J.M. Central Committee Dated 26th August 1983." The minutes listed the "Comrades Present," including Maurice Bishop, Hudson Austin, and Unison Whiteman, referring to each person as comrade so-and-so and to Bishop as "Party Leader Comrade" and to their "East German and Cuban Comrades." Forrest was surprised by this usage and thought these people watched too much TV. The minutes recorded the concerns about the situation in Grenada. The memo quoted Hudson Austin, "Comrades are in a serious state of demoralization. Comrades are saying that, at the end of five years, they are not materially better off." The proposed solution was that members of the Central Committee should "rap with party members" and "rap with leading mass organizations." Forrest laughed out loud at the thought of the "rapping comrades." A cool name for a left-wing band, he thought. Then he looked out through the glass doors at the two bodies lying in the sun and thought that those two particular comrades would not be rapping anymore, ever again—all because they'd run into some "uncultured capitalists" who shot them dead.

After sweeping the house, Forrest, Garnett, and Shields walked out by the poolside. The bodies were already starting to fester. Flies buzzed around the corpses, lighting on the wet parts. Price had patched up shrapnel wounds on the wounded PRA man, given him a shot of morphine, and laid him in the shade of a tree.

Forrest reported to battalion by radio that they'd made contact and cleared the objective without any casualties. Battalion gave Forrest the go-ahead to come down. Engineers would be sent up later to either blow up or take away the truckloads of weapons and ammo hidden in the jungle on the edge of the driveway.

Goode drove four-zero up to the house and dropped the ramp. The men loaded the wounded man in the back and laid him out on the floorboards, with his upper body propped up against the engine compartment in the forward end of the troop compartment. The men brought down armloads of documents from the house.

The Gunny walked up. "What we going to do with these bodies, Lieutenant?"

Forrest looked at them again. "I hate to leave bodies lying around. You know what we say in the Corps—always leave an area cleaner than you found it."

"I think that refers to cigarette butts and such, Lieutenant."

"We can't just leave 'em there. Anyway, they might have some intelligence value."

"Take 'em?"

"Yeah, Gunny, load 'em in with the wounded man. We'll turn 'em over to the gunner down at the POW camp."

The Gunny nodded and walked away.

On the way down the mountain, Forrest sat up in his turret thinking about what had happened. He'd aimed calmly, exhaling slowly, squeezed the trigger, and shot a bullet into the man's chest cavity. Then he'd watched the man blink as he bled to death. He remembered the contrast between sunlit concrete and dark blood and how the deep burgundy fluid inched out over the concrete slowly, pumped by the man's dying heart. He knew the killing was legal. The man was in uniform. He carried an AK-47. If not killed, he would be out there looking to kill a Marine. So it was right to kill the man. But Forrest found himself alone in his turret with the naked fact of his action—aiming in, pulling a trigger, and killing. The killing was in the foreground, spot-lit. The justifications were more obscure.

It was almost 18:00 before they finished unloading at the POW camp. When done, Forrest took his three-amtrac patrol down to the beach so Garnett and his crew could wash the blood and little gray lumps of tissue out of the troop compartment. The three amtracs pulled out onto the beach on the edge of Queen's Park. Goode backed four-zero up to the edge of the sea and lowered the ramp. The other two amtracs took up security positions on either side of four-zero. Forrest climbed down to the troop compartment. The Gunny walked up and stood on the ramp.

"This ain't so bad, Gunny. I thought it would be worse," said Garnett as he threw a bucket of seawater on the deck.

After four-zero's crew finished washing, they took a break to eat C-rats. Forrest skipped the meal. He filled his canteen cup with coffee and walked up the beach. It was late afternoon now. The heat had given way to gentle warmth and smells of the sea. The Caribbean was still and glassy. Forrest stopped and leaned against a fishing skiff that was sitting upside-down on the beach by the trunk of a palm tree. He laid his combat helmet on the boat bottom and looked out at the flat water and watched orange and yellow and pink gather in the sky and on the sea's surface as evening came.

The Gunny walked up, holding a canteen cup of coffee in one hand. "We done good today, Lieutenant."

Forrest looked over and smiled slightly. The two men sipped coffee and stared out as colors in the sky intensified.

"When I was a kid, I used to go deer hunting with my dad in the mountains," Forrest said. "One day—I was about fourteen—I was sitting by this huge oak tree overlooking a hardwood hollow. It was a beautiful spot in the woods. A little mountain stream snaked along through the bottom, and hardwood trees covered the ridges on either side. Late in the day, these two does came out of a laurel thicket on the top of the ridge and started working down the ridgeline towards me. I was downwind, so I could just sit there and let them come. Then I saw this buck, a six-pointer, up the ridge, following about seventy yards behind."

The Gunny nodded.

"Those two deer crossed the stream below me and started moving up the next ridge. The buck came in right behind them, step for step. They were beautiful animals in a perfect spot of woods. I loved watching them. When that buck moved across the stream, I had him broadside. I brought my rifle to my shoulder—I had a .308 Savage—and when I moved, that buck shot straight up in the air with his white tail sticking up, flagging me. He shot up the ridge, and I laid in on him, leading him just a little. I squeezed off a round, and that deer rolled. I got him on the run, in the heart, at about a hundred yards."

"That was a good shot, Lieutenant."

"It was a thrill. My heart had been pounding, and then everything just slowed down for me, like I was in rhythm with the deer and the trees and everything. For just a second, I was inside nature, part of it. Then that deer was dead. When I walked up, he was still alive. He was blinking his eye slowly, just like that dude this afternoon, and his stomach was moving and then there was this subtle seizure, and he was dead. I walked over, and first thing I noticed was those lifeless black eyes, like plastic. Not that there is anything wrong with killing a deer, but that feeling of killing something bothered me."

The Gunny took a sip of coffee.

"Then I killed another deer the next year, and I felt better about it. By the time I'd killed five, I didn't feel bad at all anymore."

The Gunny was silent for a long moment, looking out at the sky. "Don't worry, Lieutenant," he said, "killing people is a lot like that."

On the fifth day of the operation, Chinook helicopters began ferrying Army units into Queen's Park to relieve the Marines. By that time, the southern part of the island had been secured. Golf Company and the tanks and amtracs were ordered to sweep up the west coast of the island to secure the towns of Gouyave and Victoria. The move required the Marine column to travel up the coast road, with steep hillsides rising to the right and a drop-off on the left, so the amtracs and tanks would be unable to maneuver if ambushed. To cope with this vulnerability, two tanks were staged on a landing craft. The landing craft would then move up the coast just offshore so the tanks could fire at any ambushing force up on the hills. A Navy destroyer, the USS *Caron*, moved into position to support the column with naval gunfire.

At 08:00, Goode drove four-zero across the field at Queen's Park toward the coast road. Forrest stood in his turret. The Marine captain sat in the troop leader's hatch. The Marines of Golf Company were loaded in the amtracs, which fell into a thirteen-vehicle column followed by three tanks. It was another clear blue day, and temperature was already in the 80s. Within a few minutes, they passed the tank farm where the platoon had landed four nights earlier, and after that, there were very few houses. The column snaked along the road that curved around the terrain features—fingers of mountain that jutted out into the Caribbean. About mid-morning, the column reached an area where construction crews had been working to widen the road. To the right, there was a high, sheer cliff of tan-colored dirt that rose at least 150 feet and sloped back. Straight ahead, the road was blocked by a large, brown bulldozer that faced the amtracs. It was so big that its blade completely blocked the road.

Forrest told Goode to stop about a hundred yards away from the bulldozer. The column was bottled up now and could not move in any direction, except by slowly backing down the narrow roadway. The landing craft held its station three hundred yards out. The destroyer was a mile offshore. Forrest climbed down to the road and waited for the Gunny to come up on foot. The two of them then walked up to the dozer while the column sat waiting with engines running. They circled the dozer looking for booby traps and found nothing unusual. It was hot, and the road was bright with the sun's reflection and heat, and the metal of the dozer's hood and sides was too hot to touch. The Gunny climbed up onto the driver's seat. He looked down at Forrest and said, "No key."

The Captain walked up and stood in the blistering heat. He and Forrest just stared at the big machine wondering how to deal with it. "I'll hot wire it," said the Gunny. Within a minute, the dozer was running, and the Gunny was backing it down the road the clear the way. Within a few more minutes, the column was moving again and approaching Gouyave.

Gouyave had been named Charlotte Town by the British but was later renamed because Guava fruit grew there in abundance. It was the staging area of "Fédon's Rebellion" against British rule in 1795. Julien Fédon, a free black planter, mobilized an army that included 14,000 slaves; and for a time, he controlled the entire island except St. Georges. Fédon was influenced by the French Revolution, and he envisioned an independent slave-free state. The British killed half his army and suppressed the rebellion. No one knew what happened to Fédon. Now, almost two hundred years later, the U.S. Marines approached the town.

As the column rolled into town, hundreds of people lined the streets and cheered. The road was bordered by small wooden houses with porches and tropical plants in the yards, and the town had a neat appearance. The beach was wide and white and dotted with small fishing boats pulled up on the sand, and the palm trees along the sea leaned out over the beach and water for sunlight. Down along the beach, there stood older colonial-era buildings made of brick or stone.

The Captain dropped off three amtracs and one infantry platoon to patrol the area and secure the town, and the rest of the column proceeded north to Victoria.

Victoria was much the same as Guayave in appearance, and the welcome was the same, too. After Golf Company disembarked to run patrols and secure the town, the amtracs pulled into open spots along the beachfront, and the crews gave the vehicles thorough checks of fluid levels and updated logbooks and set a watch schedule. Forrest directed four-zero to a small palm-shaded yard by an ancient church by the beach. The church was made of stone and obviously dated well back into the colonial period. A white priest came out and politely welcomed Forrest and his crew to the churchyard. Several white-hulled sailboats were anchored in the harbor. After about an hour, a very thin and small black woman in an orange dress brought Forrest's crew a live chicken as a gift. Forrest told the old woman to keep the chicken, thinking that she needed it more than they did, but thanked her profusely.

The Marines spent a quiet night in these secluded tropical towns; and then the following day, the USS *Manitowoc* cruised in about a mile offshore and picked up the amtracs and Golf Company while landing craft picked up the tanks. The December 1983 *Life* magazine featured a black and white photograph—spread over two full pages—of amtrac four-four crossing the beach at Gouyave on its way out to the ship. The photograph showed a large crowd of Grenadians packed tightly together for a final look at the Marine vehicle driving into the ocean and, in the background, there were several small fishing skiffs on the beach.

Back on ship, the Marines planned another amphibious assault for the following day. The nation of Grenada included the island of Carriacou, which was seventeen miles north of the main island. The mission was to clear a Cuban Army rest camp on the island. So at dawn on November 1st, 1983, the USS *Manitowoc* anchored in Tyrrel Bay and launched the amtracs. The bay was surrounded by jungle-covered mountains that rose straight up from the water on two sides. A lone Navy corsair circled above in a wide circle. At first light it was mild, even cool, and the water was flat and colored by the morning's pastel sky. As the amtracs launched, they motored away from the ship and then stood by, drifting and waiting until all the amtracs were in the water. As four-zero sat, Forrest looked out over the side of his turret. He could see clearly brown rocks and colorful coral a hundred feet down, and he was astounded by the clarity of the water. The amtracs and Golf Company crossed the beach, moved down a narrow road, and then attacked the rest camp, which was deserted. The Marines of Golf Company set up a perimeter, and the amtracs staged in a column in front of the camp as they waited for further orders.

The camp itself was a beautiful and isolated hotel perched atop the ridge overlooking a bay surrounded by mountains. There were thatch-roofed bungalows in a semi-circle overlooking the bay and a main lodge. Forrest walked through the lodge to the open patio bar—all the booze was gone—that had a spectacular view. Forrest stood there alone in his combat gear and wondered if he'd ever come back to this spot for a vacation later in life and tried to imagine what that would be like. Orders received, Golf Company boarded the amtracs and the column looped around the island's perimeter, in places powering through thick thorn bushes thirty feet high. They encountered some poor farmers but no enemy soldiers. Late that afternoon, they boarded their ship and headed for Beirut.

By this time, all the major towns had been secured and the medical school students had been rescued and repatriated. The Army remained to mop up the remaining resistance, but the operation was over within a week. The government returned to the 1975 constitution that Maurice Bishop had suspended. To this day, Grenada has retained its parliamentary representative democracy with Queen Elizabeth II as head of state.

Chapter Fourteen

Life Magazine
"Farewell to the Liberators."

November 1983—"They were among the grimmest – and finest – hours in a 20 – year history. As the first coffins arrived in the U.S. from Beirut, Marines on Grenada returned to their ships amid the cheers accorded liberators."

Forrest sat up in his bunk after ten hours of the kind of sleep old people envy. He stood and walked over to the sink, ran hot water into his cupped hands, and dipped his face. Then he stood and looked at himself in the mirror. His dark, tanned face and neck contrasted with his milky white chest and shoulders. After shaving, he walked down the passageway to the head for a long hot shower. As the hot water streamed over the back of his neck, he thought of the man he killed on the island. He tried to think of home and even the girl who'd dumped him, but he could not shake the image. He would never look at a wedding ring the same way again. He dressed and headed down the passageway to the wardroom and looked out the portholes at the calm ocean gleaming in the morning sun. It was their last day on ship before landing in Beirut.

Lieutenant Stanard was sitting at the table in the wardroom. Forrest poured a fresh cup of hot coffee and then sat across from Stanard. Between them was a large plate of sweet rolls.

"Belly bomb?" asked Stanard. "Oh, yeah," Forrest answered. He picked up a warm sweet roll packed with cinnamon and raisins and white icing. He closed his eyes and smelled the warm roll. He pushed the roll into his mouth and clamped down on a mouthful. He savored the moment and chewed slowly, squeezing out every sensation of flavor. "It's good we eat such nasty shit in the field," Forrest said. "If we had this every day, we'd be as fat and pasty as the squids." Stanard looked back over his shoulder to make sure one of their Navy hosts had not heard Forrest's comment.

"We'd start taking belly bombs for granted. We wouldn't appreciate them the way we should. Before long, our whole value system would be screwed up." Forrest picked up his roll and sat back, smiling as he talked. "Wouldn't be natural to get used to something so good." He took a bite. "Wouldn't be right," he said, still chewing. "We've got to be happy with simple pleasures, like pissing outside on a starry night." He looked up and smiled as he chewed.

The list of men killed in the barracks bombing grew longer each day as more bodies were found and identified. So after breakfast each day, Forrest checked the board for Kirby's name. On this last morning on ship, Forrest walked out of the wardroom and headed down the corridor to the bulletin board. The list had grown to 229 names. Over the past weeks, back at Camp Lejeune, the Second Marine Division had to cope with notifying families that their loved one had been killed. The division mobilized teams made up of a junior officer and a chaplain to go out and notify families. It was not possible for Marines to buy life insurance, so the government provided a Serviceman's Group Life Insurance Policy ("SGLI") of $25,000 to each Marine. Lieutenants tasked with giving horrific news to wives and mothers called it the "SGLI clearing house give-away." In the dark passageway, the list was lit by a small light mounted over the bulletin board. Forrest skipped to the K's and ran his finger down the page. Kirby was not on the list.

Forrest sat on the deck with his legs out over the side and leaned on the safety railing and looked down at the ocean. He could hear the spray off the ship's bow, and he watched flying fish fluttering up out of the sea in small bunches. An early childhood memory came to him. He was four or five and was supposed to be taking a nap on a warm summer afternoon. His bed was by an open window, and he remembered how good the warm breeze off the river felt on his bare feet and the smell of freshly cut grass and the way the big oak tree in the yard cast a stippling of dark blue-green shapes across the sunlit lawn. And though he had no idea what his thoughts were at the time, he remembered a feeling of joy that he'd rarely felt since. He wondered why he had a vivid memory of that one moment when he could recall little else about those years. Perhaps it was the first moment in his life when he'd managed not to think about himself in any degree because he was absorbed completely in experiencing the river and good smells and the sunny afternoon. Whatever the reason, he remembered the feeling and he longed for it.

That evening, Forrest sat with other officers around the living room portion of the wardroom. Every other Marine officer in the room had lost one or more good friends in the Beirut barracks. There was little talk because they were all thinking about death, and that was a subject they never discussed. Forrest held in his lap a bowl of hot fresh popcorn. The Mediterranean Sea was rough, and the men leaned as the ship pitched and the room tilted. *Meatballs*, starring Bill Murray, was on the Beta-Max. The movie was a comedy set at a lakefront summer camp. For Forrest, it brought back memories of Camp Virginia in the Allegheny Mountains. He remembered sitting on his bunk bare-footed with the afternoon breeze across his toes and swimming naked in the Maury River and riding on horseback in the mountains—other joyous moments. Now, those feet were nestled inside combat boots, and he was sitting in a dark room watching a summer camp movie on a pitching ship bound for one of the bloodiest places on Earth.

After the movie, the Marine Captain called a meeting of the officers in the wardroom. He spread out on the table a large map of Beirut and another map of the Beirut International Airport ("BIA") and explained their positions ashore. The officers would fly in by helicopter the next day to meet with counterparts ashore. The units would come in the day after that and relieve in place what was left of First Battalion, Eighth Marines.

Chapter Fifteen

New York Times
"An Attack Closes Beirut's Airport."

November 6, 1983—"[Beirut Airport was closed] after the runways and nearby positions of the American Marines came under fire from unidentified gunmen that killed a Lebanese civilian and wounded a Marine and a Lebanese soldier…Shortly before noon, 12 American F-14 Tomcat jet fighters …buzzed Beirut, rattling windows all over town."

Forrest woke at 05:30 and looked across the dark room at the gray wall, just as he had every other morning on ship. But today was different. Just outside the hatchway, Beirut waited for him. He packed all his toiletries into a kit and stuffed it into his pack. As soon as he got to the wardroom for breakfast, he looked out the porthole, hoping for a glimpse of the famous city, but that side of the ship was facing out to sea. After breakfast, he left the wardroom and walked back to his stateroom. He sat on his bunk and slipped off his VMI ring. He hid the ring in the bottom of his sea bag and then pushed the bag into the locker in his stateroom. He'd not wanted the communists on Grenada to get it. He didn't want the Druse to get it, either.

He put on his "war belt"—web gear fitted with suspenders and two canteens, a first-aid kit, a K-bar knife—his flak jacket, and his shoulder holster with his Colt .45. He put on his combat helmet, grabbed his pack, and headed down the passageway to the hatch. He pulled the hatch lever down, swung open the steel watertight hatch and stepped out into the cool, early morning air. And there it was. Beirut.

The city, big as Manhattan, sat astride the Mediterranean Sea in the morning sun. Sunlight glistened off windows and flat concrete surfaces. Snow-peaked mountains floated in the deep blue sky behind the city. He'd heard about the city and seen pictures of it. He'd listened to David Brinkley and George Will and Sam Donaldson talk about it every Sunday morning on TV. He'd read the stories in the paper as each man had died, and he'd perused the death list on the bulletin board outside the wardroom. He'd trained and dreamed and thought about it. He and Ed had stood freezing on the deck atop the dune looking out at a cold black ocean and wondered whether one of them would get killed here.

The airport was south of the city. From the ship, Forrest could make out the shapes of airline hangars and the clouds of black smoke drifting across the runway. A blue mountain ran along the coastal plain.

A CH-46 helicopter flew in from behind the ship and slowed to a hover and landed. The officers, all laden with heavy packs, stepped off in single-file towards the helicopter and bent down as they walked under the rotating blades. Forrest stood by the ship's rail for a moment.

He looked at the city then turned and looked back towards the hatch that led back to the wardroom. He walked out under the blades and boarded the helicopter. He dropped his pack to the floor between his legs and pulled the seat belt across his lap. There was a Marine crewman manning a .50 caliber machinegun mounted on an opening on the right side of the helicopter.

The helicopter rose steadily, cleared the ship, then pitched and headed towards the shoreline. Forrest looked out over the rear ramp and saw the ship receding into the distance. They passed over the tan-colored beach and the coastal highway and then slowed to a hover over the airport runway and eased down. The ramp lowered, and the officers walked off under the stern rotor blade onto the runway. Forrest stepped off onto the black asphalt and walked by two old-fashioned Hawker-Hunter jets sitting side by side on the runway surrounded by sandbag walls. Across the runway, he saw skeletal hangars. The force of blasts had sheered the metal walls, leaving large holes and jagged pieces of metal curling out away from the structure like a grotesque sculpture. One of the hangars was little more than a metal frame. A Middle East Airlines jet sat on the far end of the runway. Even from a distance, Forrest saw shrapnel holes in its tail. To the south, on the far side of the runway, there were small red hills, and the clouds of black smoke were still drifting across the airport. The CH-46 lifted off and headed out to sea. The deafening noise level faded until all they could hear was the faint sound of the rotors beating the air in the distance. The old warrant officer with bad teeth and thick glasses was standing by a sandbag wall. He looked at Forrest with a yellow grin and yelled, "Welcome to Beirut!"

Forrest saw Kirby standing by his Jeep, walked over, and extended his hand. Kirby shook it, smiling. "Welcome to Beirut, Robert." Forrest glanced around the area. "Good to see you, brother." He tossed his pack in the back of the Jeep and sat in the passenger seat. "I thought you might be dead," said Forrest. Kirby looked over, smiled, and said, "That'll be the day." He was a connoisseur of John Wayne quotes.

Kirby sat behind the wheel and pressed the start button on the floor with his muddy boot. Kirby pulled out onto the gravel road and drove along the edge of the runway, headed north towards the City.

For five months, Kirby had lived in the back of an amtrac or in a hole. His face was thinned-out. It had been almost half a year since his last real shower. His uniform was covered with fine red dust. His flak jacket and steel helmet were sun-faded and smudged with red dirt. He chewed tobacco.

"What's the story on the black smoke?" Forrest yelled over the engine noise.

Kirby was hunched over the steering wheel, driving. He spit a stream of brown juice onto the dirt road and then looked over at Forrest with a gritty, tobacco-stained grin. "Burn'n shitters," he yelled.

Forrest snorted out a brief laugh and nodded.

As they rolled along, Forrest felt the excitement of a new place, like a tourist walking through a town for the first time. "Ed," Forrest yelled over the engine, "how has your platoon held up?"

"Okay, except one." He focused on the gravel road for a couple of seconds, then looked over at Forrest. "One killed."

"Truck bomb?"

"Yeah," Kirby said, "I'll take you over there."

As they rode, Forrest noticed a long pile of broken concrete, ten feet high, spread along the edge of the runway. The sunlight reflected off flat surfaces that were broken by dark, shaded recesses. Steel reinforcing bars twisted skyward, like bristles on an unshaved face. Patches of green were visible in the gaps—pieces of sleeping bags, packs, and uniform shreds. Arab kids were picking through the rubble.

"That's what's left of the BLT headquarters," Kirby said.

Forrest realized the boys were looking for souvenirs of men killed by that concrete. The Arab children were smiling and laughing—*happy Muslim children playing on graves.* Forrest felt a chill.

Kirby downshifted and steered the Jeep onto a grassy knoll overlooking the Shiite slums of southern Beirut. Laid out below them were square

and rectangle mud dwellings packed tightly in clusters. The scene present-
ed a kaleidoscope of earthy colors—the reddish dirt and tan dwellings,
sunshine brightened walls, and palms casting graceful shadows across the
dirt. The scene looked like a Cézanne' painting of a Spanish village—all
right angles and simple shapes in browns and tans and red with bluish
shadows in sharp relief. Children in khaki shorts played soccer in a dusty
opening between the dwellings. A fat lady in a plain brown dress stood in
a doorway, holding up a hand to shade her eyes as she looked up at them.
Off in the distance, over the dust and slums, city buildings stood bright
in the sunshine. Above the city, snowy peaks floated in the blue sky. In a
glance, Forrest looked out on the bold features of the place: palm-shaded
slums, a seaside city, and snow-covered mountains.

Kirby spit on the grass. "Robert," he said, "you know what that
black flag means?"

Forrest looked out over the mud houses and saw a black flag flying
from the dome of a mosque. "No."

Kirby looked over and cocked his combat helmet back to catch better
eye contact. "Means somebody will die for Allah today."

Kirby spit again and then eased the Jeep forward onto the road and
headed across the asphalt pavement of the runway towards the shot-up
hangars. They passed the MEA airliner, the deserted terminal, and a
hangar. As they passed, Forrest looked up at bullet holes in the side of
the hangar. Kirby turned right at the hangar and drove down an empty
two-lane paved road—the same road the truck bomber had used. Kirby
pulled the Jeep into a small parking lot and stopped. On the far side of the
lot stood four concrete pillars, each about fifteen feet high.

Kirby turned off the Jeep engine and sat back in his seat and looked
over at Forrest. "That's it."

"The BLT headquarters?"

"Yep."

They both got out of the Jeep and walked over to the first pillar.

"There was a four-story building here three weeks ago?"

Kirby nodded. "And three hundred men."

An amtrac was painted on a wall by the pillars. Next to the painting were the letters "YATYAS" ("You ain't tracks, you ain't shit") in black paint.

"That's where the C-7s were staged. When the building blew, some of it landed on top of the amtracs. Sergeant Jones was sleeping on the ground by his vehicle. When he heard the blast, he woke up and jumped up on top of the track over the road wheels, under the longitudinal drive shaft."

"Was he hurt?"

"Lost a finger."

"How'd your guy get killed?

"He was on mess duty. They put the mess duty guys up in the building. The troops thought it was a good deal—sleeping inside, showers."

Forrest put a hand up on the smooth concrete. It was cold. He looked around at the empty lot and thought of the Arab kids picking through the rubble out by the runway.

"What was it like?"

Kirby spat. "I was asleep inside one-zero, about a mile away. I could *feel* it a mile away while I was inside an amtrac. I stuck my head out the back hatch and saw a mushroom cloud rising. I thought it was nuke at first. It looked like one." He spat again.

"You help dig out?"

"We all did."

"Find anyone alive?

"No. Just mashed bodies. It was pretty bad."

Kirby drove the Jeep out of the parking lot and across the runway to their line along the east side of the airport, facing the mountains. He drove onto a hard-packed clay road that ran parallel to the runway. Halfway down the runway, he turned left into the company area in the middle of the line. It was the place where Golf Company would set in tomorrow.

They stopped in a small clearing by a stand of cedar trees next to a swell of ground that was about ten feet higher than the surrounding terrain. The company command bunker was dug into the center of this small hill. Sandbagged trenches stretched across the front of the position. Forrest stepped out on packed clay. The surface was hard, reddish brown, and barren. He walked over and looked down into a fighting hole. A little pool of brownish-red water in the bottom reflected the sky. The clearing itself had been soaked and baked in turn, then polished hard by boot traffic and rutted by tanks and amtracs and Jeeps and trucks. Out over the sandbag walls, there were remnants of a town and, beyond that, the mountain.

Forrest followed Kirby down beyond the CP through a patch of brown grass and cactus to the north side of the CP where an amtrac was parked behind a built-up dirt mound. There were layers of sandbags on top of the mound and on top of the amtrac. The thick barrel of the M-85 machinegun aimed at the nearest ridgeline of the Shouf, five hundred yards out. Kirby pointed up to the ridge. "The Amal—Shiite Muslim militia—is up there. Down where four-zero is going you'll be facing Druse—Progressive Socialist Party. Commie ragheads. Wally Jumblat's people."

"Amal come right up into what's left of these buildings right there." Kirby pointed to ruins of one and two-story structures a hundred yards out. "They fire heavy machine guns and rockets from those ridges up there." Kirby pointed. "Then we suppress the fire. We use the Navy guns and artillery. All these targets are in range of our 85s. They shoot first. We shoot last."

The crew chief, Corporal Rodriquez, came out of the back and greeted them. He was lean and haggard and covered with red dust. "Boy, are we glad to see you, Lieutenant," he said, with a grin flashing across his brownish red face.

Forrest nodded. "Thanks, Corporal." Forrest reached up to the side of the amtrac and sunk his finger into a shiny gouge in the armor. "AK?"

"Yes, sir."

"And over here," the corporal pointed to the side of the vehicle, "RPG shrapnel." He walked around to the ramp and pointed again. "And over here, Lieutenant, we have some cuts from rocket shrapnel." The corporal bent down and picked up a sliver of rusty metal about eight inches long. The edges were sheared razor sharp. He held it up, so Forrest could see it, smiled, then dropped it back to the ground. Kirby gestured that it was time to move on. Forrest thanked the corporal and got into the Jeep.

As Kirby drove the Jeep to the next position, Forrest studied the mountain looming over the Marine positions.

"How was Grenada?" Kirby asked.

"Easy operation. Fun, actually—if you're not a Cobra pilot."

"What happened to the Cobras?"

"They got shot down. None of my guys got hurt, though. We ran patrols…liberated some little towns. The people cheered us in the streets. Captured some commies. You know, typical Marine Corps stuff." He looked over at Kirby and smiled.

"I heard you killed a fatty," Kirby said.

Forrest's eyes narrowed—then a smile lifted the corner of his mouth. "Who told you that?"

"You can't keep a secret in the Marine Corps, Robert. So why kill a fatty?

"Garnett killed him."

"Garnett?" Kirby thought for a moment. "Crew chief on four-zero?'

Forrest nodded.

"So, why'd Garnett kill a fatty?" Kirby swerved to avoid puddles as he drove down the dirt road.

Forrest shrugged. "Dude had an RPG."

Kirby nodded.

Two hundred yards down the road, they passed an amtrac dug-in on the left. Then they passed a second amtrac and a third, spaced about sixty yards apart. All were dug into dirt berms and heavily sandbagged. Their M85 machine guns all pointed up at the mountain. The Jeep finally pulled up behind one-zero. Kirby looked over with a smile. "Home sweet home."

Behind the road and amtracs, there was an open area of uneven ground covered by patches of dried mud and stands of wild grass and bunched cactus and cedar bushes. The infantry company was dug in around a hill fifty yards behind the amtrac line. The company CP was in a building behind the hill. Out in front of the amtracs, there was a grass field, and the far side of the field was edged with silver coils of concertina wire. Behind the wire, a sluggish black-water creek meandered through thick yellow-green grass and cattails, and then a railroad bed and behind that, ruins of a town.

Forrest and Kirby walked around to the front of one-zero. The amtrac was parked inside a horseshoe-shaped dirt berm fortified with sandbags. Around the nose of the amtrac, there was a wide semi-circular parapet where men could stand and shoot over the sandbagged rim of the berm. A two-man fighting bunker was dug inside the berm with a gun port in the front. In the middle of the parapet, just in front of one-zero's nose and behind the parapet wall, there was a high-backed black office chair. Kirby sat. "We call this the Bridge of the Enterprise." He stood up and waved his arm to the chair, grinning through tobacco. "Now, it's yours." He closed his mouth, worked up a good spit, and shot a brown glob over the top of the parapet.

"Where'd it come from?" Forrest asked.

"Got it from the old American embassy downtown, after the bombing last year. The guys we relieved had to clear out bodies. They grabbed the chair and a sofa and that poster over there." He pointed to a Marine Corps recruiting poster leaning against the parapet. The poster depicted a Marine in dress blues holding a shiny saber at present arms. Forrest sat on the chair and leaned back in it. A yellow dog strolled up onto the parapet. The dog stopped and looked up at Forrest and snarled. "The boys call him Sam," Kirby said. "He wandered into our lines after the ragheads abandoned the area. I call him Abdullah 'cause I think he's a raghead sympathizer—and he hates officers. I think Abdullah had a rough childhood. We've had wild dogs in the lines. We've shot most of 'em. My guys took a liking to this one, so I've put off shooting him. He's a little wild. Mean as shit. Probably a rabies risk. You'll probably have to shoot him."

"Doesn't seem right, shooting a dog," Forrest answered.

"Well, he's not an American dog."

"Still, can't be right shooting a dog."

"You'll have to shoot him sooner or later."

"Why don't you shoot him?"

Kirby shrugged. "Been meaning to."

Forrest watched the dog disappear around a sandbag wall.

Kirby gestured towards a fifty-five-gallon drum mounted on a stand about seven feet off the ground. The top of the drum was cut out, and a showerhead was welded on the end. Kirby looked admiringly at the contraption, then looked over at Forrest. "Shower."

"You stand out here naked in front of God and everybody?"

"There's nobody around, except the ragheads out yonder." Kirby gestured over the wire to the seemingly empty ruins. "I'm so well-endowed that the sight of me standing out here naked scares the shit out of the ragheads." Kirby hooted out a laugh. They walked down the line of amtracs, checking each position and then out across the grassy field to the concertina wire. Forrest walked up to the coils of razor wire and looked over at the stream. "Smells like shit." Kirby drew in a long sniff and held it, as though tasting, exhaled, then looked over at Forrest. "That's because it is."

"Pardon?"

"Shiite shit."

Forrest looked at Kirby with a quizzical expression.

"Ragheads call this the Wadi Abu Sim'an, but it's really just a river of shit. Drains the Shiite slums up the hill there."

"Shiite shit?" Forrest said with a half-smile. "They didn't mention this on the David Brinkley show."

Kirby nodded. "It's a prime rat habitat, too. Big fuckers. Like a science fiction movie." He shot a wad of spit in a high arc over the wire and then flashed a brown smile. Then they turned away from the wire and walked back into the interior of the lines. They walked over the hill at the center of the position to the remains of a one-story rectangular brick building. An Israeli shell had knocked the concrete roof slab down on one side, making a triangular shaped space inside. "This is the general store," Kirby said as they walked inside. The merchandise was displayed on boards held up by cinder blocks. There were gas canisters for stoves, snacks, soft drinks, cigarettes, and beer. "We're going to use the profits to throw a party when we get home."

Forrest looked around the room, and studied the roof, wondering when it would collapse. He pointed at Arabic graffiti on the wall. "Do you know what this says?"

Kirby shrugged. "No, probably something about killing children."

Forrest laughed.

"No, I'm serious, Robert. That's the way these fuckers think."

They walked over to the outhouse located in an area exposed to enemy fire. It was a plywood three-seater. Fifty-five-gallon drums cut in half were placed under each seat to collect excrement. Each day the contents were burned with diesel fuel, which created a billowing plume of black smoke. Forrest walked inside the outhouse and sat. Directly in front of his lower gut there were three bullet holes in the plywood wall.

"I hope nobody was taking a crap when this happened," Forrest said.

"No. I've been meaning to get it sandbagged," said Kirby. "You can do that right after you shoot that dog." Kirby chuckled.

Forrest walked out into the fresh air. "What a way to go. Imagine the epitaph on the boy's tombstone. Corporal Joe Blow, USMC, 'Shot on the shitter.' What if Davey Crocket had been killed on the shitter? Would give a whole new meaning to 'Remember the Alamo.'" Forrest laughed silently, his shoulders humping up and down. "No," he said, "not poetic enough. It should say, 'Died while defecating.' Or better yet, a poem:

He fought with much bravery
through a bloody violent scrap.
Then was wounded gravely
while taking a large-sized crap."

They both laughed.

They walked to the top of the hill and stood in the sunlight. Spread out below on the far side of the hill was the sweeping expanse of the Mediterranean Sea, blue under a blue sky. There were three American war ships off the coast. Two helicopters were visible out over the sea. Forrest could hear the rotors chopping the air far off. He looked to his right, northward, and saw the buildings of Beirut in the sun. To the south, there was a Beirut suburb called Khalda. Then to the east, inland, there was the mountain and then a second row of higher ridges far off that were snow-covered. He'd never felt so small.

"The Israeli Army is sixty miles to the south on the Awali River," Kirby said. "The Syrian Army is in the Bakaa Valley over the mountain there. The Druse and Amal militias are dug in on the mountain right in front of us. A Lebanese Army brigade is just a few hundred yards to the south." Forrest knew all of this from briefings, but now he was standing on a hill in the middle of it looking out across a coastal plain strewn with chunks of concrete and stretches of drying red clay and stands of cactus and cedar.

That night Forrest laid his sleeping bag out on his poncho on the bare clay dirt and put his pack down for a pillow. He stripped down to his utility trousers and green t-shirt and climbed into his sleeping bag. He lay awake for a long time. The night sky reminded him of duck hunting with his father—he remembered the cold before sunrise when everything was black and they were too sleepy to talk. *They broke ice on Chickahominy Lake and rowed out across water that was like black glass. By the time the johnboat reached the blind, the sky had lightened to a dim gray that made visible the winter mist over the marsh. He and his father threw out the decoys—eight green-winged teal, eight mallards, and five black ducks—in a loose fish hook shape with a nice patch of open water in front of the blind. They'd pull the boat under the blind and climb up to the shooting box. The blind was out away from the marsh in open water that was shallow and clear and the color of tea. Forrest, then fourteen, chambered a shell and slid three No. 4s into the magazine of his Beretta twelve gauge and sat looking out over green cedar branches nailed to the outside of the blind and he remembered the sweet smell of the freshly cut cedar. Yellow and pink low in the sky brightened the water and tinged the marsh mist. The tree line on the far edge of the marsh was a featureless gray profile in the low light.*

"Pintails," his father whispered.

Eight pintails in loose formation sailed on fixed wings low and far out. The birds coasted, studying the setup, then moved their wings and gained altitude as they swung around behind the blind. The birds circled again, higher and tighter, and then moved out in a wide circle behind the blind. Forrest and his father were motionless, peeking up from under the brim of camouflaged hats. The ducks swung around in front and set their wings. They glided in towards the open water in front of the blind. Then they saw something wrong and pitched to their left, beating their wings for speed and altitude. Forrest and his father rose together, and their barrels fell in with the ducks, now flying fifteen yards out. Forrest fell in with the lead duck, swinging with him, then swung out for a lead and squeezed. The shotgun popped off one shell, and the duck rolled end-over-end and splashed into water. He looked to his left and saw that his father had dropped two pintails. Forrest remembered the warmth of being out with his dad on that cold morning. Then he heard an AK-47 clacking far off on the mountain, reminding him that he was 7,000 miles from home.

The next day, Forrest's platoon landed on the beach south of the city. One section—three amtracs—drove up through the city to the U.S. Embassy with sixty Marines from Echo Company. The Command section—two C-7s and two P-7s—went to the new battalion command post dug into high ground on the western side of the runway overlooking the coastal highway. Two amtracs went to Golf Company in the center of the Marine line. Two went to Echo Company north of the runway, and five went to the open country south of the runway, where Forrest would be with four-zero. Kirby's platoon lined up along the clay road south of the runway and staged for the run to the beach. Kirby's 14 amtracs stretched along the length of a football field or more with engines idling. Kirby's dusty Marines flashed toothy grins as they got ready to head for home.

Kirby stood by his amtrac and stared up at the mountain for the last time. Forrest walked over and shook his hand. Kirby said, "One thing I forgot to tell you. There's dead bodies buried all around this area. When it rains, heads and arms and such pop up, like rotten cabbages. It doesn't really smell at all because most of them are pretty well cured. After a rain, the troops go around and shovel dirt over the parts poking up."

Kirby turned and climbed to his turret and put on his comm helmet and saluted from his turret. His amtrac, one-one, surged forward and first platoon's amtracs rolled down the road. By that time, Gunny Coleman had walked up. They stood by the road, watching the amtracs roll by. The men's heads poked up from the driver and turret hatches—dirty faces grinning through the dust. The last amtrac rolled by them, down into the red dust-cloud then around the bend and behind the hill and out of sight. A quiet settled with the dust. Forrest turned and faced the mountain, took off his combat helmet, and rubbed his hand over his head.

The dog walked up and snarled at Forrest. "He don't look too friendly, Lieutenant," said the Gunny.

Forrest and the Gunny walked over to the Bridge of the Enterprise. They stood side-by-side at the parapet, looking out over the wrecked landscape. The Gunny said, "This place is fucked-up, Lieutenant."

Forrest nodded agreement.

"Lieutenant, sandbags out front are shot to shit. Craters everywhere. Hunks of shrapnel all over the ground." A moment passed in silence. On the far side of the wire, there were buildings reduced to piles—jagged protrusions and hard right angles, everything bent, gouged, crumbled and crushed, burned out car carcasses, and the area overgrown with weeds. Forrest laid his hand on a cold sandbag and looked up at the overcast sky. He looked to his left down the long runway and took a deep breath of cool sea air. He wondered how many people had been killed here. He looked up at the cedar-covered ridges and noticed ruins of a ranch house. Forrest focused on it with binoculars. In the window openings and places blown out by fire there were sandbags. He dropped the binoculars. "They've got a hell of a view."

"Yes, sir. They got a nice view of the *New Jersey*, too. That would scare shit out of me if I was a raghead."

This place was different, Forrest thought. There was some meanness on Grenada, but most people there were just ordinary folks. Beirut was mean right down to its broken concrete core. These people understood death. Forrest scanned the ridge five hundred meters away. There were dozens of militia bunkers on the ridge and in the ghost town over the wire. He studied and noted every concentration of sand bags. Then he scanned back to the ranch house. It was halfway up the first ridge, about 750 yards out. He reached up with his right hand to adjust focus and saw the clear form of a Druse militia fighter looking back at him through binoculars.

"You know what's strange about this situation, Lieutenant?"

"I can name five or six things, Gunny, but what do you have in mind?"

"Well, sir, we're stretched out here along a line about a mile long in the shadow of a mountain infested with hostile militia, and we really don't have a mission. Last year, the Peacekeeping Force was useful for keeping the IDF (Israeli Defense Force) and Phalange from slaughtering Palestinian refugees. But now we can't keep any peace. We'd need at least a division to do that. We can't even keep the airport open. So we're just a presence. But for what purpose?"

"Well, Guns, I don't know what the brain trust is thinking. Maybe we're just proving that they can't drive us out of here unless and until we decide to go. But our job here on the line is pretty darn clear. We need to keep our Marines alive, and that means we have to be ready to suppress those militias if they take a shot at us."

That night, Forrest ate dinner alone. The Corps had stopped issuing the Vietnam era C-rations. Now, they had "Meals, Ready to Eat," MREs, that came in green plastic pouches. On a small gas canister stove, he boiled water in his canteen cup and then lowered a pouch of chicken chow mein into the water to heat it. He then tore open the pouch and ate with a plastic spoon. He had dry crackers and cheese spread and a candy bar and dried fruit. After dinner, he brewed instant coffee and chewed Chiclets from the MRE. When he finished, he repacked his trash into the plastic bag and then leaned back against the sandbag wall and fell asleep.

Chapter Sixteen

The Washington Post
"Eight American Marines Died on Vulnerable Rooftop Post."

December 6, 1983—"Eight American Marines killed by an artillery shell last night had clustered in a vulnerable rooftop position ... the scene atop the three-story house ... was a grisly one. There was a can of spilled popcorn mixed with M16 rifle shell cases in a sandbag pillbox ... and a gaping hole in the sandbag wall clearly marking where a single shell ... had exploded, killing the eight men and wounding two others."

It rained for three days and when the sun finally lit the field, the ground was dotted with exposed body parts—there were three heads up and a crooked knee and a hand that seemed to be grasping at the sky. The Marines headed out with e-tools to cover over the shallow graves, and then they got to work filling sandbags to reinforce bunkers that had been shot to pieces. Two engineers went out to the wire to check the Claymores and make sure the wire was properly staked and laid. A Druse sniper took a shot at the engineers and missed. The engineers withdrew to the bunkers, and Fox Company called in a SEAL sniper.

Forrest was filling sandbags when the sniper and his spotter showed up fully armed. They were dressed in camouflaged utilities and flak jackets with a Navy emblem on the front. The sniper's manner was relaxed, and his hair was too long, and his mouth carried a permanent hint of a smile, like a surfer in endless summer—the easy-going contentment of a man who loved his job. His spotter was a very serious young man who carried a spotting scope. The sniper walked over to Forrest. "Lieutenant Forrest?"

Forrest nodded. "We're here to help you with your sniper problem." He smiled like a plumber promising to clear clogged pipes.

Forrest looked down at the strange rifle.

"It's a .50 caliber sniper rifle," said the SEAL.

"You kidding?" Forrest had never heard of the weapon.

"No, sir." He pulled out a .50 caliber round that was eight inches long, held it up in the sunlight, and smiled.

"What can you do with that thing?"

"I can behead a raghead over a mile away." Forrest nodded, still looking at the large bore weapon.

"If you'll excuse me, sir, I'll set up over there," he said, gesturing to a short sandbag wall behind some standing brush.

Forrest nodded and watched the SEAL walk up the hill. Forrest turned back to his task and shoveled up a spade-full of sandy red clay into a bag. After filling the bag, he stood and wiped sweat from his face with his right hand. He glanced up at the sandbag wall up the hill and did not see the SEAL.

The sniper and his spotter took a position under some small bushes and brown winter grass. About 350 yards out, there was a factory building that sat back near the slope of the mountain. The word "York" was hanging on the side of the building in large letters. The concrete face of the building was full of holes of various sizes that had been blown out of the building by the Israelis and the Marines of 1/8 and the Lebanese brigade just to the south. There were sandbag bunkers built into several of the larger holes.

Once the sniper team was in place, Fox Company sent the two engineers out again to draw fire so the sniper team could spot the Druse shooter. The engineers were not thrilled by the plan, but they walked out as ordered. When they got to the wire and began working again, a Druse sniper made the biggest and last mistake of his life—he leaned the barrel of his AK-47 on sandbags in a shell hole and aimed in on one of the engineers. The Druse's barrel picked up a glint of sunlight that was immediately noticed by the spotter. The sniper quickly aimed in on the man's head, which was clearly visible through the rifle scope. As the Druse steadied his aim, his head exploded—the wet organic remnant of his head splashed against the back wall of the building, and the man's headless body slumped to the floor. Two seconds later, the sound of the shot passed over the dead Druse.

Through November and into December, Forrest and his platoon had gotten into the rhythm of the place and sniper episodes, like the one above, and other minor firefights flared up every few days. The mission was simply to sit there under the guns of Druse and Amal militia and within range of several Syrian artillery batteries in the Beqaa Valley. Forrest and his Marines spent their days building and reinforced bunkers and standing watches and occasionally using the 50s to suppress enemy militia. There was a Lebanese Army brigade in Khalde about a mile south of Forrest's bunker, and that brigade exchanged fire with the Druse every night. The sound of gunfire would go until around 21:00, at which time everybody apparently went to bed. When Druse or Amal militia fired into Marine positions, the Marine response would escalate from small arms to 50s, to 60mm mortars, to 81mm mortars, to artillery, to naval gunfire, to air strikes. This escalation would stop when the militia stopped firing – so the tactic was to suppress the militia and then stop shooting. During this time, Forrest walked the line every morning around 03:00 and worked with his Marines to shore up the sandbags and in the afternoons, he'd sit on the Captain Kirk chair and read and then at night he'd walk the line again and talk to the troops and visit with the Gunny and drink coffee and watch the sporadic firefights between the Lebanese Army and Druse.

On December 3rd, 1983, Syrian Army units in the Beqaa valley fired surface to air missiles at two F-14 Tomcats that were flying an aerial reconnaissance mission in Lebanese airspace. The missiles missed. Early the next morning, twenty-four A6 Intruders and A-7 Corsairs launched from two U.S. aircraft carriers out in the Mediterranean, the USS *INDEPENDENCE* and the USS *KENNEDY*. As the jets launched, they paired up for bombing runs on Syrian positions in the Beqaa Valley, about fifteen miles east of Beirut. Between 06:00 and 06:15, the jets streaked low over the Syrian positions dropping bombs and then dropped heat balloons to divert the SA-7 missiles fired by the Syrians. One Corsair and one Intruder were shot down.

Anticipating a counter-attack, the entire Multi-National Force— the French, Italians, and U.S. Marines—went to defense Condition One at 06:00. This meant an enemy attack was imminent. All Marines were awake and in fighting positions, and each turret was manned. The Marines stayed in Condition One all day. Forrest spent most of the day sitting in the Captain Kirk chair with his boots propped up on the sandbag ledge. He finished reading *Chesapeake*. In the late afternoon, Forrest walked out onto the clay road. There was a strange quiet, and there was no breeze off the sea.

Starting at dusk, there was sporadic gunfire up on the mountain. After dark, enemy machinegun fire erupted from the ridges across from Golf Company. Streams of fire snaked down onto Golf's bunkers. Then a firefight broke out down in Hooterville—the small village about seven hundred yards in front of Golf Company's forward line—around a Marine forward position called Checkpoint 76. Forrest watched streams of tracers flying back and forth between buildings. The pace of radio traffic quickened—sounds of calm, radio-modulated voices with gunfire in the background. Then Forrest heard a familiar sound—the deep, rapid notes of M-85 machineguns firing. Jefferson's amtracs were firing, and two streams of bullets shot up to the mountain. After several bursts, the guns stopped. It was quiet again.

One of the Navy ships fired two illumination rounds. The shells arced in over the battlefield and popped. Two lights appeared in the sky, floating under parachutes. Light on the field in the cool night reminded Forrest of a Friday night football game—everything bright in the light and the background black. Instead of a grass football field, though, the men looked out across the razor wire at crags of concrete in sharp relief under the floating light. Spinning under parachutes, the lights made a whirling sound as they drifted. Dark shadows in and behind the ruins moved and lengthened as the lights drifted downrange. All along the line, Marines crouched behind the sandbag walls looked up with light flickering off their faces.

The tempo of the fight slowly increased. There was a burst of fire from the mountain, followed by a return fire from Marines. Then another enemy burst. Muzzle flashes in dark recesses of shell holes in the York building marked Druse fighters, and the sound of automatic weapons echoed across the coastal plain. Bullets smacked the outside of sandbags of the parapet and zipped overhead. Several AK rounds splattered into four-zero's turret armor. Forrest stood and peeked over the bags. Light from another illumination round caught his face, bringing out his tanned skin and the sun-faded camouflage of his helmet. In the last flicker of light, he noticed movement on the road up on the mountain. Then the light died, and the firing stopped again. Quiet returned.

Forrest picked up the phone and cranked it. Then, in a low voice, he spoke into the handset. "There's a gun crew on the road above the ranch house. Aim in on the road, two degrees above the ranch house and then four degrees to the left." Down the line, the turrets turned, and the barrels elevated. During daylight, the men had prepared for this moment. Forrest had given a name to twelve targets. They did not have night vision scopes, so during daylight, each gunner had sighted the targets with their eight-powered scope and then recorded the barrel elevation and turret angle using the elevation gauge and azimuth ring inside the turret. Using these coordinates now, all five M-85's on the southern end of the runway were trained on the area where Forrest had seen movement up on the road. In each turret, the gunner sat with his hands on the grips and fingers on triggers. There was a distant burst of AK fire. Then it was quiet again. The only other sound was the slurry of radio talk over radio speakers. The smell of burned cordite now hung over the battlefield.

Suddenly, the Druse gun crew up above the ranch house fired a long burst from a ZU-23-4, a four-barreled 23mm gun. A thick flow of bullets poured down onto Golf Company's bunkers to Forrest's left. Forrest yelled into the landline, "Fire! Fire! Fire!"

All five guns opened fire together and Forrest flinched at the ear-splitting noise of four-zero's M-85 firing just a few feet above and behind him. He put a forefinger in each ear as he watched the five streams of tracers arcing across the night sky into the target. Each gunner had his head up out of his turret hatch, watching his stream of fire and adjusting it in on the spot where the enemy fire had come from. The five streams converged on the enemy gun crew, hitting hard objects and ricocheting up, chewing the ground and eating whatever was there in a lead-toothed grinder. The guns maintained the fire for five long seconds, pumping nearly five hundred bullets into the small area before falling off to shorter bursts. As the M85 fire lit the sky, Lewis whooped out a high-pitched yell. His exuberance spread as the yell spread along the line that was barely audible over the deep base sound of the guns firing at five hundred rounds per minute. White clouds formed over each gun and wafted along the lines, spreading the smell of burned power. The noise filled the night air with the sound of American's fighting back—and it was exhilarating. It was rare to catch enemy militia in the open, well within range, and the hammering dished-out by the amtrac gunners sent a thrill through the Marines on that line.

Forrest joined in as the yells fused with the sound of the guns. For Forrest, the violence tapped into the pent-up frustrations of his boyhood—loss in Vietnam, the Iran hostage crisis, and the Soviet expansion in Asia, Afghanistan, Central America, and Africa. He remembered the TV images of American students cheering for the enemy, flying the Viet Cong flag, and chanting, "Ho, Ho, Ho Chi Min! Ho Chi Min is gonna win!" There was President Carter's "malaise" speech and Forrest's dad yelling at "that goddamned Walter Cronkite" on the old black and white television, and there were the assassinations and riots. All of this flashed across his mind as the streams of light shot out across the cool night sky.

The yells continued as the gunners picked up a rhythm, passing off between them to keep the fire on until every magazine was empty, and nothing was left alive on the target. After several minutes, the firing stopped. A cloud of smoke hung in the air, and hot, empty shell casings were piled on the ground by each turret's ejection port.

The battlefield fell silent again. Lewis said, "You know we hit 'em, sir."

Forrest nodded but said nothing. There was a pop high in the sky and then the light of an illumination round. The light flickered across Forrest's face and lit the smoky air and shapes of wrecked buildings over the wire and, far off, the cedar-covered ridges of the mountain. As the light passed over the target, Forrest could see the wreckage of the ZU and of the pick-up truck that had been used to tow the gun into place. The crew of every amtrac was reloading their turret's magazine.

Forrest sat down on the sandbags besides Garnett and Lewis and exhaled. He took off his helmet and rubbed his hands across the top of his head. "I heard somebody say once that there's no background music in real life. That may be true, but there's a hell of a shot of adrenaline in real life that you don't get in the movie theater."

"Well, sir," Garnett said, "we ought to get some of them bagpipe guys to play songs while the fight is on. Then we'd have both."

Forrest heard Jefferson's M-85s working down by Golf Company with long, even bursts. He stood, looked to the left, and saw streams of M-85 fire flying into Amal bunkers in wreckage of Hooterville. He waited for the M-85s to stop firing and called Jefferson on the radio.

"Dog leader, four-zero, sitrep, over."

Jefferson's voice came over the speaker. "Roger, four-zero, we have RPGs coming in on top of us"—Forrest could hear the tinny sound of radio modulated gunfire in the background—"we took out one position, another one is apparently still in action…450 rounds expended, over."

"Roger that, Dog leader, good job, out."

SSHHWWIISSSHHBBBOOOMM! The ground shuddered as waives of energy rippled through it. The rocket hit twenty yards in front of four-zero with an orange and yellow flash and sparks. Then a blast of 23-millimeter fire came in from the mountain and hit the sandbags in front of the Bridge of the Enterprise, sounding like rapid, hard thwacks of a fly swatter on burlap bags. Forrest, Garnett, Goode, and Lewis were huddled just inches away on the friendly side of the sandbags.

"I think we pissed 'em off, sir," said Garnett.

Forrest nodded.

Four-five and four-six both spotted the 23mm position and opened fire. Forrest poked his head up above the sandbags and saw the streams of bullets streaking out but ducked again when more 23mm rounds smacked into the sandbags.

SSSWWWOOOSSHHHBOOM! The rocket hit twenty yards to the left of four-zero. The impact shook dirt from the sandbag wall around the front of the parapet. Lewis leapt to his feet, screaming, "You missed again, you ass holes! Hah, hah, hah!"

Forrest rolled over on his back and looked over at Lewis. "Feel better?"

Lewis looked over with a sheepish smile. "Yessir."

"That makes me happy, Lewis. But stay behind the sandbags. What would I say to your momma if you got killed?"

"Like the song, sir, 'Tell my mom I did my best, bury me front leaning rest, ooohhhrrrahhh.'" Lewis smiled again.

"It would be easier on me if you didn't get killed."

"Yes, sir."

Forrest and the others stood again and looked out on the mountain as the night quieted down. Then, up on a far ridge, about a mile away, there was a silent short streak of light. It was the blast of a rocket launching. It streaked straight up, which meant it was coming directly at them.

"Rocket in the air," Forrest said. They all dropped down behind the sandbags and waited. Forrest was on the far left side of the Bridge of the Enterprise, with no overhead cover. He lay up against the sandbags as close as he could and hugged the cold, compacted clay ground. He breathed in the smell of clay and studied the moonlit canvas weave of a sandbag inches in front of his face and waited. As the seconds ticked by, he wondered how many Marines spent their last seconds alive with this exact smell and view.

High out in the night sky, the rocket was flying in an arc. It would hit at a steep angle. All along the line, Marines huddled close to the ground, waiting—men with good lives and healthy legs waiting in their little private worlds under the lips of their combat helmets, in the dark, smelling the packed clay ground. The last few seconds ticked by, maybe the last seconds of young lives, or legs or arms. The cold trajectory of the unseen rocket could change lives or end them. A little breeze here, a gust there, and *boom*! The good news was that if you heard the rocket hit, it had missed you.

SSSWWWIIIISSHHBOOM! The rocket hit twenty yards to the left with a shuddering thump. A hot hunk of shrapnel smacked the side of four-zero with a metallic bang. Forrest felt the sensation of the steep drop of a roller coaster—that unnerving feeling of momentum pushing your gonads into your gut.

Lewis jumped up again—"You missed again, you fuckers! Hah, hah, hah!"—and then slid back down behind the sandbags. "Sorry, sir."

The battlefield was quiet again.

All along the line, Marines crouched quietly behind sandbags, gripping M-16s. Another illumination round drifted over, flickering light across the faces of wrecked buildings and green cedars. Forrest stood and looked out again. "One. Two. Three. Three rockets in the air, coming this way." He lay down again and waited. His heart pounded in his ears. One thousand one, one thousand two …Eight long seconds. He felt the cold of the ground as he hugged down into the edge between the dirt and the sandbagged wall.

SSSWWWIIISSHHBOOM! SSSWWWISSHHBOOM! SSSH-WWWISSSHHBOOOM!

Shock waves vibrated through the ground, and dirt shook from the sandbags and fell down Forrest's flak jacket collar. He tried to scoop it out, but most of the dirt trickled down inside his utility top.

Radio traffic on the speaker indicated that Checkpoint 76 had been hit by a rocket. The checkpoint was a bunker built atop a small store in what was left of Hooterville. He listened to Golf's company commander talking to one of his lieutenants and Jefferson about moving out to relieve the checkpoint. *SSSHHHWWWWIIISSHHBBOOM!* Dirt flew. Shrapnel smacked into the side of four-zero again.

Another 23mm crew fired down on four-zero. This time, the rounds came in high and airburst directly over the bunker. Forrest lay on his back, looking straight up at the popping rounds, fireworks against a black way. Then he heard bullets smacking the sandbags out front. About three minutes later, a series of muzzle flashes were visible in the ruins two hundred meters out. The gunners in the turrets of four-four and four-nine saw the flashes at the same time and opened with long bursts of M85 fire. The bright streams of fire shot out on a line and filled the building crevice. Forrest watched with his forefingers in his ears.

Then it was quiet again, except for the radio, and automatic fire far off. Forrest leaned on the sandbag berm and listened to radio modulated voices speaking calmly.

"CP76, 50/50 over." Nothing. Static.

"CP76, 50/50, over…" Static.

Forrest listened to the radio as events unfolded. He heard Jefferson's voice over the radio, with the whine of the amtrac engine in the background as he hooked up with an infantry squad to head out to CP-76. In each transmission, Forrest heard AK-47s clacking in the background. A minute later, Forrest heard Jefferson's M-85 shooting from a forward position near CP-76. Forrest stood and looked over the sandbags but could not see the tracers because Jefferson was shooting low targets. Forrest looked up at a peaceful sky of stars and exhaled slowly.

Forrest listened as Lieutenant Sisk called in a sitrep from CP-76.

"50/50, Spiderman, over."

"Go, Spiderman."

"Direct hit. Direct…" static "…it, over. Eight Kilo-India-Alpha, over. Two priority medevacs, over."

"Kilo-India-Alpha" meant "Killed in Action."

The rocket had hit the bunker, penetrated the sandbagged roof, and exploded among the Marines inside, killing eight and wounding two. Jefferson's amtrac pulled up in front of the building and dropped its ramp. A Marine squad ran out and set up security and then started a medivac. Lance Corporal Jones manned the turret and used the M85 to hit enemy positions. Jefferson and the crew chief, Lance Corporal Dunn, ran up to help with the medevacs. The scene in the wrecked bunker was gruesome. Dunn took one look and vomited. Within ten minutes, they had loaded the dead Marines—some body parts were recovered later—in the troop compartment of the amtrac. Then they laid the two wounded Marines on top, and the amtrac headed back towards the Golf Company CP.

The time had come to end the fight. The artillery battery started firing all eight guns, and the USS *New Jersey* worked the mountain face with five-inch guns. American shells slammed into the mountain with sparkling concussions in a barrage that went on and on. Forrest and his men sat quietly behind their sandbags watching, as though watching a movie. They listened to the muffled sounds of the guns firing and watched for the hits on the mountain. A shell hit the Shiite electricity transformer and exploded in blue sparks.

Then it was quiet again. Even the radio speaker was silent.

Forrest sat in the Captain Kirk chair for the first time that night, took off his combat helmet, and rubbed his hands across the top of his stubby-haired head. His tension drained, and he felt his exhaustion and muscle soreness. It was 23:00.

The landline rang, and Lewis picked up. He took a message and hung up. "Sir, we're off Condition One. Condition Three."

Forrest looked at his watch. "Thanks, Lewis. Pass the word."

"Garnett."

"Yessir?"

"You can get Shields out of the turret. Go to normal watches."

"Roger that, sir."

"I'm walking the line."

Forrest walked down the road to four-nine, where Corporal Pizzini had just finished brewing a fresh pot of coffee. The Gunny was sitting with Sergeant Tabb on a bench built into the parapet in front of four-nine. Pizzini handed Forrest a yellow plastic USS NEW JERSEY cup brimming with good-smelling coffee. Forrest drew in the scent. "Were did you get this coffee, Pizzini?"

"Momma sent it, sir."

"Thank your momma for me."

"Will do, sir."

Forrest stepped up on the parapet and sat on a ledge built out from the sandbag wall. He stretched out his legs, felt his soreness. It was good soreness, he thought, like the feeling of a good workout. He sipped his coffee, leaned back in the darkness against the sandbag wall, and looked up at the stars. He felt the cold graininess of a sandbag against the back of his head and took in the smells of dirt and coffee in the cool air. He looked over at the Gunny and Sergeant Tabb. The two sat there in the dark against the sandbag wall, their faces smeared with dirt and gun grease, their eyes tired. They heard faintly in the distance a helicopter inbound for a load of dead and wounded Marines. Forrest felt a hollow, unsettled feeling in his chest—a sick feeling that intensified as his numbness faded and his nerves slowly reconnected. Forrest took off his helmet and laid it in his lap. He looked down at the helmet in his blackened hands and noticed for the first time a cut on the back of his right hand. Blood had dripped across his hand to his wrist and dried black.

A mile away, eight bodies zipped neatly in plastic bags lay in the darkness. In true Marine Corps fashion, the bodies were lined up perfectly, as in formation. The battalion chaplain, a Catholic priest, knelt beside each body in turn, administering last rights.

"You know," the Gunny said finally, "folks don't realize how easy this is for us and how hard it is on the families."

Forrest and Tabb sipped their coffee.

"See," the Gunny continued, "tomorrow morning every paper and TV news show is gonna report that some Marines got killed here tonight. But they won't say which ones. So everybody will wonder if it's their husband or son or whoever. And they won't know for sure till they get a letter from little Johnny. Unless, of course, little Johnny is one of the ones out there getting a helicopter ride. And if he is, then mommy or little Sally will be getting a visit from the Marine Corps. But for us, it's easy. We all know right away that we didn't get killed. And the ones who did get killed don't care anymore, anyway.

"That's one of the benefits of the Corps. If you get killed, they send somebody out to your house in blues, with a chaplain and everything. Then you get a damned nice funeral."

"I've never been to a Marine Corps funeral," Tabb said.

"It's a beautiful thing Jimmy," said the Gunny. "I did funerals on barracks duty in '70. We drilled and practiced. You fuck up a funeral detail, and the Old Man will shit in your ear."

The Gunny was quiet for a moment. They could hear the helicopters sitting in the LZ out across the runway. Then he snorted out
one of his one-note laughs. "We had this corporal. His name was Alex
Sandstone. Good boy. He'd just finished a grunt tour in 'Nam. He'd
been wounded three times, so they sent him to barracks duty. I think he
was from Georgia. Anyway, we were on a funeral up in Philadelphia for
a Marine killed in the war. The Marine's momma and daddy were there,
crying. His whole family and his high school buddies and girlfriend and
Uncle Joe and whoever. Everybody crying and wailing. Anyway, there
were eight of us, four on each side of the coffin and a lieutenant in charge.
Nice, new flag draped over the coffin. I was holding on as we inched
sideways, moving that coffin up on the rigging over the hole. Then
Sandstone, who was right across from me, just disappeared. *Wooosh!*
Dude was gone. Fell in the hole." The Gunny hooted out another laugh.
"Well, we all just stopped and tried not to look concerned. I thought
the lieutenant was gonna shit his blues. He's just standing there, not
knowing what to do. I figured we could put the coffin down and just
pretend like everything was okay and get Sandstone out of the hole
later. Sandstone was sitting down in the hole, being real quiet, like he
didn't exist. Finally, Sandstone climbed up out of the hole and took a
post in front of the lieutenant and gave a sharp salute and reported,
'The hole is clear, sir.' The lieutenant saluted back and said, 'Return
to your post,' like it was a darn parade. Sandstone did an about-face
and marched over to his spot, and we went on from there like nothing
happened. Hardest part of the whole thing was not to laugh. I damn
near bit a hole in my tongue trying not to laugh. When Sandstone
fell into the hole, well, it was a miracle I didn't fall down laughing.
Good thing, too, because I'd still be on shitter detail in Diego Garcia if I'd
laughed at a Marine Corps funeral."

The following morning, Forrest drove his Jeep to the battalion
CP. The meeting of battalion officers, company commanders, tanks,
tracks, and staff officers was at 07:00. After the Marine barracks was
destroyed in October, the battalion set up headquarters in a bunker

complex on high ground overlooking the sea. Forrest drove his Jeep up beside a short sandbag wall and stopped. He stepped out on sand and walked through an opening in the chest-high sandbag wall that surrounded the headquarters bunkers. He passed two sentries and walked down to the Command Post. About twenty yards down, he stopped where there were several objects resting on top of the wall. There was a piece of twisted black steel that, the day before, had been an M-60 machinegun, a plastic canteen with a large hole in it, and an M-16 bent into a 90-degree angle—items collected from CP76 the night before. He'd felt the ground shudder from a rocket impact, but until that moment, he had not understood the power of a rocket blast.

At the meeting, the intelligence officer reported the number of Shiite and Druse killed or wounded the night before, based on radio intercepts. The chaplain reported that he'd given last rights to the dead Marines. There was some talk of replacing the dead men, and then the meeting ended.

Forrest walked out alone and sat in his Jeep for a long time, staring out at the sea. He'd joined the Marines for adventure and thought it was a game. He appreciated the adventure, but the price was too high. Thrill seekers should engage in sports rather than combat, he thought. He watched the battleship cruising close to shore, like a hungry wolf. Little knots of shore birds flitting by in the sea breeze. He thought of the fear and exhilaration of the fight the night before and the cost of it. Then he pushed the ignition button with his left foot and drove down the gravel road, headed for Golf Company. He pulled into the Golf CP area, then turned left and rode over uneven ground to four-seven, dug in on the backside of a small red hill. There was a large pile of spent brass on the ground below the turret. As Forrest walked up, he bent down and picked up from the ground a split-open 7-Up can. There was a tiny BB-sized hole in one the side of the can.

Staff Sergeant Jefferson climbed up out of the fighting bunker and noticed the can in Forrest's hand. "Ragheads shot my 7-Up with an RPG."

Forrest looked back down at the can.

"Motherfuckers!" Jefferson said.

"An RPG made this tiny hole?" Forrest said.

"Yessir, laid that sucker right in here," Jefferson pointed to a spot in the mud next to four-seven. "Look here, sir." Jefferson was pointing at gouges in the amtrac's armor. "They splattered shrapnel all over four-seven. A tiny piece took out my 7-Up. Score one for the ragheads."

Forrest walked over and stuck his fingers in shiny gouge marks in the side of the amtrac.

"We also took some small arms," Jefferson said, pointing to some bullet gouges in the turret armor. Forrest stuck his finger in one of the holes. It was about an inch deep.

"AK-47?"

"I guess so, sir."

"How'd the boys do?"

Jefferson looked down, shaking his head. He looked up. "It was a hot ride out to the checkpoint. Dunn went up with some of the helmet heads, and they found a pile of dead Marines. They were all in pieces and smelled pretty bad. They piled everything in four-seven and laid the two wounded guys on top. Dunn threw up." Jefferson looked away, at the mountain.

"Where is Dunn?"

"He's in four-seven."

Forrest and Jefferson walked onto the open ramp of four-seven. In the forward end of the troop compartment, Lance Corporal Dunn sat in the dark, his eyes fixed on nothing in particular. Dry blood was smeared on the walls, and there were lumps of gray tissue on the floorboards and sticking to the walls of the amtrac, all the way up to the radios. The smell of organs and blood nauseated Forrest. He closed his eyes, and the feeling passed. Forrest wondered why Dunn was sitting in the bloody troop compartment. Dunn looked up from the floorboards, and then a crooked smile crossed his face. "Look, Lieutenant, Sergeant Jones' eyeball is looking up at me through the floor boards."

The following day, the battalion held a memorial service in the mess tent behind a hill south of the runway in a spot that overlooked the Med. Forrest walked over alone and found the tent full, so he walked up the hill to an empty fighting hole and sat on a short sandbag wall. A Jeep pulled up by the tent and parked. Larry Atwell stepped out, stuck his head in the tent, and then stepped back and looked around. Forrest waved. Atwell waved back and started up the hill. After greetings, Atwell sat on the sandbag wall by Forrest. They were assigned to different ships, and Larry was on the staff for the Marine Amphibious Group headquarters—the headquarters above the battalion level—so they had not seen each other since leaving Camp Lejeune.

They sat looking down at the tent, saying nothing. Forrest thought about the eight dead Marines—aged nineteen to twenty-four years. Forrest denied being an atheist and rationalized that he was merely a lazy skeptic who'd never really thought much about God. He'd made a brief appeal to God from his turret during the attack in Grenada and felt nothing. But he'd always ignored God and even the question of God's existence, and he realized his prayer had been almost vulgar and that he was like a distant relative who only calls when he needs money. It had always been easy to ignore the big questions because he was young and healthy and had no need to contemplate his own death. After his father's death, he moved quickly back into his young life and never grappled with the life-after-death question. In Beirut, it was hard not to think about death.

Even though Forrest had often scoffed at religion, he'd been impressed by the way Kirby and Atwell talked about their faith. Forrest respected both of them, and they were both true believers. They coupled sincerity and intelligence in a way that kept Forrest from marginalizing them as religious nuts. Forrest had always resisted religious discussions with them because he found the subject unsettling. He hated the idea of surrendering his will to a higher power. But now, sitting quietly with Atwell, he needed a meaningful way to think about all the young Marines who'd been killed there, and he refused to think that they simply did not exist anymore.

"Larry, what do you think heaven is like?"

"I don't know."

"I know what I'd like it to be," Forrest said.

"Seventy virgins?"

Forrest laughed. "No. I've never understood that virgin deal. They think heaven is about physical pleasure. Don't they realize that's what we're *here* for? So they spend their earthly life killing children and covering their woman with sheets, all in the hope of an endless orgy in the afterlife? Denial here and carnal pleasures in heaven. They're 180 degrees out of phase."

"Well, they do have sex. Look at all the little ragheads running around."

"And what about their wives? Do they get seventy virgins, too? And where do all these virgins come from, anyway?" Forrest asked. "Funny thing is, we probably won't have peckers in heaven. Raghead kills a bunch of kids and figures he's in for an eternal orgy, and then he finds out he has no dick. I'd love to see his face. He'd be feeling his crotch, and there's nothing there and he'd think, *Shit, I shouldn't have killed those babies.* Then all those virgins will get pissed off 'cause they've been waiting around for eternity to get some kid-killer dick, and so they'll be bitching at the raghead forever. Sounds like hell."

"Well, not all ragheads think that. Just the crazies," Atwell said.

"Yeah. I know. But it's the crazies we have to deal with."

Larry Atwell nodded. "I read somewhere that the virgin thing is a mistranslation. Some scholars studied the original text and concluded that the word thought to mean 'virgins' really means 'grapes.'"

"No shit?" Forrest said.

Atwell nodded. "So what's your idea of heaven, Robert?"

"A big, covered porch overlooking a blue-grass mountaintop. All my buddies there with me, telling funny stories. We'll laugh and drink beer in perpetuity, always having a happy buzz but never really drunk, never sober, either. That's what I'd like."

Atwell nodded. "What about your wife? She'll be pissed if she has to serve you beers for all eternity."

"Don't have a wife. Don't have a girlfriend."

"Yeah, but you probably will by the time you die."

Forrest nodded. "Maybe. If I do, she can sit with us on the porch telling funny stories, and we'll get a dick-less raghead to wait on us or maybe some of those frustrated virgins. But you know what would happen. All the women would hang out together in one room and all the dudes will be in another, if normal patterns carry over to heaven."

Atwell nodded. "If I'm there, I'd like a big bag of those Cheese Whiz things. I love those things. I could eat and eat and eat those suckers forever, if I didn't have to worry about throwing up or getting fat."

They stopped talking and sat quietly on the sandbags, both starring down at the tent.

"You believe that Jesus died on a cross and rose from the dead?" Forrest asked.

"Yep."

"You certain?"

"Well," Atwell said, "I have doubts—if people were created by God, then why are some people evil? Why do horrible things happen to good people? I understand the issues, but to me the rational case for Christ is stronger than the doubts."

"What rational case? I thought you guys relied on faith alone," said Forrest.

"You have to have faith, but how do you get there without a rational case? If you tell me to put my faith in a rock, I'm going to ask you why."

"So what's the case for death and resurrection?"

Larry Atwell stood and stretched and put one boot up on the sandbags and then looked off at the Med. "There are books about the historical validity of the Gospels with analysis of archeological finds and reports from Roman writers in the early days and other things. But for me, there are three things that push me over the top. First, look at the Gospels. What are they? They include some extraordinary claims, but they really don't fit into the myth genre of the time. There are no one-eyed Cyclopes. You know how a Marine sometimes starts off a story with, 'This is true, no shit...?' Well, Luke starts off just like that; he tells us he's writing a history. They read like histories, so I figure that's what they are. The second thing is that most of the disciples martyred themselves rather than deny the resurrection. People just don't do that."

Forrest interrupted. "Yes, they do. Those people right out there over the wire can't wait to kill themselves. What about the Kamikaze pilots in World War II?"

"You're missing an important distinction," said Atwell. "The terrorists kill themselves because they genuinely believe that God wants them to kill infidels. The Kamikazes believed the Emperor was God. But for the disciples, it was not a matter of belief in a theory—that God wants this or that. Christianity is based on a historical fact. Jesus either died on the cross or not. He either rose or not. And the disciples were *there*—they were eyewitnesses to those facts. If it was all a lie, the disciples *knew* it was lie. People don't martyr themselves for something they know is a lie. The eyewitnesses believed it and died for it.

"The third thing is the incredible early spread of Christianity despite Roman persecution. Think about that for a second. You have this Jewish carpenter who was an itinerant preacher who had a three-year ministry. The Romans tortured Him to death. He did not leave behind a single written word. Two hundred years later, Christianity was adopted as the official religion of the Roman Empire. There has never been a fraud good enough to pull that off. So it must be true."

Forrest listened carefully. He knew he'd been living a frivolous life and that he was not ready to die. He said, "I don't want to be judged or interfered with. I want my freedom."

"Robert. You're going be judged whether you like it or not. As for freedom, you've already given that up. The Marine Corps tells you how to cut your hair and a million other things. You gave up freedom for the Corps, why not give it up for the God that allowed Himself to be tortured to death just to save your sorry ass?"

As the service inside the tent drew to a close, a Marine posted outside the tent played Taps on a bugle. As the sad notes drifted across the coastal plain, Forrest and Atwell absorbed the loss, and they both knew that more young Marines were going to die there.

Atwell patted Forrest on the back and then stood. He started to walk away, and then he stopped. "Robert, you know Psalm 126?"

Forrest shook his head no.

"When the Lord calls us home, we'll think we're dreaming."

"I hope it's a good dream."

"I'm pretty sure it is, Robert," said Larry Atwell as he turned and walked down to his Jeep.

Chapter Seventeen

The New York Times
"Marines' Christmas: 'Good Try, But...'"

*December 24, 1983—"[I]n a Christmas Eve report: Three
charred bodies were found in a burned-out car whose deathly
cargo of explosives had detonated prematurely... Near Beirut,
the wooded hills of the Shouf Mountains resounded with the
thumps and bangs of an artillery battle between the Lebanese
Army and Moslem Druse opponents."*

To celebrate Christmas Eve, Forrest arranged to play dominos with
the officers of Golf Company at their command post about a half-mile

down the line. They'd captured weapons and soldiers in Grenada but also a set of dominoes from the Peoples' Revolutionary Army. During the ship ride from Grenada to Lebanon, they played with the "commie bones" every night, and a game now seemed the perfect way to celebrate Christmas. So after an MRE breakfast of chicken chow mein and instant coffee, Forrest stepped out of his bunker and headed for the Jeep. He took a few steps and noticed that rain had partially uncovered the dead woman in a blue dress that was buried behind his bunker—a victim of some Phalange or Druse execution squad. She peered skyward with eyes as small and black as raisins, and her mouth cavity held a little pool of water. She was part of the ground now, and she seemed comfortable, as in bed under a blanket of red clay with one thin, yellowed arm out over the covers.

The Golf Company command post was set-up in a forty-foot cargo container buried under a small hill. There was a sandbagged observation post atop it, and the company's platoons were dug in across a front that covered about a mile. On the hill's east side, there was a line of bunkers and fighting holes occupied by an infantry squad. The concertina wire was about a hundred yards out, and beyond that stood the remnants of a town that the Israelis had shot to pieces. Pockmarked half-walls stood about randomly, like an abstract sculpture garden. Beyond the ruins, nearly a mile out, stretched the bluish range of the Shouf Mountains. In the far distance, snow-covered peaks stood out sharply against the blue sky.

Forrest parked the Jeep and headed for the sandbagged command post entryway. Before heading down, he paused and watched a civilian cameraman and reporter wandering around the company area. They were making holiday messages for local TV back home—"Merry Christmas from Lance Corporal Schmitz from Albuquerque" and the like. The woman was pretty, but when not talking, she kept her mouth so drawn that it was little more than a dot below her nose. Her cameraman was just as pitiful. He was thin and bony, with a long neck and prominent Adam's apple; long, thin blond hair; and a face as white as wall paint.

His blue jeans were worn through at the knees, and his long, skinny legs were anchored by giant brown Frankenstein boots. The camera was suitcase-sized and mounted on a tripod. After interviewing a corporal, the two journalists stood side-by-side on a barren patch of dried mud, unhappily gazing up at the blue mountain.

The reporter noticed Forrest and walked over.

He smiled. She did not.

"Hi, there," she said listlessly.

"Merry Christmas," Forrest said.

She didn't respond. The cameraman hustled over.

"Ever seen *How the Grinch Stole Christmas?*" Forrest asked.

"Yes," she said with a curious twist in her face.

"Well, you know the Who sing joyfully even without presents and roast beast."

Her mouth tightened so much it almost disappeared.

"We're taking shots for the home folks," she said flatly.

"That's funny, we do the same thing here," Forrest said.

She didn't get it. She asked whether he'd like to send a holiday greeting. The dead lady in the blue dress was more animated.

As the cameraman moved into position, Forrest imagined the woman thinking about her parent's big house in Connecticut and a glittering Christmas tree. There'd be a wreath with pears and apples on the front door, and in the living room, a white bowl filled with silver pinecones and there'd be snow. He glanced down at her L.L. Bean boots on hard red clay and then her manicured hand holding the microphone. She had red-painted fingernails, and she looked healthy and smelled clean. There was no wedding ring.

He moved around and stood in front of the reporter. About seven hundred yards behind Forrest, a fire smoldered from an artillery hit on an Amal bunker the night before. The smoke was thick and nearly white and drifted low along the ground. Several palm trees were silhouetted against the smoke, standing out like black paper cutouts.

The cameraman lined up the shot and gave the reporter a thumbs-up.

The reporter got Forrest's name, hometown, and then, in a suddenly cheerful voice asked, "Okay, Lieutenant, do you have a message for the folks at home?"

Forrest stared into the lens. "Yes, ma'am, I do. Children in the United States are no doubt worried about Santa Claus getting shot down when he comes in here tonight."

The reporter's eyes narrowed.

"Don't worry, kids. Marine jets are going to escort Santa, and we're going to cover him with our .50 caliber machine guns. The United States Marine Corps will protect Santa. He'll *probably* make it out alive!" Then Forrest grinned.

"You're an asshole," she said. Then she and her cameraman turned and trudged away. Forrest shrugged and headed down to play dominoes.

That night, the Colonel sent out a Christmas message. "If you're hit, follow battalion SOP. Keep your heads down, and Merry Christmas!" Forrest passed the message down the line. Then he sat alone in the small fighting bunker in front of four-zero and missed his family. This was the first Christmas he'd been away from home, and he knew that was true for many of the young Marines in his platoon, especially the teenagers. He crossed his arms to stay warmer and thought back to the first Christmas he could remember, when there'd been GI Joes under the tree, with lots of extra gear, including Marine Corps dress blues. He was five that year. Then he thought of the Christmas tree, a cedar cut out on the marsh, with silver icicles and red lights, a fire in the fireplace, and the good feeling of being home with the family. He and his dad and brothers would hunt ducks the week before Christmas, and by Christmas Eve, Forrest had been very cold every day and was happy to be warm by the fire.

A gunman opened fire with an AK-47 up on the ridge, far off. The clackity-clack of the automatic fire took Forrest's mind off Christmases past and grounded him in the dark bunker. When the shooting stopped, he was thinking of the Marines killed so far that month. He wondered about their families celebrating Christmas. Then his mind shifted to the man he'd killed by the pool. He had a vivid image of the bloodstained photograph of the man's wife and baby and he wondered how they were handling Christmas without their commie daddy … Though commies were generally atheist, so maybe it was just another day. Then he thought of the giant, fat corpse laid out in bright sunlight and the too-white concrete in the sun and heat beating down on the bright poolside. He turned on Radio Beirut and closed his eyes and listened to Burl Ives sing "Have a Holly, Jolly Christmas."

On Christmas Day, Forrest stopped by Corporal Haynes's bunker. His position was comprised of several sandbag bunkers built into the slope of the hill. The amtrac was dug into a horseshoe-shaped bunker in the backside of the hill, and a fighting bunker was dug into the slope facing the mountain, and there was a living bunker off to the side. The hill abutted the shit stream in which black water oozed through stands of green marsh grass and cattails. Forrest immediately detected the smell of the ditch. A radio on top of the bunker played a beautiful female voice singing "Silent Night" in French. Corporal Haynes climbed out of the fighting bunker. He wore a red Santa Clause cap. His lower lip bulged with dip, and he had a cigarette in his mouth. "Merry Christmas, Lieutenant," he said.

Haynes brought out an ammo can that contained a large rat he'd shot by the ditch. As they stood admiring Haynes's trophy, an ambulance pulled up and stopped. The ambulance was a cammo-painted truck with an enclosed back end. Forrest walked over and opened its back door. The chaplain was sitting there in a Santa Claus outfit, surrounded by presents. Forrest reached out to pick one up. "No presents for officers, Lieutenant," Santa Claus said. Forrest looked up and smiled and then dropped the box back in the pile and backed away from the ambulance. One by one, the Marines of Corporal Haynes's crew went to the ambulance and each got a gift.

Jack Stanard, a nineteen year-old lance corporal from Virginia, sat on a sandbag ledge and pulled away the silver ribbon and ripped the red and white Santa Claus paper away and then held in his hands a used paperback book. He looked up at Forrest and smiled. "Look Lieutenant, I got a book." He held it up for Forrest to see. It was *Fields of Fire* by James Webb.

"Have you read it?"

"No, sir."

"It's about Marines in Vietnam."

Stanard smiled and looked down at the pages as he thumbed through them. Forrest watched the boy's joy and knew from his reaction that he'd always had joyful Christmases.

After midnight, Forrest walked the line. As he walked alone, he looked up at stars splashed across the black sky and smelled the sea and relished the quiet. *This is the good part*, he thought. He worked his way along the line, from amtrac to amtrac. All was quiet except the sound of his boots on the hard clay road. He got to four-nine's sandbagged berm and said in a clear voice, "Lieutenant coming in," so he wouldn't startle the man on watch. He ducked into the small fighting bunker and found the Gunny and Lance Corporal Wise sitting on the bench looking out through the gun port. The Gunny was wearing a Santa hat.

Off to the left, a Golf Company Marine popped a hand-held illumination flare. It flew up in a trail of smoke and popped. Out over the wire, ugly concrete faces flickered up from the darkness. The men in the bunker sat silently, looking out through the narrow gun port. In the middle of the gun port, a small American flag fluttered in the cool breeze. The flare finally died out, and the dead buildings sank back into the dark. Forrest breathed in the smell of dirt and wondered if their mission there was accomplishing anything. Another flare popped out over the broken town. As the flare drifted, light sifted through the gun port and lit their faces.

The men sat in the quiet, staring out at the mountain.

"You know what I'm gonna do when I get home?" asked Lance Corporal Wise, mostly to himself. The Gunny and Forrest looked over in the dark. Wise was barely visible, his voice floating out of the dark corner of the bunker.

"What's that, Wise?" asked the Gunny.

"I'm gonna eat a near-raw steak."

The Gunny and Forrest nodded.

"When I get home," the Gunny said, "I'm taking my old lady to the opera up in Norfolk."

Forrest looked over at the Gunny and cocked his helmet back to get a better look at his face.

"No shit, Lieutenant."

"Opera?"

The Gunny nodded.

"What do you like about opera?"

"The stories are good. The music. The sets. You ever been to an opera, Lieutenant?"

"No."

"Go see *Madama Butterfly*, Lieutenant. You'd like that one. It's about this Japanese woman in Nagasaki who is selfless and honorable—the model of Japanese culture and character. But she falls for a squid."

"Opposites attract," Wise said, chuckling.

"So, what happens, Gunny?" Forrest asked.

"Well, sir, she converts to Christianity and goes all in, thinking the squid is in for the long haul. He knocks her up. Then he shit-cans her. He goes home and marries an American woman. After a few years, he returns with his American wife to take his son away from Madame Butterfly. Madame Butterfly sees that her existence makes for an awkward situation, so she kills herself. The squid takes the child and his American wife and lives happily ever after. Then thirty years later, we nuke Nagasaki and kill everybody in the city." The Gunny hooted out a laugh.

"They got a nuke in the opera?" Wise asked.

"No, but I can't help but think of it every time I see it."

They sat in silence for a moment. Another flare popped over Golf Company.

"It's a perfect story," the Gunny continued. "Here's this squid that cares about nothing but himself and this Japanese woman who is selfless. He's shit. She's not. Both get what they have coming. Madame Butterfly has honor, but she's dead. The squid has a wife and boy and a white picket fence, but no honor. It's self-indulgence versus self-denial."

Forrest and Wise stared at the Gunny for a moment. Forrest took off his helmet and scratched the stubble on the top of his head.

The Gunny continued. "So, there's two points. One, it is impossible to fulfill both our selfish passions and spiritual perfection at the same time. You either live for the world or live for eternity. Miserable in life, happy in death, and vice versa. So, the point of the opera is that you always have a trade-off. You cannot be truly happy in this life."

"I'm happy, Gunny," said Wise.

"That's because you're ignorant, Wise."

Wise shrugged. He popped open a 7-Up and propped his feet up on the sandbag wall.

"What's the second point, Gunny?" Forrest asked.

Gunny spat tobacco juice into a plastic cup, fixed his eyes on Forrest, and paused to reflect. "Never trust a fucking squid." He hooted out another laugh.

"I saw an opera once," Wise said.

Forrest leaned out and looked over. Wise's face was concealed in the darkness in the corner of the bunker.

"My momma and daddy took me."

"Which opera?" asked the Gunny.

"Don't know, Gunny. It was about a clown who kills his old lady."

"*I Pagliacci*," said the Gunny.

"Is that it?" asked Forrest. "A clown kills his wife?"

"I think she cheated on him," explained Wise.

"Oh."

"I was around fourteen. My folks wanted me to have some culture. Towards the end, the clown got up on his wagon, and it was dark except for this violet light shining down on him. He stands there with the light real bright on his white clown face, and he's looking up into the light. What made it weird was that they had him made-up with this red smiley face, so he had a cheerful face but with sadness showing through and that sick color, and he was singing with this awful despair, like a wounded rabbit. And he had these blood-shot eyes, like he'd been crying. The clown's arms were stretched out in that light, grasping. You could see the shape of his hands and fingers out-stretched and shaking a little as he sang out long pitiful notes. I'd see that face in my dreams, and I'd wake up scared." Wise reflected for a moment. "You know how dead people wash up in the rain here? The sun comes out, and we find a hand or a foot sticking up, and we shovel dirt on it. And sometimes we find a head or a face coming up from the clay. That doesn't bother me at all anymore. But that clown still scares me."

Chapter Eighteen

The Washington Post
"French Paratrooper and Marine Killed in Beirut."

January 10, 1984—"Gunmen killed a French paratrooper here tonight and wounded two others in the second assault in two days on the multinational peacekeeping force. ....Yesterday, a U.S. Marine was killed and two Lebanese soldiers wounded when unidentified gunmen opened fire on two U.S. helicopters that had just landed a 12-man work party at a beach adjoining the Lebanese Army officers' club, near American Embassy offices in northwest Beirut. Marine spokesmen said the gunmen were in nearby apartment buildings on the west Beirut seafront."

The New York Times
"Druse Don't Forget."

January 31, 1984—"One chilly morning, after enduring a night of heavy shelling from the United States Marines, a young Druse leader stalked around his dingy office, jumpy with coffee nerves, eyes streaked red... 'See that guy over there,' he said, jabbing at a small boy with an automatic rifle, 'He's 11 years old. He can shoot and fight, like all our children. We are fighting for our people and our land. Our people don't forget our deaths. We will let our sons know that their fathers were killed by Marines, and the sons will go on for 10 generations killing Marines. The Marines are going to be killed by the families of the people they have killed. Our people won't forget.'"

January 31, 1984—"A United States Marine was killed and three others wounded today when their compound at the international airport was bombarded by anti-Government militiamen...the Marine was ...the 259th American serviceman to die here since the arrival of the Marines in August 1982."

On New Years' Eve, as midnight approached, Forrest sat on the forward edge of the roof of his bunker, looking out at a black moonless sky. The Gunny walked up. Forrest could only see his dark shape.

"That you, Lieutenant?"

"Hey, Gunny."

The Gunny leaned on the bunker. "Dark as the inside of my asshole, sir."

Forrest chuckled. "You think the ragheads are taking New Years' off?"

"Been quiet tonight, that's for damn sure. Maybe they'll light us up at midnight. Happy motherfucking New Year."

The two men stared out, saying nothing for a moment.

"I've never seen it so dark," Forrest said. "You have nights like this in Vietnam, Gunny?"

"Vietnam was a beautiful place, Lieutenant. People think of Vietnam as a hot jungle. I damn near froze in Vietnam. It would rain and get cold."

"I never heard that before."

"Folks watch too much TV news. So they don't know what's really going on."

"You've got two years of college, right?"

"Yes, sir." The Gunny looked over at Forrest, "Berkeley." He snorted out a laugh.

Forrest nodded. He knew from the Gunny's Service Record Book that he had two years at Berkeley. He'd been curious about it—Berkeley produced few Marines—but he'd never gotten around to asking the Gunny about it. "So how'd you end up in the Corps, Gunny?"

"That's a long story, Lieutenant."

Forrest nodded.

The Gunny sat silently for a full minute.

"Well, Lieutenant," the Gunny said finally, "I was a sophomore at Berkeley in '68, and I was safe from the draft. My old man had graduated from Berkeley back in '45. Then he'd gone to law school. He was a lawyer in Memphis. He was big on me following in his footsteps, and I planned on doing just that. Grades were good. All systems green and go. Then I got mixed up with all the campus bullshit. Now, don't get me wrong, Lieutenant, I appreciated the finer points of the movement." The Gunny chuckled softly. "I was nineteen, wandering around with a nice buzz in a place where it was impossible not to get your dip-stick wet. I had a good time."

"So what was the problem?"

"Well, Lieutenant, I don't have any problem with people having fun. But those people took themselves way too seriously. It wasn't enough to just enjoy the booze and the drugs and the sex. Those people just loved themselves. Everything was about them. They were the most self-obsessed people I ever saw. There's a word for that. What is it, LT?"

"Narcissistic."

"Yessir, that's it. Those people were narcissists. Anyway, they thought themselves noble. Now, drinking and drug'n and fuck'n are fun—but not noble. That's for damn sure."

Forrest took off his helmet and felt cool night air easing across his Marine Corps haircut. They could see millions of stars scattered across the black sky.

"In January of '68, there was this big event at Golden Gate Park. They called it a 'human be-in.'" The Gunny chuckled again. "It was one of those sunny days in California. I was never into dope or LSD, so I drank Tennessee whiskey all afternoon. There were thousands of people there. Everybody fucked up and wandering around in tie-died t-shirts and bell-bottoms and dressed like Indians and Hell's Angels mixed in. It was a sight, Lieutenant."

"You, in a tie-die, Gunny?"

"Naahh. I was fucked-up—but not *that* fucked-up." The rattle of an AK echoed out from a far mountain ridge.

"I was okay with the foolishness of it," said the Gunny. "What the hell? I was nineteen and having fun. But like I said, those people took themselves very seriously. They talked about revolution and renaissance of compassion and awareness and love and how violence was going to be transmuted and submerged in rhythm and dance and poetry or some such horse crap. All those people on dope and LSD were planning to take over the world. It was like a circus where the clowns don't know they're clowns."

"Then the speeches started, and it got nuttier and nuttier. That's where Tim Leary gave his famous line, 'Turn on, tune in, and drop out.' Dude was a Harvard professor. Since that day, it's been mighty difficult to take Harvard seriously. Of course, we don't see Haaah-vaahd men in the Corps. Get a few from Princeton, but not Harvard. Anyway, after the be-in, it got freakier and freakier. Jane Fonda had something she called her 'Fuck the Army' tour. Then she went to North Vietnam on her morale-building trip for our enemy. Protesters started flying the North Vietnamese flag and burning the American flag. That ruined it for me. As much as I liked the drinking and the sex and the freedom of it, I just snapped when I saw that. Thing was, I'd been to a bunch of their rallies and protests. I was associated, know what I mean? I'd been dipped in shit."

Forrest nodded in the dark.

"When I realized how fucked-up it was, I had to do something drastic. I sort of cracked-up, truth be told."

There was another burst of AK fire on the mountain. The Gunny stopped talking and listened and then waited to see if anyone fired back. No one did.

"So I dropped out, like Leary said. But I didn't drop out of regular society to be a freak, like he was talking about. Hell, no. I dropped out of freak society to be a United States Marine." He snorted out a laugh. "Poetic, don't you think, Lieutenant?"

Forrest nodded in the dark. "And the rest is history?

"Yes, sir."

"Any regrets?"

The Gunny thought for a minute. "Well, Lieutenant, I suppose it's a mixed bag, like everything is. To most people, the word 'Vietnam' means 'fucked up.' I'm sure they're saying our operation here is 'another Vietnam.'" He infused the words with sarcasm. "Probably some asshole's saying Grenada was 'another Vietnam,' even though we won. Hell, Lieutenant, you take a crap and run out of ass-wipe and somebody's gonna say, 'Hey man, that crap was another Vietnam.'" He laughed again. "People think of Vietnam as a name for all monumental fuck ups or wasted lives or whatever. I don't see it that way at all. When I hear somebody say something is 'another Vietnam,' I just remember how much we loved the country and that the country did not love us back."

The Gunny stopped talking. Forrest waited for elaboration.

Forrest looked down at his watch. The tiny glow-in-the-dark hands told him it was almost midnight.

"You could talk to people all day and not run into an original thought. They all dressed alike. They all said exactly the same things with exactly the same words. Thing was, they all thought they were nonconformist and revolutionaries 'doing their own thing.' But the truth was that they were the most uniform bunch of people I ever saw—do anything to fit in. If it was cool to pretend to be a nonconformist, they'd put on tie-dies and bell-bottoms and headbands and drop acid or whatever else to conform. If it had been 1942, they'd all volunteer for the Army then try to get a library job on Staten Island."

"I never understood why any American would side with the communists against us. That always puzzled me," said Forrest.

"Well, like I said, Lieutenant, those people thought they were nobler than George Washington. So if you're a 60's freak, you can't admit that you refuse to serve because you're scared or don't like working outside or don't like being bossed around or whatever—wouldn't be noble. There's a draft, so you're going ape-shit. You've got to deal with it, one way or the other. So you have to say the war is immoral and that your nobility requires you to protest and dodge the draft—you're courageous for standing on moral principle, and the guy who carries an M-16 into the jungle is an immoral coward. You can't honor the troops 'cause that would make your claim of moral superiority a sham. That's why they called me a baby-killer when I got home. That's what you do when you think you're noble, but you're really just a dollop of dog shit."

Forrest nodded in the darkness. "Well, Gunny," he said finally, "don't you think there were some sincere conscientious objectors?"

"Sure, Lieutenant. I just don't think you'd find many of them at an LSD party."

"So it was the draft?"

"That got people excited."

"Well, there's no draft anymore."

"So now those people don't have to justify draft dodging. There's no obligation, just a choice. So they'll point their noses in the air and say they oppose our mission but support the troops. You can see it in newspapers right now, about us. The Hanoi Jane types. They support us but want us to lose." He snorted out another laugh.

The two men were silent again.

"Were you ever tempted to get out, go back to school?" Forrest asked.

"Yes, sir, but I couldn't do it. I love the Corps, and I love these boys. They're the opposite of what I saw at Berkeley. If the protestors were the 'me' generation, then these boys are the 'you' generation. They care about you, Lieutenant. They care about me and every other Marine in this platoon and battalion. They care about their families and our country. They even care about the ragheads in a strange sort of way. These boys care. And they have the dedication and the guts to risk everything to make their families proud and to serve and to take care of each other. These are good boys."

The Gunny stood to stretch. Then after a minute, he continued. "You walk around a mall and look at all the fat slobs. Then look at these young Marines. All we've got to do is feed 'em and lead 'em." The Gunny paused for a moment. "You know, Lieutenant, somebody like Hitler shows up, and it's boys like these who kick his ass. No, Lieutenant. I'm staying with these boys as long as I can. Because when we get out, we'll never again be among such people. We'll not find anywhere else the courage and devotion and valor and originality and humor and friendship that we find right here, in a Marine Corps platoon." The Gunny paused for a moment. "You know, Lieutenant, those people at Berkeley thought they were noble, but they weren't. These boys on this line don't think they're noble, but they are."

At midnight, the mountain lit up with streams of fire shot straight up into the sky. Ribbons of light reached up in crisscrossing patterns. The sound of the guns echoed across the coastal plain and out over the starlit Mediterranean Sea. When the bullets fell back to earth, it was 1984.

Chapter Nineteen

The New York Times
"Polls Find Most in U.S. Want the Marines Out."

*January 6, 1984—"A majority of the American public want the
United States Marines pulled out of Lebanon, according to two
national polls conducted by ABC News and issued last night.
Those results were the first in any major national public opinion
surveys to record a clear public desire for withdrawal."*

On the afternoon of January 5th, 1984, Forrest drove the Jeep over
to the Golf Company area to play dominoes with the officers. He parked
and stepped out on hardened mud and looked around. It was a typical

winter afternoon, clear and cool. The command bunker's profile stamped a dark shadow on the sunlit ground. An AK-47 clacked just across the wire. It was close. Marines to the left fired back with M-16s. He listened to the weapons firing and then walked down the stairway into the underground bunker that was Golf's headquarters. The Captain was sitting at a bank of radios, monitoring the firefight. Several radio operators and a runner stood by. The Captain looked up, saw Forrest standing in the entryway, and nodded. "We've got a fight. Let's play tomorrow," he said. Forrest nodded, turned, and walked up the stairway and stepped out on hard-packed clay.

Forrest stood by his Jeep, looking out across the line of bunkers around the CP and the wire and the wrecked buildings and the bluish mountain ridges. Marines were firing M-16s and shooting an M-60 machinegun at militia in a wrecked building a hundred yards beyond the wire. Forrest walked up to an observation post, which was a two-man open bunker dug into the top of a hill behind the CP. The lance corporal on watch there just nodded at Forrest and then went back to observing the fight through binoculars. Four-seven let go a burst of M-85 fire—the burst was much louder than small arms and added a new level of violence to the fight. A smudge of white smoke from the M85 fire drifted across the field. Forrest saw an AK-47 poke around a corner about 150 yards out. The weapon fired a long burst while the gunman stayed safely behind the wall. A Marine machine gunner fired a stream of bullets at the gun, hitting it and chipping the wall. The gun flew into the air in a cloud of masonry dust. To the left, two amtracs and a tank sat behind sandbagged berms with only their turrets above the berm. The three armored vehicles were quiet, like predators waiting to pounce. A burst of fire came from a second story window of one of the wrecked buildings. One of the amtracs fired a burst of .50 caliber fire into the window, the bright tracer rounds tracking the stream of bullets into the window, and the sound of bullets smacking a concrete wall echoed back.

Forrest looked over at the lance corporal. "Those people ever shoot at you up here?"

"Not yet, sir. I don't think they've noticed us yet." The man gave a half-smile that dimpled his right cheek.

An Amal fighter burst into the open, running hard. At the same instant, the tank main gun fired. It happened fast and all at once, and man and projectile met in a puff of reddish-gray smoke. When the dust cleared, the man was gone—vaporized. Forrest and the lance corporal looked at each other and nodded approval. "That was a nice shot," the lance corporal said.

Forrest left the observation bunker, got in his Jeep, and headed down the road to four-zero. He parked and walked onto the fighting bunker. It was late afternoon.

"We're at Condition One, sir," said Lewis.

Forrest nodded. "You pass the word?"

"Yessir."

Forrest walked into the fighting bunker and looked out through a gun port. The Druse were quiet, but the Amal was still fighting with Golf Company. Forrest listened to the exchange of fire down the line. The sound was clear in the cool air—M-16s popping, AKs clacking, M-85s drilling long bursts, and the tank gun firing. It finally settled into a rhythm. Sporadic firing would build to a crescendo when the tank gun and 85s would fire, followed by quiet, and then the enemy firing would start again, slow and sporadic at first, and then build intensity. Lewis stood by Forrest in the bunker, a handset rigged to his flak jacket, so he could hear the traffic. From a few feet away, Forrest heard the faint, inaudible sound of radio-modulated voices in a firefight.

The sounds of jet engines echoed across the airport. At the far end of the runway, down by the skeletal hangers, two MEA 727s were lined up, engines running. Forrest walked over and sat on the edge of the sandbag berm with his arms crossed and waited. The sound got louder as the first airliner roared up the runway towards him. The airliner lifted slowly up and passed low and loud over them. The wings dipped, and the jetliner cruised out over the Med. As the noise of the takeoff subsided, the sound of the other jet grew as it, too, came down the runway and lifted off.

It passed low over the Marine bunkers, then dipped a wing as it veered sharply and flew out over the Med.

Forrest looked over at Lewis. "I guess the stockholders of Middle East Airlines are happy now."

"I guess so, sir."

Just as the second jetliner pitched to the right and began its curve out to sea, a line of 23mm bullets poured down from the mountain into the dirt berm in front of four-five, 150 yards to the left of four-zero. Four-five, four-zero and four-six fired back with M-85 bursts, but they each shot on a different target, firing blind. Forrest stepped into the fighting bunker and looked up with binoculars, trying to find the 23mm gun. Quiet returned as the last light drained out of the western sky. The Navy fired two illumination rounds that popped high over the field, and light danced across the cedar-covered face of the mountain.

Now in dark, Forrest's mind wandered again. He saw himself as a young lawyer in a dark suit—wife, children, house, and dog. He'd have a boat and fish with his sons on Back River every summer weekend and hunt ducks with them in the fall. They'd grow up near the river and love it and they'd know what a peeler crab looked like and the best place to catch speckled trout in September. They'd eat crabs and clams outside by the water, and his wife would love him, and it would be a good life.

"Sir!" Lindley pointed to the ridge. "Rocket in the air."

"What direction?"

"Coming this way, sir."

The rocket was out in the night, arcing in on them. Forrest sat down in the corner of the fighting bunker. It was dark and quiet and strangely serene in the dark corner, under the lip of his helmet. The seconds ticked by slowly—*SWWOOOOSSSHHHHHBOOOM!* Dirt flew over the berm. Forrest stepped back up behind the berm and scanned the dark ridge. Small arms fire was popping away in the distance, but the Marine line was quiet again. Forrest listened to the radio voices. The Naval Gunfire Liaison Officer, a lieutenant, call sign "Caveman," was transmitting a fire mission. He'd received a grid coordinate for the rocket launcher from an Army radar-tracking unit. Forrest listened as Caveman called in the mission.

The destroyer offshore fired three three-inch rounds. From four-zero's bunker, it sounded like a far-away popgun. Then the shells hit out on the mountain about 3000 yards out. Then Caveman was back on the radio.

"Fire for effect, over."

The destroyer responded, "Fire for effect, out."

The destroyer fired ten rounds in rapid succession. The shells shrieked over the Marine lines and saturated the target with sparkling concussions. The crunching sound of the impacts echoed back.

All across the front, tracer streams shot back and forth between the ruins and Marine bunkers. The amtracs and a tank down by Golf Company opened with their 50s, and the tank fired several main gun rounds at a Druse bunker on the ridge. Forrest watched each glowing tank round arc out across the night sky and impact the bunker. Then he heard the Marine M198 Howitzers firing, followed a few seconds later by silent, sparkling explosions out on the mountain and a few seconds later the crunching sound of the shells impacting. Then the pace of the fight slowly ebbed, and finally the battlefield fell quiet.

Two Navy illumination rounds popped over the battlefield. Lights appeared under parachutes and drifted from right to left. The Marines looked out across the concertina wire at standing lumps of concrete and burned-out car carcasses. Spinning under parachutes, the lights made a whirling sound high overhead. Dark shadows in and behind the ruins moved and lengthened as the lights drifted downrange.

Every few seconds, muzzle flashes winked from shell holes out in the ruins. Bullets smacked sandbags on the face of Forrest's position. A few rounds dinged four-zero. Then the Druse launched a rocket barrage against the Marine positions south of the runway. One after another, the rockets hit, their energy shuddering through the ground, dirt rattling from between sandbags and razor-sharp hunks of shrapnel smacking amtracs and sandbags. Rockets hit all around the Marine bunkers.

When the barrage ended, smoke hung low all across the battlefield, a thick fog that smelled like fired bottle rockets.

Then it was quiet again.

All along the line, Marines crouched quietly behind sandbags, gripping M-16s. Another illumination round drifted over, flickering light across the faces of wrecked buildings. When the light had drifted downrange, there was a burst of AK fire from behind a short, mud-brick wall just across the wire. A yell came from down the line—"Corpsman!"

Corporal Haynes came up on the landline. "Stanard's hit."

Forrest ran down to Haynes's bunker. By the time he arrived, the Gunny was already there. Stanard's body lay on the side of the road. The corpsman, a Navy man named Page, was kneeling beside Stanard's body. Page reached up a bloody hand and closed Stanard's eyes and then looked up at Forrest. "He's dead, sir."

The shooting had fallen off along the line.

Forrest stood there with the others looking at the dead boy. The boy's helmet was gone. His face seemed peaceful, like a smooth, clay bust of a child. Under moonlight, his skin was blue-tinted, and the clay ground was purple. The boy's flak jacket was open, and his utilities were wrinkled. Forrest focused on the American flag sewn on his left shoulder and his worn boots and then looked up at the Gunny and the Marines standing about. In that light, he had only an impressionistic image of them, as though each Marine had been painted with a thick brush in hues of blue and sienna, lighter tones highlighting the hard crests of helmets, the tops of shoulders, and the curved folds in the sleeves of their utilities. Upper faces were hidden in inky dark under the lips of combat helmets. Dashes of moonlight highlighted chins and jaws. They stood silently for a long time.

After Stanard's body was medevac'd, Forrest went back to his bunker and sat alone on the sandbagged roof. It was after midnight and quiet. The moon lit the ground back to the wire and the ditch, and in the ruined town, moonlight reflected brightly off flat surfaces in piles of broken concrete and standing half-walls, making the town look like scattered heaps of sun-bleached bones. He looked north and thought it strange how the whole city, big as Manhattan, was dark. The city was like a wrecked stage, the coastal plain like an empty theater, all under one blue light projecting down through dust. He pondered the fact that the lady in the blue dress was cold in her grave just a few feet away. The bitchy reporter and Frankenstein were probably huddled in one of those dark monoliths in the city. The Gunny was probably drinking coffee in his bunker.

Stanard had been zipped into a black plastic bag and was with the other bodies now by the landing zone just north of Forrest's bunker. He heard a helicopter out over the Med, inbound for its load of dead Marines. As the sound of the rotors of the CH-46 got louder, he closed his eyes and saw the boy again, dead on that purple clay. The image was not at all like the waxen corpse of an old man in a funeral home. Forrest thought that when you see the old man in his best Sunday suit, all stiff with eyes sewn shut, you think that old men die and that this one had a very long, good life, and you know that one day far away, when your body is withered and shrunken, you, too, will be on display, but only after having kids and grandkids and enjoying many cool mornings in the duck blind and days casting for speckled trout and evenings sipping scotch on the back porch. The dead boy makes you know your mortality and also that his mama and daddy and brothers and sisters will suffer and that his whole life and the lives of his children and grandchildren have been skipped with one shot from an AK-47.

Looking north, Forrest saw the unlit hull of the helicopter slide in low and land in the LZ. The helicopter sat with rotors turning while Marines loaded the cargo. At that moment, he realized that he didn't care if people said the mission was another Vietnam. He was grateful to be there. Grateful for the good men along that line and the cool night air and the moon and the smell of the sea, for his well-worn boots and steel combat helmet and Kevlar flak jacket and a .45 that rattled when he shook it. He was grateful for his bunker and the gas lantern and diesel stove down inside and the look of the Marines' lamp-lit and powder-stained faces.

And he was grateful for the memory of a very good boy who got shot in the chest while standing watch in the red hill country of Lebanon.

Forrest finally dropped off the roof and pulled aside the tarp covering the entryway and stepped inside the bunker. Garnett and his crew sat on the black sofa, on stools, and the sandbag ledge in front of the stove. The light of a gas lantern flickered across faces darkened by smoke and dirt and gun grease. The smells of the Coleman light and the diesel burning in the stove and the dimness of the light gave the bunker the feel of a tent at winter camp during deer season in the mountains. He remembered hunting with his dad and brother in the snow and then coming back at night to the cozy tent that held the exact same smell. Forrest walked to his corner and tossed his steel helmet and flak jacket and pistol on his bunk. As he dropped his war gear, the tension drained from him. He headed for the stained tin coffee pot on the gas canister burner, then paused and turned to his men. "I could use a beer." He went to the stash of Heineken in the back corner of the bunker—the beer was a gift from the French Legionnaires in the city. He gave a can to each man, sat on a stool by the stove, and reached out a cold hand to the warmth. Forrest popped open his can and raised it—"To the French Foreign Legion." The men raised their cans and drank. Forrest took another sip and raised his can again. "To our heroic dead." The Marines nodded and drank.

Forrest warmed by the fire and finished his beer. Then he stepped outside and leaned on cold sandbags and looked up at the sky of stars and thought of *her* again. He knew he didn't need her and that she didn't care about him, anyway. But there was the lingering sadness—not so much from lost love as lost friendship. And now she was with some boring service station attendant or whatever he was. But it didn't matter. There'd be somebody else. He'd go to law school and meet new people, and he'd walk around campus with law books and read all night and go to class and drink beer on Friday night like all the other college boys. But through it all, he'd be alone with his memories of nights like this night and the glow of the stove fire on grease-stained faces and the glitz of tracers shooting the night sky and rocket impacts shaking the ground and the sound of the helicopter coming in for a load of dead Marines. There would always be a memory of the two dead men on the poolside concrete—the image burned into his mind in sharp swaths of black and white and burgundy. Late at night over the books, he'd remember that twitching finger and the wedding band shining up through a coating of blood. How do you talk about that with college boys? He decided he'd keep it all to himself and bring it up only with himself and only when he was alone, outside, at night.

The following morning at sunrise, Forrest stepped out of his bunker and looked across the field to Haynes's bunker that looked like a sad sodbuster's redoubt on the prairie. The wall facing the mountain was well-lit by the sun peeking over the ridge, and the bunker cast a long, burgundy shadow back towards the sea. Forrest stared at the bunker for several minutes and pondered the fact that Stanard had been living there the previous morning. He knew he should walk over and talk to the crew, but he hated grief, and he wanted to put it off. Something inside spurred him forward, and he took a step and then walked out across the open ground to the bunker to talk to Standard's crew chief, Corporal Haynes, a short and stocky Marine with a face pockmarked by old acne scars. He'd never be on a Marine Corps recruiting poster, but there was no better field Marine. He kept his amtrac spotless, and he took good care of his crew.

Forrest found Haynes sitting on a sandbag ledge. Forrest sat down beside him.

Haynes said, "I guess Jack's folks will find out today."

"Yes, probably," answered Forrest. "They'll send out an officer in dress blues and a chaplain to tell his momma and daddy."

"Jack has two little brothers and a sister."

Forrest nodded.

Haynes said, "When you sign up, you know the risks in your mind, but you don't know them in your heart. You assume you won't get killed and none of your buddies will get killed, and then Jack gets shot dead." Haynes snapped his fingers. "Just like that." Haynes stuffed a wad of tobacco in his mouth and then spat in a cup. "I guess now I understand. Anyway, we're good, Lieutenant." Haynes looked over at Forrest. "How about you, Lieutenant?"

Forrest smiled and nodded. "I'm good, too, Corporal."

Chapter Twenty

The Washington Post
"Bodies Found in Druse Village Said to Be Victims of Christian Massacre."

February 16, 1984—"Decomposed bodies of scores of men, women, and children were found in a mountain village today, a Druse militiaman said they were among 100 people massacred by rightist Christian militiamen five months ago. There were corpses in bedrooms, living rooms, and around dining room tables. Dining rooms that appeared to have been set for breakfast could be seen, the rotten bread, jam, cheese, and tea cups still on the tables."

On a sunny February afternoon, Forrest drove down the dirt road by the runway towards the MAU headquarters (the headquarters one level above the battalion). Leaning over the wheel and staring ahead as he passed the infantry bunkers of Fox Company and then the sandbag walls of the Battalion Command Post, he cut through a checkpoint and drove into a parking area in front of the MAU headquarters. On the front of the building, a large red "M" and an "A" were separated by a space. The "E" had been shot off long ago (Middle East Airlines). The windows were mostly missing, and there were bullet gouges in the concrete wall. By the front door, there was a sandbag wall manned by a sentry. An American Flag flew from a pole out front.

Forrest parked and stepped out on gravel and walked to the doorway. The sentry was a tall hound-dog of a man, raw-boned and lanky with freckles. He wore a dusty flak jacket and a war belt laden with two full ammo pouches, two canteens, and a K-Bar knife. His chinstrap was buckled. As Forrest walked by, the sentry gave a sharp, "Good afternoon, sir," but did not salute. Saluting tended to mark targets in combat zones. Forrest walked inside, climbed the steps, and then walked down the hall to the Combat Operations Center ("COC").

There was a shell hole in the side wall of the COC that was five feet wide. Steel reinforcing rods twisted out of the crusty concrete into the opening, and a tarp used to block the hole at night hung from the ceiling. Sandbags were stuffed in the lower part of the hole. There was a large map on one wall that showed the positions around the airport and in the city at the embassy. Numbers grease-penciled on the map gave the numerical designations of pre-plotted targets. A bare light bulb hung dark in the center of the room. Muted light filtered in through the shell hole. Larry Atwell, the duty officer, sat alone in the light of the shell hole, reading a paperback. He looked up. "Robert, you being sociable?"

"I guess." Forrest took off his helmet and plopped it onto a desk. He unsnapped his shoulder harness and .45 pistol and clunked it on the desk. He pulled his flak jacket open in front, letting cool air in.

Atwell tossed his book onto the desk and leaned back on his chair. "You shot that thing since we got here?"

"Rats. Shot a dog."

Atwell nodded.

Forrest walked over and looked out through the shell hole.

Atwell stood by Forrest, and they both looked out across the Marine lines stretching to the south. "Look out there, Robert. The whole Marine Corps is right here. All Marines that ever lived are right here."

Forrest looked over at Atwell, nodding slowly.

"Hear the news?" Atwell was still looking out across the lines, his features vaguely highlighted by winter light.

"No," said Forrest.

"We're pulling out."

Forrest looked back at Atwell, then shifted his stare to nothing in particular. Then he looked back out through the shell hole at the bunkers to the south. Down along the line, he could see at least a dozen American flags. Small plumes of smoke rose from diesel fuel stoves warming bunkers. He could see three tanks dug into the long berm inside the lines. There were two more down there somewhere, but he couldn't see them. He saw four-zero, a mile away on the far end of the runway. The mountain loomed long and blue and quiet. "We've lost almost three hundred men here," Forrest said.

Neither man spoke for a long minute. The sound of a helicopter pitching into the runway LZ broke the stillness.

"This is like Vietnam," Forrest said.

"I don't know what that means," said Atwell.

"Well, it means the politicians were committed enough to risk our lives, but not committed enough to win. The politicians send us into these situations and then, when it gets tough, they quit. So we show up and die or get maimed or whatever, then the survivors pull out. If it truly doesn't matter—if it's not worth the trouble of winning—then I'd rather stay home. I'd rather go duck hunting."

"I don't look at Vietnam like that," said Atwell.

"No?" Forrest looked over with his eyes squeezed down to slits. "We came here to help stabilize this place, and now it's worse than ever and we've lost hundreds and we're gonna quit. It is *exactly* like Vietnam. We lost 58,000 people trying to save that place, and we failed there, too—because we quit. All those people killed. Nothing accomplished. The politicians jump in with both feet—*our* feet—and then when it gets tough politically, they don't lead, they cut and run. These damned politicians…" His voice trailed off, his face red. "It's a shit sandwich, Larry."

"Well," Atwell said, "we never jumped in here with both feet. We're just a toe. A pinky toe. We tried to stop some of the bloodshed. Mission turned to shit. So we either send in a Marine Division to take over the whole screwed-up place or get out. A few hundred Marines can't do any good here now. It would have worked out just fine if we pulled out when the Israelis moved south. Circumstances changed, and we got caught up in the civil war. The head-shed was a little slow reacting. It's a miscalculation, not a malignancy."

Forrest sat at the table. He leaned over and put his elbows on his knees, looking down at his mud-crusted boots on the concrete floor. "I keep thinking about Lance Corporal Stanard."

"We're Marines, Robert, what do you expect? These are the risks we run to give the brain trust in D.C. options. So people aren't perfect. Mistakes happen. That's life. The whole operation on Peleliu in World War II was probably not necessary—a miscalculation. Eighteen hundred Marines got killed in that battle. It's just tough shit. Stanard knew the risks. So do we. If we're gonna get killed, we want it to happen on Mount Suribachi, raising the flag. But it doesn't really matter. All honorable service is the same. Everybody killed in Vietnam and our guys killed here and all of our people ever killed in action were doing exactly the same thing: serving the country. As far as I'm concerned, they all died on Suribachi. That's what I love about the Marine Corps—we're all on Suribachi every day."

Forrest nodded slowly. Then he closed his flak jacket and slipped his holster back on. He dropped his combat helmet on his head and turned to the doorway, then he stopped and looked back at Larry.

"My old man put his faith in the Corps and the country. After the country betrayed him, he drank himself to death."

Larry Atwell nodded. "Robert, it's depressing to think that about half of our people admire Jane Fonda. But a lot of those are decent people who don't understand what she did. Hell, Jane Fonda might even be a decent human being today. And our half of the country is pretty good. So we have a good country, and its virtues mark it as extraordinary, but we can't expect perfection."

Forrest nodded. "Semper Fi, Larry."

"Semper Fi, Robert."

Forrest sat in his Jeep in the parking lot for a few minutes thinking about Stanard and the others. He felt the magnitude of the waste in his chest, like a mild nausea. He drove the Jeep back along the road parallel to the seaside runway, by the long pile of concrete chunks and slabs where hundreds of Marines died in the barracks attack and then stopped near the LZ as a CH-46 took off, raising a cloud of red dust. As the helicopter flew off and the sound of its rotors faded, a quiet settled over the LZ, and before the dust settled, three Marines walked by on the road. In the dust cloud, their forms were obscured to mere shapes of men moving—the smooth, hard curve of helmets, M-16s slung over shoulders upside down, magazine pouches and bandoliers, canteens and K-bars, all hanging from their war belts. Forrest watched the men walk down the road. As the dust settled, sunlight brought out the color of their faces, tanned and black, and he thought it was a picture that no one would photograph—an image that would never make it into the conscious mind of the country. He would always remember it, though, even though it meant nothing. Just three Marines walking through a cloud of Lebanese dust and emerging into sunshine with the blue Med stretching out behind them. He thought that photo journalists always tried to snap the dramatic picture—somebody crying or dead bodies or dead stares, like the iconic shot of a wounded black Marine reaching out to help a wounded white Marine on a muddy hill in Vietnam or the dead stare of a Marine on Guadalcanal or the flag shot on Iwo. They were good pictures that told stories. Three Marines walking down a dusty road overlooking the Mediterranean didn't say much, he realized. But still, there was something about it that drew him away from himself.

He took off his helmet, settled back in his seat, and stared out. There was a winter thunderstorm moving in from the Mediterranean. He could smell it in the cool sea breeze. Forrest drove the Jeep up to his bunker and stopped. Lewis was sitting on the ramp of four-zero, reading a book.

"What are you reading?" Forrest asked.

"*Chesapeake*, sir."

"Good book."

"Yes, sir, I think it's yours."

Forrest nodded. "I've finished it." Forrest stood up on the ramp and faced the dark sky. "Another storm coming."

"Yes, sir. Supposed to rain all afternoon and tonight," Lewis said, looking up from the book.

"Lewis, I got word we're back loading to the ships."

"Really, sir? When?"

"Don't know. Probably another ten days."

"Shall we pass the word on the landline, sir?"

"No. I'll walk the line in a little while. I'll pass the word then."

Forrest walked up the hill and stood at its crest. Out over the sea, lightening shot across the sky. He had always loved watching thunderstorms in summer on the Chesapeake Bay. He would stand on the beach just beyond the rain line watching the lightening, or he'd sit on his parents' back porch as the wind heaved through the leafy branches of white oaks and black gum trees. The massive green foliage would heave high in the air, and leaves would break free and twist awkwardly in the warm wind. He loved the feel of a storm breeze on his tanned face. Proximity to a storm was one of those simple pleasures, he thought. Like cavemen, who must have reveled in these same things: shelter from a storm, a well-balanced club, meat on a spit, and a warm fire. All good things, he thought. He stood in his flak jacket and combat helmet with his boots on red dirt, looking out on the Mediterranean and the storm, and he felt at home. Maybe this *is* Suribachi, he thought.

The rain started in large droplets that hit the ground like water balloons and then increased in intensity as the sky closed in. Forrest walked down the hill and ducked inside his bunker. He dropped his helmet on the sandbag ledge and sat on the sofa. There was a fire in the diesel stove, and it was warm and dry inside. Forrest lay back and closed his eyes and fell asleep. In time, he woke and moved over to the ledge inside the entryway. He leaned over and fished through extra pouches of MREs. He picked up a pouch of freeze-dried fruit and held it up in the light to see what it was. Apricots. Forrest lowered the pouch to his lap and looked outside, thinking of the Gunny. He smiled and pulled out his canteen and poured water in the pouch to hydrate the apricots, and then he ate them with a white plastic spoon. He dropped the empty pouch in the cardboard trash box, then sat back on the ledge and closed his eyes. After a few minutes, it stopped raining, and Forrest looked up into dust floating in a beam of weak winter sunlight. He put on his helmet and flak jacket and poncho and rose out of his bunker. He paused and looked around. Through broken clouds, sunlight shined down on the Marine lines, and the wet ground sparkled. Brownish-red bunkers on the hillside stood out clearly in the cool air. Puddles in tread tracks reflected the sky and stretched across the red clay ground, like luminous claw marks. Out on the perimeter, water droplets hanging on concertina wire glistened. To the north, Beirut stood in profile, like so many gray blocks.

Everyone was still underground, and the position seemed deserted. He walked over to the fighting bunker. PFC Shields was on watch, leaning on a sandbag ledge, looking out through the gun port. Forrest paused and looked out, too.

"Everything okay, Shields?"

"Yes, sir. Lord's making more mud."

Forrest looked out, nodding.

Soft light fell on the lower part of Shields's face. The whites of his eyes were visible in the shadow of the wide lip of his combat helmet.

Chinstraps dangled on both sides of his boyish face. He cradled his M-16 rifle, with his left hand resting on the curved full magazine. It hadn't been too many years since he'd cradled a teddy bear in just that way. They talked for a few minutes and then Forrest headed out to walk the line.

Forrest walked down the slope towards the perimeter. Thirty yards out, he stopped for a moment by a tank sitting low behind a berm, its mud-colored reflection visible in the creamy puddle covering the bottom half of the tank's wheels. A small American flag flapped from the tank's radio antenna, colorful against a small stroke of blue in the sky.

Near four-six, he stopped and pulled out a pouch of Red Man. As he fished with cold fingers for a chew, he noticed a corpse in the mud by his right foot. He wasn't surprised. The rain had exposed this one's face and shoulder. The eye sockets and mouth cavity held pools of brown water. As he stared down at the face, clouds sealed off the sky, casting darkness as though the Almighty had hit a light switch backstage, and the whole position fell into shadow. Then rain moved in across the field and enveloped him, pattering his helmet and surrounding him with its noise on the ground. He stood motionless, sucking tobacco, and watching rain hit the dead face—he almost expected a blink. Then he noticed a Marine in the distance walking towards him. At first, the man appeared as though rendered by a few lazy brush strokes of green watercolor, with streaks of wet paint bleeding off with the wind. With each step, the man gradually gained substance until he held together in solid form, looking like they all looked: old-fashioned American combat helmet, poncho flapping in the breeze, wet legs, and muddy boots. It was Gunny.

"Afternoon, sir," Gunny said loud enough to be heard over the rain on their helmets. Down under the wide lip of his combat helmet, his face was dark, and his features were barely visible.

Forrest nodded. "Won't be shooting today, Gunny."

"No, sir."

The two men stood in the downpour, looking up at the mountain.

Forrest spat tobacco juice and finally asked the Gunny if he'd heard the news. He had not.

"We're redeploying," Forrest said.

"Sir?"

"Pulling out. Back-loading on ship."

The Gunny's eyes bulged for an instant, and then he stared down at the ground. After several seconds, he looked back up. "There's a dead raghead by your foot there, sir."

Forrest looked down again and spat. The Gunny watched the brown glob spin out through rain and splatter into the mud by the dead face. "When we leaving?"

"Not sure. Soon."

The Gunny looked up at the mountain. "What about our dead? We lose all these people, and we just gonna leave?"

Forrest nodded.

The Gunny stared into the rain for a long minute. "This is like Vietnam."

"Maybe."

While the Gunny and Forrest talked, a Druse militiaman was using the cover of rain to work his way in close to the Marine line. He moved carefully through concrete rubble in front of the York building—a cinderblock factory building shot full of holes and infested with Druse bunkers. As he moved in a hunched over posture, the downpour obscured everything, like varnish. Around him were dark shapes of car carcasses and piles of concrete rubble, and the ground was covered by knee-high weeds. He worked his way out through the rubble and moved up the back steps of a mud brick one-story building just over the wire and railroad bed, and he set up on the roof. The Druse rose up and peeked over the wall. About a hundred yards out, there were two figures standing in the rain in easy range. One of the Marines finally walked off, but the other man just stood there in the rain. The Marine seemed to be looking at something on the ground. The Druse militiaman chambered a round and raised his

AK and rested it on the wall. He aimed in on the shape of the Marine and squeezed.

Forrest never heard the shot that killed him. After he fell, the sound of the shot echoed over. But he couldn't hear it. He lay there alone in the pouring rain, bleeding out into the wet ground, just a few feet from the local corpse. The last animating sparks flickered through him as his life faded into the wet clay. In his brain, faint electrical impulses moved across nerve paths that carried the memories of his lifetime. He was twelve again with no shirt, skin sunbaked brown, his khakis rolled up to his knees and wet, a crab net in his right hand, looking across the vast flat marshland to a stand of pine trees far off, the sun hot on bare shoulders, and then he walked along the mud bank by the bay's edge, and he could smell salt in the air. The smell was good, and he shaded his eyes and looked out, wondering where the boat was. And then he was home, on grass in his parents' yard, shaded by white oaks. Sunlight filtered through the leaves and formed on the freshly cut lawn a painter's stippling of bright yellow-green stamped within purple tree-shade. He smelled the grass and saw his father riding the mower in the distance. His father looked over and smiled, waving. His brothers passed a football nearby. He saw his mother, smiling and calling his name with open arms. He wanted to answer, reaching for her, but she faded slowly, losing color and tone and resonance in increments, until she was gone.

Chapter Twenty-One

October 1984
The Washington Post
"Fighting Terrorism."

October 28, 1984 – "Secretary of State George P. Schultz is a man preoccupied by international terrorism... Thursday in New York, he went out in front a step further, declaring that the United States should stop playing 'the Hamlet of nations' and use force as necessary abroad, to preempt and to retaliate, even if the evidence is not of 'courtroom' caliber and even if American servicemen and innocent civilians are killed."

It had snowed all night and all day. In the late afternoon, the snow stopped, and cold sunlight projected down through a gap in the clouds. A cadet stepped out of Scott-Shipp Hall and stood for a moment in the late-afternoon light. He breathed in cold air, listened to the silence, then stepped off, snow crunching underfoot. On his way back to the barracks, he stopped at the edge of the Memorial Garden and looked across smooth virgin snow streaked with blue shadows.

He hesitated, not wanting to disturb the perfection of the snow-field. Then he walked into it, plowing powder that almost reached his knees. He walked by plaques etched with names and places and dates, all dark and weathered, until he reached a shiny new plaque. There in gleaming gold was a name he knew, Robert E. Forrest. Glancing up, he saw in the classroom window the shape of his professor looking down on him. The cadet looked back at the plaque and pulled his black glove off his right hand. He reached up and touched the letters of the name. He felt the cold bronze and remembered the face and the sound of the now-dead voice. A sound never to be heard by anyone ever again.

He remembered Forrest in town on Saturday night and at Goshen Pass where he'd sit with his feet in the stream and drink beer and tell stories while "Free Bird" played. He would lean back on a flat rock mid-stream with sunshine on his face. He remembered how the cadet had gotten barracks confinement for swinging from the lanyard on the flag pole in front of barracks one night after drinking too many pitchers in town. He'd stuck his foot in the cable and swung out in a wide arc, singing the third verse of the Marine Corps Hymn—*if the Army and the Navy ever looked on heaven's scene, they would find the streets are guarded by United States Marines.*

Now he was on heaven's guard team.

The cadet standing in the snow was in his first year when he'd worked on the school newspaper with the boy on the plaque. He remembered how the older cadet had talked about duck hunting on the river by his house and that girl he'd dated, what's-her-name. And now it would all slip away with time, the cadet in the snow thought. The life story never to be told. He looked across the plaques and realized there was a life's story behind each one.

The cadet in the snow remembered the newspaper article reporting this death. All it said was that one Marine had been killed by a sniper in Beirut. A hard-edged fact, nothing more. Nothing of the dead Marine or his dreams or the things he cared about or how he affected other people or the grief of his mother and brothers. Nothing of the empty place at Christmas dinner or the family he would never have. Of the children who would never exist. The hard fact just lay bare in newsprint that would be shuffled off to the archives to yellow and be reduced to microfiche. The newspaper story was just an emblem, really, like the plaques. There were dozens of plaques here and thousands of newspaper stories; and for each, there were untold dramas lost forever.

The cadet stepped back from the wall and looked up at the window again. It was empty. He stood in the snow, staring up and thinking of his professor's words in class that afternoon. "Many good boys get killed. Sometimes for a lost cause." The professor had uttered the words so matter-of-factly—like he was teaching calculus. The cadet felt a chill from the cold breeze across his neck. He crossed his arms to hold in warmth and then stared up at the empty classroom window again.

He slid his hand back into his glove and looked back across the wall. To his left, through the snow, was *Virginia Mourning Her Dead,* with her dark bronze face highlighted by the reflected light of the snowfield. He studied her feminine profile: a mother's face. As the remaining natural light dimmed, he watched her fade to a dark shape. He finally stepped back and looked up at flakes sparkling in the glow of a streetlamp. In the distance, spruce trees faded to bluish shapes, like unlit Christmas trees in a dreamlike snow-world. He was alone, and it was deathly quiet.

THE END

John E. Holloway grew up in Williamsburg, Virginia. He graduated from the Virginia Military Institute in 1981 and was then commissioned a Second Lieutenant in the United States Marine Corps. He deployed with Second Battalion, Eighth Marines, in October 1983 and participated in the invasion of Grenada and operations in Beirut. In 1987, he graduated from the George Mason University School of Law (now the Antonin Scalia Law School), where he was the editor-in-chief of the law review. After clerking for a federal judge, he has practiced maritime law in Virginia since 1988. He has been published by *The Sewanee Review* and the *Tulane Maritime Law Journal.*